Chapter One

Janet Zwingel sent a glance and a sigh toward her chirping phone. No doubt, the office was sending another message. Today was Friday, but the end of a long week remained out of sight. While at the stop sign, she picked up the phone from the cup holder and read the text.

—*Mandatory overtime. Full crew until 2200+?*—

"Welcome to August." She tossed the words to echo around the interior of the van. Air conditioners were failing all over the St. Louis area. Six days of afternoon temps in triple digits stressed equipment, owners, and HVAC techs alike. She'd be working into the night—again. Tomorrow she had afternoon plans. An engagement party without the hostess, a.k.a. the mother of the bride-to-be, wouldn't be much of a party. She scanned the sky, disappointed to spot nothing other than one, white wisp of a high cloud.

Parking on a flat area of withered grass at the edge of a narrow street, she triple checked a house number. She needed to concentrate on the job now.

While buckling on her tool belt, she listened to the neighborhood. No voices disturbed the air. No watchful or welcoming dogs alerted owners. Only the soft drone of traffic from two blocks away and the dull hum of electric motors disturbed the silence. The street was in the doldrums of a summer afternoon.

A few moments later, she stood on a tiny concrete porch and pushed the doorbell. Every window on this side of the ranch-style house stood open. Only a combination storm and screen door, in full screen configuration, blocked her entrance. She focused on maintaining a small smile for a positive first impression.

"In a sec." A male voice sounded, immediately followed by approaching footsteps.

A trim man with short, silver hair unlatched the door, began to push it open, and froze. His mouth paused with the lips parted a few millimeters as he stared from hazel eyes. After a long moment, he straightened to his full height, an inch shy of six foot, by her estimate. "Janet. From Comfort On Call. I'm here to repair your air conditioner." She pointed to the logo on her dark blue cap and then to the white van with the same red symbol.

As he nodded, she increased her smile one size. *Probably expected a man.* As the only female field technician for Comfort On Call, and one of very few in the region, she collected all sorts of first reactions. They ranged from relief by some young women to demands for a "real tech" from a few of the older clients.

"Of course. I'm Rich Taylor. Come in. You're late." He backed one large step, his expression turning into a frown.

"I'm here now." She hid her sigh. Precious minutes had been spent with a gas stop for the van and finding his almost-hidden street. Taking a quick glance at her watch, she verified her arrival was within twenty minutes of the confirmation call. Nevertheless, she avoided voicing any further explanation, which could

"Do you have one of those cube things so I can pay with my credit card?"

"Absolutely. Is an email receipt okay? If not, I can write up a manual one." She reached into her back pocket and retrieved the case with the credit card reader. The rest of the transaction proceeded without delay.

"Hate my fingertip scrawl, signature never comes close to my real one," Rich muttered while returning her phone.

She gulped ice water and studied his face. Those hazel eyes, they tickled at a memory. They also hinted this man could sort truth from lie better than most. She laid a red and white card on the table. Best to stay with only one break from protocol and keep the conversation on task. With a few seconds of thought, she could list multiple reasons the only visible sign of a woman in the house was the photo. She pressed her lips tight for an instant. "We appreciate your business. You have a warranty. Call if the unit gives you another problem. Please feel welcome to share our name with your friends."

"Janet Zwingel." He tapped the edge of the card on the table. "Good to do business with you."

Standing, she extended a hand, expecting a quick, bland press. At his touch, she blinked in surprise, glanced down, and willed her fingers to slip out of a handshake. His grip was comfortable, genuine, and a stark contrast to his early attitude of "hurry up, I've got important things to do."

Praise for Ellen Parker

"Reading the *COMFORT ZONE*, I was very intrigued how Ellen built the happy and disturbing coincidences drawing Janet Zwingel and Rich Taylor together. They are older real people, set in their ways, wanting stable lives. Ellen expertly wove conflict between them when Rich, a police detective, investigated fraud, theft and murder disrupting Janet's personal and professional life. Could their attraction continue to a life of gusto?"

~*Lois Scorgie*

~*~

"*COMFORT ZONE* is another example of Ellen Parker's outstanding talent in creating real characters we'd all love to know. She writes of family, heartaches, and second chances with honesty and understanding. Don't miss her stories."

~*Barbara Bettis*

~*~

"*COMFORT ZONE* is an engaging romantic suspense book for those wanting a realistic story with mature characters. The characters' behavior and judgment was down-to-earth and true to their personalities. Family relationships were important to the story and enhanced the plot. *COMFORT ZONE* kept my attention from beginning to end."

~*Diane K. Peterson*

~*~

"Ellen Parker delivers another solid read with *STARE DOWN*. From start to end the author put you in the story with two dynamic characters."

~*June Ashland*

Comfort Zone

by

Ellen Parker

This is a work of fiction. Names, characters, places, and incidents are either the product of the author's imagination or are used fictitiously, and any resemblance to actual persons living or dead, business establishments, events, or locales, is entirely coincidental.

Comfort Zone

Cover Art by *Jennifer Greeff*

The Wild Rose Press, Inc.
PO Box 708
Adams Basin, NY 14410-0708
Visit us at www.thewildrosepress.com

Publishing History
First Sweetheart Rose Edition, 2020
Print ISBN 978-1-5092-3165-2
Digital ISBN 978-1-5092-3166-9

Published in the United States of America

Dedication

In memory of my parents:
Bert and Grace
By instilling a love of reading,
You made this whole thing possible.

be taken as confrontational. Even in the middle of a heat wave—especially during a long heat wave—the customer was always right.

"Yes, I see that. Unit's out back. Follow me." He pivoted and led the way through a living room.

The room, with traditional style furniture, impressed as tidy. A flat screen TV dominated a space at one end. Clean, cream walls were void of wall decoration, aside from one framed photo. The picture was of a family, the man with a remarkable resemblance to her customer, except with mahogany hair. He had an arm around the waist of a petite blonde. Two children, a boy and a girl in their late teens, completed the group.

Scanning the walls and making a mental note of the thermostat location in the hallway, she followed his long strides.

"Inside part." He pointed to a gray, wall-mounted evaporator as they reached the entrance to a small utility room.

She stepped inside and ran her gaze over the unit beside an open electrical panel. This opportunity to give a quick check was too good to delay. She examined the exterior connections and pulled the filter halfway out. "The filter looks good. Did you change it recently?"

"Couple of weeks ago. Before that?" He shrugged.

"General recommendation is every two to three months." She slid in the filter until it was tight. Add a smile and this customer would be handsome. The woman in his life, if he had one, should feel lucky.

He continued out the back door, halted one step off a bricked patio, and gestured to the compressor sitting on a small concrete pad. "I think the problem's with the compressor, or whatever you call the square thing. It plays dead—no matter how many times I reset the circuit breaker or thermostat."

As she walked across a dozen feet of browning grass, she kept her voice even. "Do you happen to know the age of the unit?"

"No clue. The system was here when I moved in last October. Your company sticker was on it."

She nodded before squatting down next to the connections. In a moment, she found the factory label, including a serial number indicating the unit was manufactured seven years ago. Being one of the more popular models, the most common parts should be in her van. She pulled out her voltmeter and tested the first circuit. "I'll be going back and forth between the circuit breaker and here. I'll let you know what I find."

"I hope you find it soon and fix it on the spot. I've got things to do." He pulled a phone from the pocket of dark gray workout pants.

As Janet removed the cover and followed the memorized troubleshooting flowchart, she sneaked the occasional glance in his direction. His stance as he talked on his phone at the other end of the patio tickled a faded memory. He rested one hand against his hip while the other, between phone calls, stayed a few inches away from his body. She knew him from somewhere. *Don't gawk. Mind belongs on my work.* The sooner she completed this repair, the sooner she could get to the next—and the next. She wiped sweat off her forehead and replaced the company cap over her short hair before approaching him with the repair description and estimate. Most of an hour later, Janet held her hand to a vent and smiled. "We have success."

"Not a minute too soon." He emerged from a bedroom, phone in hand.

"I'll be a couple minutes cleaning up and figuring the bill. Then you'll be good to go. I need to offer you the broken motor."

"No thanks. Recycle it or something." He started to make another call, abandoned tapping the screen, and turned to her. Hesitating, he curved his lips into a hint of a smile. "You may as well figure your bill in here. I'll toss a glass of ice water into the offer."

Has he suddenly remembered good manners? She skimmed her tongue across her lips. Ice water. Tabulating the charges inside the residence and accepting a drink wasn't following company protocol, or her personal safety standards, but it was exactly the cure for working in the heat. "Thanks. You got a deal. I'll get the paperwork from my van."

A short time later, she faced him across the corner of a rectangular dinette table and turned her phone toward him. Using her index finger, she scrolled down the invoice on the small screen. "The work is broken down into service call, parts, and labor. Questions?"

"Do you have one of those cube things so I can pay with my credit card?"

"Absolutely. Is an email receipt okay? If not, I can write up a manual one." She reached into her back pocket and retrieved the case with the credit card reader. The rest of the transaction proceeded without delay.

"Hate my fingertip scrawl. Signature never comes close to my real one," Rich muttered while returning her phone.

She gulped ice water and studied his face. Those

hazel eyes, they tickled at a memory. They also hinted this man could sort truth from lie better than most. She laid a red and white card on the table. Best to stay with only one break from protocol and keep the conversation on task. With a few seconds of thought, she could list multiple reasons the only visible sign of a woman in the house was the photo. She pressed her lips tight for an instant. "We appreciate your business. You have a warranty. Call if the unit gives you another problem. Please feel welcome to share our name with your friends."

"Janet Zwingel." He tapped the edge of the card on the table. "Good to do business with you."

Standing, she extended a hand, expecting a quick, bland press. At his touch, she blinked in surprise, glanced down, and willed her fingers to slip out of a handshake. His grip was comfortable, genuine, and a stark contrast to his early attitude of "hurry up, I've got important things to do."

"Zwingel. I don't expect that's a common name."

"I think all of them living in St. Louis are related in one way or another." She started for the front door, aware he followed without crowding her. The comment on the name got her to thinking. As far as she knew, her ex, their daughter, and she were the only Zwingels south of Dubuque. Almost to the door, she threw caution out the window and tipped her head to the photo. "Nice looking family."

He glanced at the picture and gave a tiny shake of his head. "That photo was taken a long time ago. Before…well…everything changed."

Okay. She continued to the entrance, aware her comment prompted his eyes to cloud for an instant.

Hope he forgets my blunder before he fills out the evaluation.

"Thanks again. Stay safe," he commented through the screen.

As she stepped off the porch, she lifted a hand in acknowledgement of his words. *Taylor. Rich Taylor.* The common name circled around in distant memories as she checked in and drove to her next call. They had crossed paths before. When and where? The old neighborhood? One of the co-workers or casual friends Greg, her ex, brought home to eat their food and drink their beer? She shook her head. No, the beer buddy scenario didn't fit. Maybe he was a parent to one of her daughter's friends.

With a sigh, she pushed his image out of her mind. Thinking about a person she'd never see again defined a waste of time.

****

Rich walked from room to room, closing and locking each window with sure, practiced motions. When he reached his bedroom, he changed into black slacks and a pale blue golf shirt before picking up his phone. He selected the number for his father. According to his last call to the Amtrak station, the train should be thirty minutes out.

"Hello."

"Dad. This is Rich. I'm running late. The HVAC tech just finished. Don't leave the station." As he spoke, he secured gun, badge, and handcuffs to his belt.

"I've extra luggage this time. Hope you got room in your trunk."

At the words, Rich curved his lips into a smile. His father, Henry, considered more than an overnight case to be excessive luggage. "Don't worry. I talked to Sis. I've plenty of room in the car for two checked bags."

"Rode through some pretty country. Could use a spot of rain for the farmers."

He glanced at the thermostat in the hall as he walked past. "I agree. Well, I've got to go. Remember, stay in the station. Today's a scorcher."

"Yes, sir. Mr. Detective, sir." Henry disconnected.

Rich laughed. He imagined his father sitting by the generous train car window snapping off a salute. A moment later, he slipped his phone into a pocket, double checked the back door, and went to his car. He looked forward to Henry living with him again. In all sorts of ways he could see more benefit for him than the older man. Coming home to a quiet, empty house night after night got stale. Talking with a real person over the supper table or during the breaks in a baseball game would be an improvement.

Mary, I miss you. As he drove toward downtown, he allowed memories to visit.

Walking into the house, wrapping Mary into his arms, and enjoying delightful smells from the stove.

Haircut night, when she worked magic with comb and scissors while passing along comical stories from the beauty salon.

Mary, lying too still and pale after cancer claimed victory.

****

Later that night, Rich removed his shoes and stretched out on the sofa. He laced his hands behind his head, pressed them into the square throw pillow, and closed his eyes. No sense in watching another commercial during the late-night news.

Janet's image, squatted beside the compressor and intent on her work, swirled in. Five-eight. One thirty. Brown. Blue. He gave a mental shake and forced his mind from a formal description. Pretty brunette HVAC techs didn't belong in his brain. He opened his eyes and glanced toward his dad. "Do you think you're here to stay?"

Henry muted the TV. "I like to think so. Chicago's nice. Living with Betty during the hip replacement and therapy worked out well. Some days, I think your sister spent as much time behind the wheel for me as a full-time taxi driver. Without the tips."

"I'm sure she didn't complain." He thought back to how often the phone discussions with his sister centered on transportation and her offer to continue past the usual number of physical therapy visits.

"St. Louis is home." Henry patted the arm of the worn black recliner. "I'm looking forward to getting back together with some of my friends. Did you pick up bus schedules? Remind me where the stop is from this house."

"Short two-block walk gets you to the arterial. Light to cross the main street. Schedules are on your nightstand. I feel as if I forgot something." Rich blinked up at the ceiling. "Oh, I didn't ask where to buy the monthly pass. Remind me tomorrow, and I'll check the web site again."

He scanned the room, surprised at how bare it suddenly seemed. The bookcase held a mixture of hardbound and paperbacks. Gone were the colored glass vases interspersed between them. *Mary's.* The table lamp sat dark, sharing the oval stand in front of the big window with a neat stack of magazines. Each thin volume contained one or more of Rich's word search puzzles. He needed a better place for them. He made a mental note to stop at the office supply and purchase a package of proper storage boxes. "Are you coming to the party tomorrow?"

"Who's doing what?" Henry turned his face and leaned toward him.

"Mary's nephew, my nephew, Daniel, gave his girl a ring and set a date. The bride's mother wants to celebrate." Rich thought back to the only time he'd met the young lady. A call from work interrupted and pulled him away from the gathering before he had a chance to really talk to her. All he remembered at the moment was an attractive brunette with a wide smile. *She reminded me of someone—not from work.*

"Are you sure I'll be welcome?"

He pushed up to a sitting position and rested his hands on his knees. "Daniel said I could bring a guest. I think it starts at three."

"Then I'll plan on it. Takes me a little longer to get going in the morning than before the surgery. Should have all the necessary stuff unpacked and my room organized by the time to leave."

Rich tipped back his head until it brushed the wall beneath the family photo. "It's decided then."

"Right now, my bed's calling to me. Glad you got the A/C fixed. I don't do as well in the heat as I did years ago." Henry pushed up and out of the recliner, releasing a sigh when he was steady on his feet.

"Yeah, me too. I'll be up early, so ignore my noise. Okay?" Rich ran a mental list of errands delayed during the wait for the HVAC tech. Losing most of his day off rubbed the wrong way against his sense of organization.

Interruptions, impromptu changes, and controlled chaos belonged at work, not home.

"Got it." Henry walked from the room carrying a cane he didn't need inside the house.

Rich retrieved the TV remote and rolled the name and image of the HVAC tech around in his head. *Zwingel. Janet Zwingel.* The name refused to wander away. He tested it against different sectors of his life. Within a few minutes, he'd eliminated knowing the name from work, friends in the old neighborhood, and businesses he currently frequented. As he stood and made a final check of the doors and windows, he thought of one other place. Years ago, when his kids were in elementary school, he'd been involved in a community athletic association.

After checking the window in the small third bedroom used as a home office, he squatted in front of the storage crates turned on their sides as a makeshift bookcase. He pulled out one of three thick, blue binders. Team photos, from his years as a youth soccer coach, were inside. First, he drew a deep breath to fortify himself against the onslaught of memories. A moment later, he opened to the first page.

In the second year's photo, he found a player named Ashley Zwingel. She sat cross-legged in the front row, second from the left. Dressed like the others, in the team shirt, and with her brunette hair in a pony tail, she was remarkable only for her wide smile. He flipped the page to the next year and found her again. She was gone from the team in the third picture. *Two years. I wonder what happened.*

Studying the photos, he thought back to his coaching days. Recalling his daughter, Rachel, and a few of the other girls was easy. He could visualize them doing drills or attempting steals. He returned to the second page and tapped Ashley's image. She didn't stand out in his memory.

"They have to be related. Zwingel's a rare name and the smile is distinctive." He relaxed in the office chair and recalled the wide, brief smile on Janet Zwingel's face when she drank ice water in his kitchen. Daniel's fiancée was named Ashley. He closed the binder and smiled. Tomorrow, at the engagement party, would he be given an opportunity to speak with a certain brunette?

Chapter Two

After pulling off her work boots, Janet placed them beside the other footwear reserved for outdoor work. *Late to my own party.* Correction—she wasn't late yet. And technically, the engagement festivities were not her party. Today she was hostess, not guest of honor.

"You can't plan the weather." She mumbled one of the standard mottos of her profession as she hurried up the steps to the main floor. Her co-workers would handle the rest of the weekend calls—emergency only since noon.

A memory from yesterday's most unforgettable service call surged forward, warming her neck. She shook her head to banish the image of the homeowner with short, silver hair and hazel eyes emphasized with smile crinkles. At least, she preferred to think of such lines being the result of smiles instead of anger. Did he wear a ring? *Don't go there.*

The safe assumption, in her experience, remained to speak and act as if any new acquaintance lived in a happy marriage. The only evidence to the contrary was the almost-bare living room walls. She failed to recall any woman who would live in a house for close to a year without hanging more than one family portrait. She thought for a moment and remembered a clock and a corkboard in the dining area. Had she missed anything? A man certainly had the right to live alone, or with another male, and keep decorating sparse and functional.

Mr. Taylor's decorating habits were not her business. She had plenty of activity in her own life and shouldn't waste time trying to analyze customers.

She stepped into the kitchen and smiled the instant she saw the note from her daughter.

I'm gone to get the balloons and extra tablecloth. Eggs are cooked, cooled, peeled, and await your magic touch. Ashley.

Opening the fridge, Janet found the eggs on the bottom shelf. She did a quick scan of the other shelves to confirm the deli bowls of coleslaw and potato salad were on site. *Hope we have enough.* Heading for the shower, she ran an estimate of the guest list through her mind. Would the visitors total over twenty? She'd estimated twenty-five when ordering the cupcakes. She hoped not all of the single friends would bring a guest. Daniel, Ashley's fiancé, never gave her more than a rough estimate on his relatives.

A short time later, fresh from the shower, she pulled on clean, worn red shorts and a faded T-shirt. She slid her feet into flip-flops and picked up a wide tooth comb to tame her short, dark hair. She heard a sound at the front door and paused the comb mid-stroke. "Is that you, Ashley?"

"Good guess," her daughter called back. "The party store was hectic. Have you been home long?"

"Long enough to wash off the morning." Janet laid the comb beside her dresser clock, a 1910 Seth Thomas in a walnut case, and headed to the kitchen.

"I'll do the cheese and meat trays." Ashley pulled containers from the fridge.

"Good. We have time if we don't dawdle."

"We have more than an hour. Daniel will be here in thirty minutes. Neither of us have any qualms about putting him to work."

Janet chuckled. "He's family now. Your ring made it official. In practice, nothing changes. I've treated him like family for a couple of years."

A companionable silence filled the room as they worked. Janet sent a few quick glances toward her daughter, thinking again how lucky her students were. They enjoyed a kindergarten teacher at the beginning of her career. She easily imagined a cheerful, energetic, atmosphere in the classroom.

While her multiple shelf clocks ticked in the background, Janet mashed, spiced, and tasted the egg yolk mixture before spooning the rich, yellow filling into a disposable pastry bag. She didn't speak until she was piping the filling into the first egg white. "Did your father ever reply?"

"He finally called late yesterday. He'll be here."

Janet pressed her lips tight for an instant. Conversations involving her ex, Greg, ranked as necessary with a tinge of unpleasant. "Did he specify with or without wife number three?"

"Without. For future reference, her name is Pam." Ashley overlapped cheese triangles on a large oval tray.

"I know her name, and I'll be pleasant if we ever end up in the same supermarket line." If Janet took a few seconds to think, she could add his second ex-wife and at least two live-in girlfriends by name, occupation, and a few trivial facts. When she didn't think about them, days were more pleasant. "Trouble in paradise?"

"Possible…I'm pretty sure Dad's gambling again.

He had the nerve to ask Daniel and me to meet him for lunch at the casino last Sunday."

Janet studied her daughter's profile and classified it as thoughtful before filling the next egg. Gambling, and the resulting financial losses, shattered their family fourteen years ago. The shards scarred both her and Ashley deeply. Ashley avoided any wager involving money. As far as she knew, her daughter even abstained from charity raffles. "I'll file the new tidbit under interesting."

Ashley tipped her head and raised one eyebrow. "Will you be nice to him? Daniel's parents need an opportunity to form their own opinion."

"They haven't met Greg? I assumed they got acquainted at graduation last spring." Janet exchanged the pastry bag for the paprika shaker. Ashley and Daniel were college sweethearts. She met Daniel near the end of their freshman year. The next fall, during homecoming weekend, she'd been introduced to his parents.

"By the time Dad arrived at graduation, Daniel and his family had left campus. And you moved Gram and Gramps into air conditioning."

She paused her work and thought back to the hectic moments between long periods of waiting. "I remember now." Greg marred his daughter's day. His behavior fit a pattern he developed early. He either neglected important details or stole the spotlight. "I never did believe he got lost in road construction detours."

"Neither did I." Ashley smiled.

"Smart girl." Janet watched her daughter put the finishing touches on the first meat and cheese platter. Snapping a plastic lid over the eggs, she turned to put them in the fridge. "What's next?"

"Why don't you get dressed? Daniel will be here in a few minutes. I'll give him balloon duty."

"I am dressed." She inspected her daughter and saw her younger self for a moment. At five nine, Ashley was an inch taller than her mother. Her dark coffee hair fell down to her shoulders today, with loose curls brushing the neckline of a red-and-white sundress. Mother and daughter shared the same sturdy bone structure, dimpled chin, and high cheekbones. Medium brown eyes were the only obvious feature the young lady inherited from her father.

"Party clothes, Mother. I meant, go put on your party clothes."

Washing her hands, Janet chuckled. A moment later, as she turned to go down the hall, she caught a glimpse of Daniel's dark blue compact pulling up. *A new dress awaits—a dress I'll never have occasion to wear after today.*

****

Rich slowed his full-size, silver sedan until a small kid on a bicycle could have kept pace. "I patrolled this neighborhood years ago. I don't see many changes."

"Are you saying this is one of the safer areas?" Henry gripped his cane with arthritic hands.

"According to last year's statistics the entire zip code east of the freeway ranks in the top ten." He admired the neat homes covered with brick siding. On his right, the ground sloped away from the street enough for the houses to have walk-out basements. Narrow driveways curved around the back and led to lower level and rear garages. Two lots ahead, just before the corner, a bunch of red and white balloons bobbed above the mailbox. He drew a quick breath of anticipation and reviewed the half dozen snappy openings he'd rehearsed during morning errands. If…when…he saw Janet Zwingel. He planned to improve on yesterday's first impression.

Parking on the edge of the street ahead of a dark blue compact, he shut off the engine and glanced at his dad. "You okay? Ready to meet new people?"

Henry stilled with one hand on the seat belt buckle. "I feel like the third wheel. I'm an old man crashing a young people's party."

"You're invited, as my guest. You know Daniel and his parents." Rich opened the driver's door.

"What's the girl's name again?"

"Ashley." He adjusted his gait to stay beside Henry crossing a lawn turning brown from too little rain and too much sun. "She met Daniel in college. The family will be gaining a teacher."

Henry made a guttural reply.

Standing on the small, covered porch, he pressed the doorbell and listened to the first portion of the Westminster chimes.

"I'll get it." The female voice was quickly followed by a shadowed figure moving beyond the gauzy curtains in the large window.

The instant the door opened, Rich froze. Every witty phrase conceived during sleepless early morning hours or Saturday errands flew away faster than a bullet speeds from muzzle to target. He swallowed.

Henry opened the storm door.

He hunted for words and enough moisture to speak. "Janet."

She smiled and gestured them inside.

"Henry Taylor." His father presented his hand.

He scrambled for a sensible second introduction. "I'm Rich. Daniel's uncle. Henry's my father. I was told I could bring a guest…uh…nice neighborhood."

"Pleased to meet you, Henry. I'm Janet, mother of the bride-to-be." She shook his father's hand while looking the older man full in the face. A moment later, she turned her attention to him, her smile stiffening. "We meet again. How's the unit working?"

He flicked his gaze from her face as her neck reddened. A blush looked good on her. So did her dress, a blue and white creation which showed off curves her uniform only hinted at. He blinked at her white sandals with medium heels before lifting his gaze past one of the uneven-on-purpose hemlines to eyes bluer than the sky on a clear day. "The unit's fine. The entire house was cooled to the comfort zone by the time we got home from the train station."

"Excellent." She smiled wider, and her eyes sparkled. "I'd like you to meet my parents, Joe and Marie Johnson. They've opted to stay in the cool house, at least for the present. The other guests are out back."

Rich nodded a greeting to the couple sitting in the living room and fumbled for a proper phrase.

Henry went over, shook Joe's hand, and started talking about the fields he'd seen from the train yesterday.

Rich turned to Janet. "I think he's found a kindred spirit."

"New acquaintances are a good thing. Follow me, and I'll introduce you around."

"You've got a deal." He held up an envelope. "Where do the cards go?"

"Basket." She led him across the room and pointed out a wicker container with red and white ribbons wrapped around the handle.

He dropped the sealed envelope into the collection without breaking step and almost bumped against her when she stopped at the table. He shifted his weight away after his arm brushed her back. "Oh. Pardon me."

"No problem, I need to learn to signal before stopping." She scooted half a step away and picked up two bowls of salsa. "If you'd be so kind as to bring the chips."

He glanced down at a table covered with several dishes of finger foods and two large platters of cupcakes. "Yes, ma'am." He picked up both large bowls and followed her out a sliding door, across a modest deck, and down wooden steps. Glancing around the yard, he spotted several familiar figures among the twenty or so guests.

Janet made a sharp turn at the bottom of the steps and set the appetizers on a picnic table shaded by the deck. She snatched a corn chip and dipped it in red sauce. "As you can see, my yard is modest. On a positive note, we don't have to be elbow to elbow in the house."

He started to open his mouth and closed his lips before hasty words escaped. Touching elbows with her in a crowded room might be interesting.

"Hey. You've arrived." Daniel walked toward them extending a can of diet cola to Rich.

"You had doubts about my attendance?" Rich nodded silent approval at his nephew's blond hair in a fresh high and tight cut.

Daniel shrugged. "Considering your occupation,

work schedule, and history of missing social events—questions always exist."

"Once in a while, management slips up and gives me a day off. Now, I'd like you to introduce me again to your future bride. I'm looking forward to more than a thirty-second conversation today." He turned to say a word to Janet and discovered she'd already gone. *I'll catch her later.*

A few minutes later, when a college friend pulled Daniel away, Rich found himself alone with Ashley. "Do you remember me?"

Ashley looked him over before taking a sip of her drink. "We met this spring, briefly."

"Think back to youth soccer." He waited a beat before adding. "I was the coach. My daughter, Rachel Taylor, was a teammate."

She drew a quick breath and closed her eyes for an instant. "Soccer was forever ago."

A lifetime. He didn't want to get into a conversation of how either of their lives had changed between then and now. She'd grown up, and now he could see a strong resemblance with her mother. He wondered again why he couldn't remember Janet on the sidelines. "I tend to agree. I hope my coaching wasn't responsible for you dropping out."

"My parents divorced. Mom and I moved." She shook her head.

Rich paid attention to the trace of pain in her voice. Family separations could be difficult to talk about—almost like a death. "Divorce can be rough on the whole family. Daniel told me you're a teacher. But he didn't get into specifics."

"Kindergarten. This year will be my second in the

city." She smiled wide and brief before adding the name of the school and this year's starting date.

He caught a note of excitement in her voice and observed a sparkle in her eyes as she described getting ready for the new school year. As he listened, inserting a key word here and there, he made mental notes to ask Daniel about the security at her apartment.

A few minutes later, another young woman walked up.

He found a pause and backed away a step. "I've enjoyed our chat. But I think I've taken up enough of your time for now."

For the next hour, he mingled with the other guests. During short, friendly exchanges, he picked up tidbits of their interests and opinions on more than the current heat wave. At irregular intervals, he scanned the yard out of professional habit and to locate Janet. She moved among the guests, appearing at ease among all of them. When she came down the steps carrying a bowl of salad, he started over to assist until he noticed three other women already bringing out and arranging the food.

Rich popped the top on another can of soda as he chatted with Daniel's dad, John Latin. "I'm impressed with Ashley."

Nodding, John took a quick swallow of his craft beer. "She's sensible. I think they'll be good together."

Glancing up for a routine scan of the guests, Rich stalled his gaze on a new arrival. The man swaggered down the driveway toward the gathering as if he owned the place. Five ten. Two forty plus. Dark hair and eyes. Clean shaven. Red over tan over black. He followed him with his gaze like he'd watch a suspect cross a street.

The man walked toward Janet chatting with two other women in the shade of an umbrella.

The stranger tapped Janet on the shoulder.

She startled, pivoted with a hand raised, and stalled with her palm an inch from his cheek.

Rich leaned into the first of three, long steps necessary to reach her.

"Ashley's father. Recognize him from his picture," John commented.

"His name?" *Carries trouble like I carry my badge.* Rich committed the man's features to memory.

"Greg."

He blinked and recalled Ashley's face during her brief statement. *My parents divorced.* If he were a betting sort of man, he'd put his money on the non-friendly sort of parting. "I'll remember."

Chapter Three

Facing the bright sunshine, Janet blinked. The action failed to banish an unwelcome shiver crossing her shoulders. Greg, standing closer than was welcome, sighed behind her. Inching her feet forward, nearer to Ashley, she pressed her lips tight.

"Relax, people. Smile. You're happy today." Matt, Daniel's brother, the designated photographer for the afternoon, waved for the back row to spread out a little.

Janet waited but didn't sense Greg following directions. Arranging her body into parade rest, her favorite pose for long periods of time, she curved her lips into a smile. *Think happy.* Today's photo session was practice with an amateur. In December, at the actual wedding, a professional photographer would be doing the directing. She refused to think of the number of different ways the wedding party and immediate family could be arranged.

"Everyone say pickles," Matt called out and began snapping a series of photos as Daniel, Ashley, their parents, and Ashley's grandparents reacted.

Janet contained a sigh as the photographer signaled the desire for more shots. Perhaps the professional in December would be quicker, more confident, and require fewer forced smiles.

"We need to talk," Greg whispered into her left ear.

"Not now—smile for the camera." She'd like to

delay any conversation with Greg into the next millennium. However, the realist within her knew the delay would be a matter of minutes, not days or weeks.

"Today—I have an important question."

Everything was important and urgent in Greg's world. His air of compelling action was one of his characteristics which she'd found exciting at first. Her opinion soon changed to irritating. Now, after courtship, twelve years of marriage, and fourteen years divorced, his attitude of emergency in routine matters was past exasperating. "Follow directions—smile."

"I mean it, Janet."

Finding a reserve of restraint, she spoke through her smile. "I believe you think the topic's urgent. I don't want you to spoil Ashley's party. Put your concern in an email."

"No can do." He brushed a hand along her arm.

She shivered in the sunshine.

"Thank you, everyone. Now, I'll take just a few of the happy couple. Then I heard a rumor of food." The photographer waved a hand to dismiss the group.

"Take a couple with only mother and daughter."

Janet darted her attention to the speaker. *Rich?* A specific photo appeared an odd request from him. She would have understood the same request instantly from either her mother or Ashley's godmother.

"Three generations," Ashley replied. "I want to include Grams."

"Good idea." Janet spoke without hesitation.

While Daniel and Ashley posed for a few more, Janet turned her gaze and thoughts to Rich. Since greeting him at the door and escorting him into the yard, she'd not spoken to him. More times than she wanted to count, she'd lingered her gaze on him. She'd stayed aware of his location when moving among the guests or going in and out of the house. She knew he'd had a conversation with Ashley. He'd been difficult to ignore when escorting Henry and her parents down the wooden steps a few minutes before the photography session began.

"Janet." Greg stepped in front of her. "I need a little help."

She inspected her ex from hair to toes and back again. "No, Greg. I've told you over and over. The only time I'd help you is possibly on your deathbed. You look like you have at least a few days of normal life in you."

"My health is fine. I'm here to offer an investment opportunity." He crossed his arms and scowled.

Resisting the urge to rub at the sudden gooseflesh on her arms, she clenched her hands. Was he guessing, or did he know for a fact, about her recent inheritance? "I'm not gifting, loaning, or investing money with you."

"Come on, Janet." He extended one hand, palm up. "The venture is low-risk. I've done my research better than when I almost opened a diner."

"My answer is no." She eased away another half step. "Why do you have trouble believing me?" With a sigh, she banished memories of the largest of his past business proposals. Facing him, she touched the center blue-and-white disc of her favorite summer necklace and looked at his soft, larger-than-last-year waistline. In addition to, or perhaps because of, his gambling addiction, he wasn't aging well. Not like…she lifted her gaze beyond Greg's shoulder and encountered Rich.

Mr. Taylor looked trim and fit as a gym rat. Aside from the silver hair, and perhaps a few of the character wrinkles around his eyes, he could pass at first glance for mid- to late-thirties. Snatches of conversations overheard this afternoon actually placed him at the half-century mark—give or take a couple years.

"I'll go ask Ashley."

"No, you won't." Janet snapped out the words and gripped Greg's wrist. "Our daughter is a second-year, public school teacher with student loans. She doesn't have money to waste on your schemes."

"You make my proposal sound malicious before you've even listened." He leaned forward and ground out the accusation.

She silently listed a few of the adjectives which she usually applied to her ex: leech, liar, selfish, clueless. No, malicious was not on the list. "Have you paid back her college fund? Or the child support shortage accumulated during your second divorce? By my reckoning, you owe Ashley thousands. Why would she give you money?"

"Investment. I'm not asking for a gift." He lifted off her hand and walked away.

"Mom. We're ready for the three generations." As Ashley looked toward her father's back, her expression shifted from cheerful to serious. "Are you okay? Do you need a referee?"

She turned to her daughter, who had too much experience as peacemaker between her parents. "I'm fine. Let's get the photo done so Grams can get out of the direct sun."

A short time later, after the photography session ended, and Marie sat in the shade with a plate of food,

Janet took a seat on the steps next to her daughter.

"Have you talked to him?" Ashley lifted a forkful of potato salad.

"I think I've talked to almost everyone. Exactly who do you mean?"

"Mr. Taylor—Daniel's uncle. I didn't recognize him. He told me he was my soccer coach and his daughter, Rachel, was on the team. I've been thinking about it since we spoke. I sort of remember her." Ashley spilled out her words with only tiny pauses between her sentences. She pointed her fork to where Rich chatted with Daniel's mother.

"Soccer. I thought he looked familiar yesterday." Janet tucked in her lower lip. The mental puzzle pieces assembled. The coaches for the youth teams were usually parents. Due to her work schedule, she hadn't attended entire games but caught the end of most.

"Yesterday?"

Janet swallowed a bite of ham. "Service call on a Model 829D—I replaced a failed compressor motor and topped off the coolant. You did say youth soccer."

"You're talking about before—"

"I know exactly when we paid sports fees." She closed her eyes for a moment. Snapping at her daughter was counterproductive. Pulling in a deep breath, she jabbed a black olive. "In answer to your original question—not yet."

"I was going to say the service call in your ramble was before today's party." Ashley shielded her smile with her dollar roll sandwich.

Janet shook her head, one of these days she'd listen, think, and reply in the proper order. After finishing her meal, she walked over to the ice chest. On the way back, she paused within range of a conversation between Greg and Rich. She didn't eavesdrop often, but since Greg was cruising the guests for funds, she'd made an exception.

"Ashley's a lovely young lady. You must be proud of her." Rich lifted his drink.

"I am. She turned out fine." Greg straightened his shoulders.

Rich turned his head and scanned the yard. "Is your wife here? I'd like to meet her."

"No. She…another obligation."

Janet twitched her lips. His hesitation signaled trouble in marriage number three.

Rich shrugged. "Guess I'll wait until the wedding to meet her. What are the duties of the father of the bride these days?"

Greg lifted his drink and swallowed.

"I'm merely gathering information. I've got a daughter of my own."

And a son. Janet thought back to the photo in his house. No wife—according to a comment by Daniel's mother earlier today, her sister died nearly two years ago. *Rich took Mary's death hard. I'm pleased to see him getting social again.*

Greg took a final bite of sandwich. "Ashley just told me to follow directions."

Rich chuckled. "No different from any other day then. Daughters," he lowered his voice. "They grow up and move away. Some people would say you're lucky she's not moving far."

"She's pretty independent. She got a wide stubborn streak from her mother."

It's a survival skill. Women develop all sorts of

traits when the men around them break promises. Janet took pride in her daughter's abilities.

"Strong women can be difficult to live with." Rich nodded.

"Sounds like the voice of experience." Greg shifted his drink to the opposite hand. "Would you be interested in a business opportunity? I'm asking for a minimal investment."

"I'm cautious with my money." Rich turned his head a tiny amount and glanced at Janet.

A polite person would move away. Instead, she remained still and quiet, curious how the proposition would unfold.

"We'll be almost family after Christmas." Greg took a swallow of his beer.

"I need a loan—I go to the bank."

"You'd be getting in at the beginning of a new thing. Well, the concept has a track record, but the specific would be new." Greg pulled out his wallet and handed over a business card. "Ignore the corporation name. I'm ready to go out on my own—have one partner already. One more investor, then great things will happen."

Rich accepted the card and tucked it in his shirt pocket.

Janet stepped over and tapped Greg on the shoulder.

Greg flinched and fumbled his wallet halfway to his pocket. "Hey. Oh—you."

"About time you experienced the receiving side." Janet pressed her lips tight. Only a very few people would understand the importance of the moment. For years, Greg thought sneaking up on her when engrossed in conversation or work was clever or funny. His reaction a moment ago gave a small, but deep, twinge of satisfaction.

"No big deal." Greg stood stiff.

She smiled small as a blush crept up his neck.

Rich backed up a step. "I'll leave you to sort out the winner of your private game."

"You've no need to go." Janet glanced between the two men. Once again, Greg practiced poor manners by putting his interests first. She addressed Rich. "Greg's made his rounds. I believe he's asked most everyone over thirty for a loan."

"I have not." He tapped one foot and crossed his arms.

She raised her eyebrows and stared her ex straight in the face. "I'll not have our daughter's party turned into a way for my guests to lose money."

"You make me sound evil, Janet." He chopped the air in front of her with one hand. "I always thought better of you."

Evil? She regarded him closer to clueless and forced her next words to be slow and clear. "You picked the wrong descriptor. I speak the blunt truth rather than flatter you. Really, now is a good time for you to leave."

"I need to talk to Ash first." Greg turned his head and scanned the crowd.

"Ash? Our daughter outgrew that nickname a decade ago." She glanced toward Rich. He appeared to be studying the other guests, but she suspected he paid attention to her exchange with Greg.

"I still need to talk to her."

"Will you keep the conversation short?" Janet

worried her bottom lip. "I don't want to find out later you even mentioned money."

Rich waited in silence for a long moment while Greg walked out of easy hearing. Then, he gestured with his drink can. "You've no need to explain why he's got ex in front of husband."

"Contrary to today's performance, once he was rather charming. Something happened along the way to cause bad manners and other vices to surface. We ended up going different directions in life." She smiled. "Have you had a cupcake yet?"

"Dessert's an excellent idea. But first, I want to apologize."

"I don't understand why. You and Greg had a conversation. I was the eavesdropper."

"The apology is for my behavior yesterday. I was rude. My mind was preoccupied with half a dozen things. Letting my concerns spill over to you was unfair." He extended his hand. "Are we good?"

She hesitated only an instant. To her surprise, the feel of his hand surrounding hers was more comfortable and reassuring than yesterday's brief touch. "Apology accepted. I wasn't holding a grudge. In the big picture, what you saw as rude was a tiny brush stroke."

"You speak like a woman of proverbs and wisdom." He curved one side of his mouth into a brief smile.

She shook her head and released his hand. "Don't over-rate me. I'm a simple HVAC technician wearing an extra hat embossed mother-of-the-bride."

"I'd bet you don't have a simple bone in your body."

"I don't—" She sealed her lips before "bet" slipped

out. He used the word in casual conversation, like a great majority of people. Only a select few, people deeply wounded by the gambling addiction of others, avoided it. "I think"—she gestured toward Greg walking up the driveway—"now is a good time for cake."

Janet walked at his side toward the dessert. She searched for a conversation topic other than the weather or baseball. *Ignore the gossip snippets.*

Chapter Four

The heat wave collapsed late Sunday afternoon with a thunderstorm. After the initial, brief downpour, an hour of light rain brought relief. Dust vanished from the air, leaving behind a clean summer scent. Every plant in the region sighed with pleasure, then perked up a little taller. Lawns, parks, and vacant lots developed a blush of green among tan grass.

On Monday morning, Janet drove to work with the truck windows down. Life was good. Today's list of blessings scrolling in her mind included a steady job, a mortgage within her budget, and a daughter launched to the next step. She felt stable, ready to face life with confidence. Neither her parents nor her child expected explanations for every tiny decision. The future stretched out before her, an a la carte menu. For the first time in years, certainly since her marriage, she felt truly independent.

But first, she anticipated getting home from work before dark.

Half a mile from the Comfort On Call property, her musing was interrupted by her cell phone's chirp. She glanced at the device but did not reach for it. Any message could wait until she was safely parked.

At her employer's gate, she turned in and skirted a large, shallow puddle. While making a mental note to ask if the gravel would be topped off, she glanced at the garage portion of the building. A water stain beside a downspout reminded her that the roof leaked. Since the first of the year, the company had lost precious storage space. She sighed, aware roof repairs had greater priority than gravel.

Janet's phone chimed. "Okay, okay, I'll look," she muttered and reached for the phone. A moment later, she glanced at the number, blinked, and stared. "Carter? Why is she texting? We talked yesterday morning." Snippets of the recent video chat session with the entire group from Navy boot camp darted into her memory. The five women spoke often and planned joint vacations. "Everyone was well."

She retrieved the message and read the text in a whisper.

—Call me ASAP. Regarding Sims. Carter—

After reading the message a second time, she tapped in the programed San Diego number for Carter, one of her best Navy buddies. If Sims, another of their close-knit group, forgot to give a bit of news yesterday, why not make her own call? Sending information secondhand was out of character.

Carter picked up in the middle of the second ring. "Thanks for calling back."

"What's going on?" She opened the truck door and watched a gray cloud, heavy with rain, grow on the horizon.

"Are you sitting down?"

Janet stayed in her seat. "Affirmative. Getting ready to walk from my truck into work."

"Sims is dead."

Dead? Sims? The formerly friendly air turned into a great invisible weight pressing on Janet's chest. She looked down at her feet, counted to three, and found her voice. "Say again."

"Sims died last night."

Janet stilled, the only sounds a stuttering heartbeat and a groan of unknown origin.

Silence—no—more like a struggle for breath, came from the phone for long seconds. "She was killed by a drunk driver late last night. Her husband called an hour ago."

"And he asked you to notify the rest of us." Janet finished the sentence and leaned against the head rest. *Sims*. Her buddy was gone in a moment due to a careless drunk. Didn't the world know she needed her friends—all of them? She blew out the breath she'd been unaware she held. "The others? Do they know?"

"Holt hasn't responded yet. I expect the delay is due to the time zone difference."

Janet nodded. Holt remained the only one of the quintet on active duty, currently stationed on a Pacific island near the International Date Line. "She'll get back to you."

"I don't have details yet. I'll be connecting with Sims' husband later today. Paul…well…he sounded in bad shape."

"I imagine." She blinked away the urge to cry and sought distraction by scanning the parking lot.

Pat Maguire, one of the two brothers who owned Comfort On Call, exited his dented pick-up and approached. "My boss is headed toward me. I've got to go clock in. Will you send me the details via email?"

"Affirmative. Take care, Johnson-Zwingel."

"Back at you, Carter." The sign-off spilled from her lips automatic, perfected and polished during hundreds of calls during three decades. She disconnected the call and closed her eyes for a moment. Five of them held their regular video conference session less than twenty-four hours ago. Sims had been alive—vibrant. She'd shared a joke currently going around the San Francisco police precinct where she worked.

"I can't believe she's dead." Janet drew a shaky breath and reminded herself Carter would never lie. "I don't want to believe Sims is dead."

"Hey, Janet. Are you all right?"

She struggled to a higher level of alertness and brought Pat's lanky frame into focus. "Affirmative."

"Are you sure? You look like your dog died."

She concentrated on breathing normal and moistened her lips. "I don't have a dog." For an instant, looking into the familiar face, she was tempted to share the general contents of the phone call. A glance behind him, at another of the technicians arriving, squelched the idea. Sharing details of her private life with co-workers, or bosses, seldom turned out well. Working in an occupation dominated by men, she'd learned early to keep her break room conversations limited to baseball, the weather, and road construction. "I'll be fine."

"If you say so." Pat shrugged and waited while she locked her truck.

"The phone call…contained bad news. Let's drop the subject." She squared her shoulders and gripped the handles of her lunch bag and purse.

"How about I share good news to balance the bad?" He pulled a stick of gum from his uniform shirt pocket and unwrapped it. "Our deal with Sleep E-Z Motel went through. First of the units are scheduled to arrive in two weeks. Do you want dibs on the project?"

She clicked her mind into HVAC tech mode. "Motel unit replacement—sounds interesting. How many rooms?"

"Forty-six."

"Put me at the top of the list." Commercial installations beat dealing with hot, short-tempered homeowners anytime, even handsome men who apologized the following day. The only sort of work she enjoyed more were installations in new construction. But the contractors weren't accepting many of Comfort On Call's bids this year.

The instant they crossed the threshold into the building, Janet secured her invisible professional armor. She greeted the other techs as if the break in the heat wave was the only thing in the world which mattered. She half-listened to the banter about weekend parties. After greeting the receptionist/dispatcher, the only other woman employee, she picked up her first assignment for the day.

As she tapped the address for her first service call into her phone, one of Sims' favorite mottos blossomed behind her workday mask. *Live with gusto and soar.* If I can figure out the "how."

****

Easing the black police sedan in front of the ambulance, Rich pushed the transmission into Park. The first call of the day arrived while he studied the overnight reports and promised a busy Monday. Three regular patrol cars crowded at the edge of a modest parking lot. A fourth marked vehicle pulled to a stop across the two-lane road as he opened his door.

His new partner, Cal, looked at him over the roof of the car, his height and build consistent with a professional football player.

Rich gestured for Cal to begin with the victim and ambulance crew. He strode toward the uniformed officer directing traffic. "Are you the first officer on the scene?"

"Yes, sir. A mechanic arriving for work made the initial call. I arrived three minutes later."

"And the mechanic is…?" He scanned the growing number of personnel at the scene.

The officer pointed to a thirty-something man in dark blue coveralls next to the building. "He's shaken but cooperative. I told him to stay put until detectives arrived."

"Good first step. Tell me the rest of the situation."

"Victim is middle-aged, white male. He was laying at the edge of the parking lot. I noted bruises on his face and blood soaking through his pants. No weapon was visible in immediate area. He was semi-conscious when I arrived. Paramedics arrived on scene six minutes ago." The officer paused and pointed toward the narrow shoulder on the road. "A blood trail comes up the hill."

Rich nodded in the appropriate places and jotted a few notes. "Take another officer…" He beckoned over a new arrival. "I want the two of you to follow the blood trail and mark it without disturbing evidence. Keep a sharp eye out for a weapon. I'll talk to our witness. Consider handoff complete."

A few minutes later, Rich completed the mechanic's preliminary statement. Pressing a business card into the witness's oil-stained palm, he looked the man in the eye. "Thanks for your assistance. We'd appreciate you staying available for follow-up."

"I don't plan on going any farther than home." The

mechanic pulled off his dark cap and skimmed a forearm across his brow before he gestured to an arriving pick-up truck. "My boss just drove up. Do you want to talk with him?"

"Absolutely." Rich intercepted the owner before the wiry man entered the tire and auto repair shop. Three questions into the interview, Rich acknowledged his partner's arrival with a nod. Keeping his attention on the local businessman, he moved to the next question. "What's down the hill?"

"Not much until you get on the other side of Butler Creek. Only one building between here and the cluster of freeway exit stuff up on the flat."

"What sort of building?" Rich set his pen against the paper.

"A vacant warehouse sits in the valley on the near side of the bridge. Used to be a carpet and flooring outfit. They moved out six, maybe seven, months ago." He tapped a cigarette from a pack. "You fellas gonna let me open for business?"

Rich glanced toward the uniformed officers and newly arrived crime scene technicians setting up a taped perimeter. "Aside from the lot on this side of the building, you should be clear." A moment later, he summarized his interviews as they walked toward a cluster of small, bright cones marking evidence. "My information's pretty generic. What did you find out?"

Cal flipped to his first page of notes. "Our victim is Ken Robard, white, forty-four, address in an unincorporated pocket of the county. He told the medics and me the entire thing is an accident. His background information should be arriving at the car's computer any moment now."

Accident? The statements from both the mechanic who'd reported it and the first officer on the scene indicated a crime. "Injuries?"

"Medics identified one gunshot wound to the left buttock. He has obvious bruises on face and hands. We'll know more after the docs at Meramec assess." Cal skimmed a hand over his shaved head. "Want my opinion?"

Rich nodded.

"All injuries were several hours old, not received at this site, and in no way are we dealing with an accident."

Rich allowed a brief smile. A concise opinion properly labelled was the best kind. "I sent two officers to follow the blood. Let's go see what they've found so far." He pulled out his gloves and gestured for a crime scene tech to join them as the first rain drops hit their shoulders.

The blood trail stopped a dozen feet in front of a gate in a ten-foot high chain link fence. While the crime scene tech photographed the blood already dissipating in the light rain, Rich continued to the barrier and looked toward the warehouse beyond. "Today's our lucky day—gate's open."

After obtaining photographs of the chain, unsecured padlock, and the "For Lease or Sale" sign, Rich swung the gate wide and led the group into the property. He started searching on the right side, Cal the left, and the tech remained ready to photograph, bag, and tag any evidence discovered. Rich spotted the first solid evidence halfway to the warehouse office door. "Here—shell casing." He patterned his gaze out in a circle from the spent cartridge. "A second one."

"Got it." The tech positioned a numbered marker before clicking a photo and transferring the evidence to a plastic bag.

"Cigar," Cal shouted from beside the loading dock.

Rich squatted near the second shell casing. He sighted toward the gate and studied the line of fire. From here to the closest blood drops would be an easy shot—in adequate light. Glancing up, he pivoted and counted the lights on the exterior of the building. Lighting would be sufficient—if they all worked.

For the next half hour, Rich and Cal inspected the crushed gravel and broken asphalt around the empty warehouse. They collected a few items, including a disposable lighter, but no additional shell casings or weapon. Rich checked the doors, found them locked, and made a note of the exact address and basic description in case they applied for a search warrant later.

Walking up the hill to their car, Rich stripped off his gloves and tucked them into a jacket pocket. "You can read me Ken Robard's biography on the way to the hospital."

Meramec Medical Center—thinking the name sent a chill up his spine. He acknowledged the hospital was a fine facility with a top-notch trauma center. But each time he conducted interviews on the premises, he fought an internal battle. He'd spent too many hours in the institution—worrying and watching.

****

Janet turned the porcelain table clock and studied the grime-coated brass back. Overhead, the dining area ceiling fan turned at medium speed, helping the A/C unit combat a hot Monday evening. She pressed her lips and discarded the notion of starting a Sims memory conversation. Speaking too much would bring tears. She reserved crying for late nights when she was alone.

At the other end of the table, Ashley assembled construction paper apples for a classroom bulletin board and hummed the alphabet song.

The tranquility was only a thin coating over inner turmoil. Inside Janet's head, images and memories of Sims raced each other in tight circles.

Laughter, instigated by Sims, during the group video chat. The sound, from little more than twenty-four hours ago, repeated clear in her mind.

Trying on hats beside her in the tourist shops of El Paso ten months ago.

Janet swallowed back a memory and set the screwdriver in the first slot. Images of five women invading restaurants off the beaten path after long, morning hikes put a tremble in her hand. Five—we are a group of five—not four. The rational portion of her mind knew a group of four would gather in San Francisco on the date of the memorial service. "Cremation followed by burial at sea," she whispered the highlights of the most recent email. "Live with gusto and soar."

"Was that comment for publication?" Ashley rubbed a glue stick across a green paper leaf.

"No." Janet shook her head. During her hours of troubleshooting A/C units and calming nervous clients, she stayed focused in the present. The activity and immediacy of her job cooperated to keep the recollections brief and infrequent. But her workday was over. While fixing supper, she'd read, reread, and replied to Carter's email. The reality of her close friend's death slipped through her defenses, dragging in a new wave of memories. She started the clock's repairs to keep her hands busy and the recollections brief.

"Where did you get such an ornate clock? It's not your usual style." Ashley gestured toward the cherub and flower decorated timepiece.

"Same place I buy most of my clocks—an estate sale. This one happened to be in Ballwin—back in March." Janet switched to a different screwdriver from her array of tools. "Before you ask, yes, the sale was in one of those subdivisions where I can only afford their discards."

"I thought your taste ran to wooden cases. Are you showing a new facet to your personality?"

"I saw a challenge. The works should be similar to the one behind you." She poked her tool in the general direction of a walnut and brass mantel clock ticking softly on the small buffet.

Ashley glanced over her shoulder toward the timepiece. "After you restore a couple more, you can hold your own sale."

"I'm considering selling on one of the computer sites. What do you think?" She focused her gaze on Ashley's face for a long moment.

"You should be careful. Don't let potential buyers come to the house." Ashley met her mother's look.

Janet dropped a tiny brass screw into a paper cup. "Good idea. I'll suggest a parking lot with decent lighting and camera coverage."

"Dad called yesterday."

Stilling her hand, Janet pressed her lips until the cold wave in her stomach ebbed. "Did he ask for money?"

Ashely met her mother's gaze for a brief moment. "Not directly. On at least some level, he knows I don't have any to spare."

Janet settled the screwdriver into the slot of the next fastener. "I reminded him of your general financial status on Saturday. He hinted for me to invest in his next project, but I cut him off before he went into details."

"He has his eye on a food truck." Ashley glued two green leaves to a red apple shape.

Twisting her tool counterclockwise, Janet broke the next screw loose. "I hate to think how much money that business will swallow. Does he have a partner? Or does he think one person can manage the entire operation?"

"He claims to have one person willing to work with him, but he avoided giving me a name. They need funds to convert a panel truck. I tuned him out when he asked me for possible investor names."

Janet ignored her growing interior iceberg while aware knowledge was her best preparation and defense. "He was asking around on Saturday. Did you hear any comments from Daniel's relatives?"

"We stayed on other topics." She paused with the glue stick poised above another leaf. "Oh, one of those subjects was the rehearsal dinner. Elizabeth plans to contact you about venues."

Janet nodded. Working with Daniel's mother for the wedding was one of the brighter spots on the horizon. She could think of two or three possible venues for a rehearsal dinner near the church. Perhaps together, she and Elizabeth could figure out a way to involve her own mother in more of the planning. "I'll add consulting on rehearsal dinner to my growing task list."

"Topic switch—tell me your opinion of Mr. Taylor. I saw the two of you talking over cupcakes."

Janet missed a breath. Why couldn't her daughter find a more soothing topic? She focused on the tiny maker's mark engraved into the clockwork assembly and worried her lower lip. "We talked. He's pleasant. He was a lot friendlier than on Friday."

"Friday? I thought—"

"Service call was on Friday. I broke my own and company protocol when I figured up the bill in his kitchen and accepted a glass of ice water." She blinked away an image of him standing on his patio with the phone almost an appendage to his ear. After the mention of the soccer coach connection at the party, she could almost picture him in a similar stance with a whistle around his neck and a clipboard in his hand.

Ashley glanced toward the ceiling and tapped the side of her head. "Now I remember. You mentioned it after the photo session. Did you know he's available?"

Available. She lost control, and the screwdriver clinked against the porcelain. "What are you telling me?" She thought for a moment to recall any reference to Rich's marital status.

"His wife died. I'm not sure of the date, I could check with Daniel, but I get the impression it's been well over a year. I think you should become friends with him."

"Who are you? Did your grandmother give you this idea?" Janet narrowed her eyes to slits and stared at her daughter. By silent agreement, neither pried into the other's dating life. The pact was easy to keep. Since Ashley started dating Daniel in the second semester of college, she'd kept other males as casual friends only. Janet kept her private life…well, private. She didn't feel any need to broadcast the rare first date which never lead to a second.

"An effort at friendship, Mother. I'm not asking you to elope next week." Ashley's exhale ruffled the stack of completed apples.

"New relationships get complicated at my age. Our histories, those long, convoluted personal events of our past, get dragged along into everything." Janet pulled the flattened, softball-size works free of the ornate case and set it on the white butcher paper. A glance at her hand revived the memory of Rich's handshakes, both of them, and sent a tingle to her fingers. She didn't dare let her daughter suspect the effect. She moistened her lips. "Widowed—explains why he brought his father to the party."

"Was he the man with the black cane? The one who had Gramps laughing every few minutes?"

"I believe so." Janet smiled and recalled the two elderly men holding an animated conversation in the shade of the deck.

"Then you definitely need to get acquainted. After all, Daniel's family celebrates holidays and milestones by inviting the entire clan." Ashley pressed the final paper leaves into place and reached for a plastic container.

"Just for my own information, did you tell your dad about the inheritance?" Janet pulled Greg's plea for investment from the bag of topics resting one layer below the subject which refused to exit—Sims' death. The entire family knew Janet's Great Aunt Lois, a rather wealthy woman, died six months ago. The inheritance being split between Janet and Jeremy, her brother, was not generally known.

Ashley shook her head until her ponytail swished. "I don't go around talking about your finances. Dad could be poking around in public records. He does follow the scent of money."

"Remind me not to smell like dollars." Janet cut her laugh short. Greg could cause real problems. The financial mess left in the wake of the divorce took her most of a decade to untangle and move beyond. After years of careful spending, and many letters to credit reporting agencies, she'd obtained a mortgage in her own name. Closing day, five years ago, shined as one of the top ten days of her life.

"Do you want to talk about Sims?"

The memory of Sims modeling her new summer haircut during their June video chat popped up in Janet's mind. An instant later, she blinked it away. "My mind's too unsettled, and the emotions are still raw."

Ashley packed up her project supplies and snapped the lid. "Will you listen to me?"

Janet sighed and nodded.

"After you told me, I've been thinking about her. Do you remember when she helped us move?"

"How could I forget?" The bank foreclosed on the house a few months after she filed for divorce. While specific days were a blur, she remembered being half-paralyzed due to the number of decisions forced upon her. Then Sims, with energy and keen organizational skills, arrived. Within a few days, Sims helped Janet find an apartment in the same school district and sort out which furnishings went to Greg, into storage with Janet's parents, or into the new place. "Live with gusto and soar."

"Is that a new bumper sticker slogan?"

"No...maybe...Sims signed greeting cards that way." Janet placed a small drop of fine oil on a stubborn screw.

"Do you remember the first night in the new place?" Ashley crossed her arms on the storage bin. "You were getting ready to fix peanut butter and toast for supper. While I was hunting for the plates, Sims comes in with a whole car load of groceries. I don't think I've seen you cry since."

At her daughter's words, Janet cringed. Now there was no possibility of ignoring the memory she'd pushed away a dozen times today. An hour before starting a simple meal, she'd hugged Sims farewell.

Instead of starting for home and getting a few hours of driving done before finding a motel, Sims went to the supermarket. She brought back enough groceries to stock the cupboards to overflowing with staples and fill the small freezer with chicken and ground beef. *I hide my tears better now.*

To disguise the tremble accompanying the memory, she drew a deep breath. She should give thanks. Her daughter was launched. Her own life was in order with a stable income, dependable truck, and adequate house.

"Well, I'm finished with my project. The teacher part of me advises you to take Sim's advice." Ashley pushed back her chair and stood.

Janet wrapped the cautious portion of her personality around her like a cozy blanket. *Live with gusto. Make friends with Rich.* Both...either...piece of advice seemed daring and dangerous.

Chapter Five

Flicking her gaze from mirror to mirror, Janet backed the company van across the threshold of the warehouse door. One more day, twenty-four hours of keeping her grieving for Sims in the shadows and the weekend would be here. She needed to hold it together for another half hour to chalk up one more work day.

She licked her lips and imagined a tall glass of tea, heavy on ice and lemon. After she unloaded the broken unit and tidied the van for tomorrow, she'd clock out and make a cool drink a reality.

Walking around the vehicle, she glanced up to see her boss, Mike Maguire, accompany a tall, thin, balding man out of the office entrance. The older and heavier of the Maguire brothers, Mike spent the majority of his time dealing with the business portion of the firm. The way she understood the division of labor, Mike dealt with contractors and prepared the bids for commercial projects. With an outgoing personality, he was more suitable for public relations than the taciturn Pat.

After securing the portable ramp into place, Janet stepped into the van. A moment later, she eased a broken residential unit down the incline and into the storage area. After stowing the broken compressor beside the other recyclable equipment and parts, she rolled her shoulders. She released a sigh, shedding a large portion of recent physical stress. Next, she gathered an assortment of fasteners and tubing to re-stock her vehicle.

Across the parking lot, Mike and the stranger continued in conversation beside a new model, black SUV.

Janet closed her van, climbed into the driver's seat, and studied the men. The stranger stood with his suit coat hooked on a finger while the wrist rested on his shoulder. His face, elongated by the lack of hair, appeared dominated by a generous mouth. *I need to stick with my own business.* After parking the van at the end of the row of operational company vehicles, Janet walked back into the warehouse and pressed the door control.

"Zwingel."

Pat's voice reached Janet an instant before the clatter of the descending metal door drowned out normal conversation. "I'm over here—getting ready to clock out and go home. What's up?"

"Mike wants to see us."

Us? Me? Her recent fantasy—a large cold drink—vanished at Pat's words. She thought over her work reports for the previous week. She couldn't recall anything out of the ordinary—certainly not something worthy of Mike's attention. "Did he say why?"

"Not exactly." Pat tucked his thumbs in his back pockets and shrugged.

Janet skimmed one hand across a pallet of crated residential units as she walked past. Maybe Mike was assigning her to one of the few, new construction projects. She discarded the notion an instant later. The situation reminded her of being ordered to report to the squadron commander for a reprimand. She glanced down at her dirt-smeared hands. "Can I take a minute to wash first?"

"Good idea. I'll snag a soda for each of us out of the management fridge."

She almost laughed. The fridge in Mike's office held a variety of soft drinks and bottled water. The public reason was to offer a cold beverage to salesmen and other visitors. She always suspected the majority of the beverages ending up diluting the liquor Mike kept in his lower left desk drawer.

Pat loped off toward his brother's office.

As she washed her hands and checked her hair in the small, restroom mirror, she allowed her mind to contrast the Maguire brothers. In addition to their different duties around the shop, they displayed distinct personalities.

Mike enjoyed flash. He presented a larger-than-life image to outsiders. With his new, large home, luxury car, and younger second wife, she felt a little of the same unease around him which she experienced when interacting with her ex-husband.

Pat, in contrast, worked beside the other techs during heat waves, cold snaps, and whenever projects called for an extra hand. He drove an older model, pick-up truck and lived in the same house, with the same wife, going on forty years.

Pausing to draw a deep breath, she steadied herself, and exhaled before opening the antique wooden door with a frosted glass panel and the single word, *Office*. Pulling the door behind her until she heard the soft "click" of the latch, she advanced to Mike's desk and assumed parade rest. "You wanted to see me."

"Have a seat, Janet. You're not in trouble. The

situation is exactly the opposite." He gestured toward the visitor's chair.

Picking up the soda from the chair seat, she obeyed and studied him. Mike was past the typical retirement age. According to company lore, Maguires didn't retire. Stories circulated of the founder, Mike and Pat's grandfather, dying while working in this same office. Today Mike's cheeks appeared more blushed than usual and either his shirt was a size too small or he'd gained weight. However, his expression was genial, a thousand times better than any of the displays of Irish temper she'd witnessed during the years. Out of habit, she glanced at his hands. *He's been boxing again.* The knuckles on his right hand displayed fresh bruises in addition to his 2011 World Series replica ring. She glanced at Pat and experienced an ease of her tension.

Pat straddled a plain chair, his favorite way to sit during informal meetings. He broke the seal on his bottle of soda and looked at his brother. "So, are you ready to tell us? Did you work out the details?"

"Not all of them." Mike drew a cigar from a ceramic humidor on his large, antique wooden desk. Examining the cigar and palming a gold toned lighter, he turned his attention to Janet. "As you probably realize, we've outgrown our facility. Proper repairs would be costly and not add much-needed space."

"I'm aware of our tight quarters." She held back a plea to get to the point. Every employee knew the vans hadn't been garaged for the last three winters. She muttered prayers and curse words at the vehicles along with the other techs on cold mornings.

"Roof leaks—we find a new one each rainstorm." Mike held the flame in front of the cigar and drew in the first mouthful of smoke. "We've been looking at other properties. Recently, Pat and I found a dandy. I understand you might help us—financially. In case I'm not clear, this is an invitation to purchase an interest in the company—ten, maybe twenty percent."

Did he know of her inheritance? How? Well, Greg found out. Someone along the line must have dropped a hint in a public place. She hid a swallow behind her soda and delayed a response for precious seconds. "You know my wages. My savings are modest. What made you single me out? Why not approach Tim? He's been with you longer."

"We found the ideal property. Vacant warehouse—sound condition—loading dock. and the building's got plenty of garage and warehouse space. Site's located a mile and a smidge from the freeway." Mike continued speaking, ignoring her questions.

"Are you talking of the Butler Creek property?" Pat rested his soda against the chair back.

Mike nodded. "We need to move on our proposal. Another party is interested. Real estate agent can only hold the site for a limited time."

Pat wrinkled his brow. "A competing offer is news to me. Is the bid real? Or are you repeating a rumor Al brought?"

"Al and I discussed the property—and other topics." Mike shot a stern look at his brother before turning to face Janet. "What do you think? You've been with us what—ten years? You know the business better than most."

"Twelve years." The words of his offer tumbled in her brain among a forest of caution signs and the word "gusto." The sensible course of action would be to step back and look at this business deal without emotion. She needed time for research. "You've surprised me. I thought Comfort On Call was a family company."

"Yes, we're the third generation. The next one's not interested. Only grandson showing potential is still in school. This building will fall into rubble before he's ready to take over." Mike toyed with the lighter, tipping the metal rectangle over and over against the oversize blotter calendar.

"I need information—hard facts and figures. I require some time to weigh the options." She listened to her heart pound at near double time, uncertain if excitement or panic fueled her interior. Holding tight control over her hands, she capped her drink and set the bottle on the floor.

Pat adjusted his arms across the chair back. "We know your work ethic, Janet. Your organizational skill is top notch. I'll confess"—he lifted his hands and displayed his palms. "I heard scuttlebutt of an inheritance back in May—when you took off those half days. Did you have other plans for the money? Are you eager to travel? Retire?"

"I'm fifty-one—too young to retire." She stiffened her already straight spine. The Maguire brothers didn't need to know her current plans for the inheritance were firm as fog. Comfort On Call was an actual, legitimate business. The evidence of years serving the community surrounded her on the office walls. Framed certificates from technical schools and one university business degree hung above the file cabinets. Dealership awards emblazoned with the Silver Star Enterprises logo shared wall space with half a dozen calendars distributed to customers throughout the decades.

In contrast, Greg talked of an idea and an unnamed partner. Knowing her ex, the entire project was heavy on dream and light on actual plans.

For a moment she steadied her gaze on Pat before she returned her attention to Mike. "The only promise I can make today is to consider the idea. I'll need to see tax returns, balance sheets, and bank statements. I'll want to review them with my accountant." She spun comments about Daniel's schedule through her mind. "I'm thinking a minimum of two weeks."

"One week would be better." Mike set his cigar in a heavy glass ash tray and pulled a thick manila envelope from a top desk drawer. "Here's a packet of papers to start with. Our accountant's card is included. I'll instruct him to release other reports on request."

Way too prepared. She stood and accepted the documents. Opening the flap, she pulled the bundle of papers out a few inches and scanned the column headings of the top sheet. She realized it was the proposed budget for the next fiscal year and nodded satisfaction. Ruffling through the papers, her tension eased when she spotted income and expense reports. "About the new property you're looking at—I'll need exact information."

Mike sorted through a short stack of business cards. "Give the realtor a call. I'm sure he'll be glad to show you around and give his spiel."

"I'll give an answer, either way, in two weeks." She tapped the papers back inside and fastened the metal prongs on the envelope.

"Sounds fa—" Pat flexed one hand.

"One week." Mike picked up his cigar.

"Two." She held up two fingers before turning for

the door. On her way out of the building, she couldn't ignore Sims' favorite motto making another lap in her brain. *Live with gusto and soar.* She stepped up into her truck, tossed the documents on the passenger seat, and voiced one of her own alternate endings, "Or crash and burn."

****

Thursday evening, Rich inspected each cell across the bottom line of a new puzzle. Checking for stray, unwanted words was the final stage. Soon, he would send the puzzle, a Missouri geography-themed search-a-word, to the magazine publisher.

What's that smell? He sniffed again. Smoke! Rising so suddenly he sent the desk chair careening into the treadmill in the cramped home office, he sprinted toward the kitchen. "What's burning?"

"Supper." Henry bent over in the center of the kitchen, both hands on his knees, coughing. "Blasted stove—" Another cough cut off his speech.

Rich ignored the blood pounding in his ears and glanced at the appliance where a skillet on the back burner poured smoke. He grabbed the handle with both hands. A moment later, he half-dropped, half-tossed the hot pan into the sink. A sizzle and a hiss filled the air. Bumping on the tap to full, he doused his hands first, then directed the water to the blackened lumps in the pan. "Gheeze, Dad. You know how to scare ten years off our lives."

Waving one hand in the general direction of the stove, Henry coughed once more. "I thought the burner was cold."

"You thought wrong. Why didn't…?" Rich stepped into the hall and eyed the silent smoke detector.

Henry turned away and pulled the string on the ceiling fan. "I took out the battery. Considering my cooking skills, I figured we'd have an accident. I don't need a squawking alarm adding to the confusion."

"You"—Rich snapped shut his mouth. The guilty party was neither a child nor a new recruit in clear violation of the rules. He and Henry would both be better off if he gathered some self-control. With a muffled curse, he jerked open the kitchen window and strode off to open the back door.

A few minutes later, Rich offered Henry a glass of water. Staring at the mess in the sink, he shook his head. The pan's non-stick coating appeared to be hanging tight to cubes and circles fused together. "What was supper…before?"

"Potatoes and sausage—one of your favorites."

Rich shook his head. "I'm on a low charcoal diet." Keeping a tight rein on his tone, he faced his father. "You climbed and removed the battery. Didn't your last fall and all the medical procedures which followed teach you anything?"

"Last tumble taught me plenty. I took my time. You've a dandy ladder in the garage. I even set the cell phone right at the bottom—just in case." Henry took another sip of water.

"Don't go climbing again." He still broke out in a cold sweat when he thought of finding his dad crumpled up in the bathroom. Rich wanted to wrap him in blankets—put him under house arrest—anything to keep him safe—and alive.

"Did someone give you a God badge?" Henry raised his chin.

Staring at his shoes, Rich silently counted to five.

Henry was a stubborn old man prone to ignore advice from children, doctors, and friends. "When the smoke clears, I'll put in the battery. I expect the smoke alarms to stay functional. If you get ambitious and want to clean the ceiling, put a long handle on the dust mop or whatever."

Henry grunted.

"No ladders—no climbing at all when you're alone. I want to keep you around and in one piece. Is concern for your safety hard to understand?" Rich kept eye contact with his dad.

"I tried to be useful. You shouldn't have to fuss with cooking after a full workday."

"The freezer's full of quick meals." He moved the trash can closer to the sink and transferred soggy, charred food into the garbage.

"Where the food and the carton taste the same." Henry thumped a chair.

Rich grinned. "They've gotten better. But you have a point." He opened a lower cupboard and grabbed a kettle. "Let's move on to Plan B. Supper tonight will be the one dish I feel confident cooking—pasta plus sauce from a jar."

Half an hour later, Rich pushed his fork into a mound of long spaghetti coated with marinara. The jar label claimed the sauce was roasted garlic flavor, but his palate categorized the taste as spiced tomato, just like all the others he'd purchased.

"I've been thinking." Henry speared a piece of lettuce from his salad.

"Should I be frightened?"

"You've delayed long enough."

Rich lowered his fork. He didn't need to ask for

specifics. For the previous year, Henry and other family members, plus several co-workers, expressed concern over his social life. The invitations got more difficult to turn down—come over and meet my sister, cousin or… He shuddered at the memory of one Friday. Three months ago, a fresh-from-academy officer suggested a popular happy hour spot to meet his mother.

Well-meaning people pushed him to find a companion and break out of his social slump. His son, Brian, was the only exception. The young man went the opposite direction, objecting to every change away from their tidy life as a complete family.

Rich viewed storing or donating an abundance of Mary's things and moving into a smaller house as positive steps.

Brian grumbled about the changes during every visit.

"Are you going into the matchmaker business with the rest of the world?" Rich picked up his ice tea.

"You could use more social life."

Henry's tendency to state a situation plain and simple was a mixture of comfort and curse. Rich understood the problem. He enjoyed social events with his friends. But too often, since Mary's death, he felt like the odd man out. He also didn't like being pushed. No matter how often he looked at the situation, the time failed to feel right. "My co-workers and I socialize. I know my neighbors, at least by sight. I'm not a hermit."

"I saw the way Ashley's mother looked at you on Saturday. Bet she'd accept if you asked her out for a drink—or coffee." Henry stared for a long moment.

"Janet was probably still placing me. The party was winding down, and we were eating cupcakes before I found an opportunity to tell her of the coaching connection." The memory of her smile, with a dot of white frosting at the corner of her mouth, flared like a welcome flame in his core.

"Janet." Henry twirled his fork in the spaghetti. "She's an attractive woman, divorced, available, and the right age."

He studied his dad and raised an eyebrow. He decided not to mention the additional facts he'd acquired at the same party. "Do I even want to know how you gathered this information?"

"Her father, Joe, and I have a lot in common." Henry paused with a fork full of spaghetti half an inch from his mouth. "I'd guess she cooks better than either of us."

Rich refused to look at his father. "Middle school students cook better than Taylor men." He concentrated on eating. He couldn't see any reason to admit the lady under discussion visited in his imagination every night. Last night, he dreamt of her laugh. The night before, she twirled on a sunny lawn until the uneven hem of her skirt billowed. Of all his casual female acquaintances, why did Janet invade his dreams?

Chapter Six

Janet adjusted the tote bag on her shoulder and stepped into the Quill Plaza Café. Drawing a deep breath, she savored the mixture of fresh coffee, cinnamon, and bacon. A person could gain weight from the Saturday morning air in the bakery cafe. She placed one hand on her yellow, fitted T-shirt to urge her stomach toward patience. *Good thing I worked out first.*

Avoiding the order counter, she glanced at the wall clock. The timepiece featured different bakery items instead of numbers and showed the current time as a muffin before bagel o'clock. She was five minutes early, exactly the sort of timing she aimed for. After a deliberate scan of the dining area, she exhaled relief. She liked being the first to arrive. Working her way past tables with adults waking to strong coffee and children hyped on fruit juice, she selected a small window table. The view, strip mall parking lot, wasn't special, but sunshine on the other side of the glass brought out her inner optimist.

Unzipping her tote, she pulled out a folder, ruler, pencil, and calculator. She slipped on a pair of rainbow-framed "cheater" eyeglasses and directed her attention to Comfort On Call's financial reports. Last night, during a phone conversation with Daniel, she'd received advice on how to compact the numbers into groups her layman's brain could grasp. He'd also provided the names of some additional reports to request and promised to look over the papers with her early next week. The addition of an accountant to the family already proved useful.

"Good morning." Rich rested his hands on the back of the opposite chair. "You're prompt."

She warmed at the voice and glanced at her watch before lifting her gaze to his face. The man arrived exactly on time. "Promptness is an old Navy habit."

"Explains a lot."

Matching his brief smile, she breathed deeply and detected a trace of mint. "Such as?"

"Efficiency...organization." He blinked and shifted his gaze off her face.

She made a quick mark on her paper, closed the folder, and removed her glasses. The numbers could wait. Rich deserved her attention. In an unexpected phone call last night, he'd invited her to breakfast at a place of her choosing. Perhaps if she got to know him better, she could squash Ashley's budding busybody tendency.

"Have you decided what you want for breakfast?" He slid his fingertips across the smooth wood of the chair back.

"Affirmative."

"Is your selection a secret?" He settled his mouth into a slight smile.

She forced her gaze from the open collar of his blue, button-down shirt and felt her lips curve into a grin. "I'd like a large black coffee, cinnamon roll, and fruit cup."

"Coming right up." He brushed back his windbreaker and reached for his wallet.

Is that? She blinked, and made a mental note to ask later. Perhaps he had a rational explanation for wearing a gun to breakfast. As she packed her papers, she watched him place their orders. Thinking back to conversations at the party, she realized no one mentioned his occupation. She'd heard comments about irregular hours and frequent overtime. How many occupations require wearing a handgun? Did he bring a firearm to the party? A shiver skittered across her shoulders.

He turned and looked in her direction.

Forcing a smile, she gave a tiny wave. She switched her thoughts to possible conversation starters.

At his arrival, she lifted the two large coffees off the tray. She took a quick inventory of the food as he transferred small platters to the table. He set her roll and fruit cup in front of her. A whole wheat bagel and cream cheese occupied his place, and an order of bacon claimed the center.

"To share." He pointed to the meat.

She licked her lips. While a favorite treat, bacon went direct to her hips. "Should I call you a mind reader or a tempter?"

"My name is Rich."

After the first, wonderful sip of coffee, she set down the cup and picked up her fork. "You have me at a disadvantage, Mr. Taylor."

"I prefer Rich among friends." He stirred one packet of sugar into his coffee.

"Are we friends?" She waited for his nod before picking up her suspended thought. "My occupation is known while yours remains a mystery."

"The relatives didn't blab?" He opened hazel eyes

wide. "Let's categorize me as a government worker, local government." He blew across the surface of his drink.

She regarded his short haircut and athletic physique plus the ability to talk in full, coherent sentences. Physical appearance and vocabulary left a myriad of careers. But she couldn't ignore the weapon. She interpreted the glint in his eye as humor and played along. Before her next sip, she voiced her second choice. "Are you a fire fighter?"

"Try again." He lifted his coffee.

Leaning back in her chair, she tipped her head and pressed an index finger against her chin. For only a moment, she pretended deep thought. "Since your hair is shorter than mine, I'll cross rock band drummer off the list."

He spewed coffee. Grabbing all the napkins on the table, he covered his mouth, swallowed, and mopped the spatters. After a moment, he rested an elbow on the table. "You get a point for blindsiding me. Last time I checked, the county didn't keep a rock band on the payroll."

"Points—I like that idea." She broke a strip of perfectly cooked bacon into two. "County is a nice clue. I can cross off the city and any of the dozens of municipalities." She took a bite of bacon and savored both the treat's flavor and the light verbal exchange. However, she didn't want to give the impression of being mentally slow. "Do I need to keep my hands above the table? Should I confess the last time I ran a stop sign?"

"You may skip the confession. Your hands…well, they're nice to look at." He peeled foil from the cream cheese container.

A self-conscious wave of warmth climbed her neck. She inspected her hands and didn't find anything special about short, rounded nails void of polish. Tiny scars, a result of working with sheet metal in close quarters, decorated the skin. Traces of grime and oil worked into the fine lines and caused stains, no matter how often she scrubbed. She resisted the urge to hide at least one hand. "So, you'll confirm law enforcement?"

He gestured toward the ceiling with one thumb. "I recently completed twenty-two years. I'm currently assigned as a detective."

"You have enough years to retire." She speared a cantaloupe cube. Another second looking into his eyes and she would lose control of hands, tongue, or both.

"Our...my...the plan was for me to retire after twenty-five. Then"—he glanced down for a long moment and drew a breath—"things happened."

His wife died. Ashley's words from early in the week rushed. For an instant, she thought of the photo on his wall, tried to date the picture, and failed. She reached across the table but stalled without touching him. "I'm sorry for your loss."

"Thank you. Although, after meeting your ex, I feel obligated to offer you condolences."

She shook her head. "My marriage ended a long time ago. On the other hand, you won't get an argument if you cross Greg off any sort of 'I'd like to know you better' list."

He leaned back. "I hear Henry hit it off with your dad."

"According to my information, the new friendship goes both ways." She appreciated a note of teasing in his voice. "However, returning to our previous topic—will you retire in three years? Do you intend to travel the world? Or are you more the sort to find a new career?" She cut off a bite of cinnamon roll.

"I haven't decided. My personal life got tossed into a fog bank, and I'm still working my way out. Life's temporary. Too much future planning gets messy...and disappointing."

Nodding, she chewed and turned her thoughts to the spring trip with her Navy buddies. The five of them...four of them—everything changed the night Sims died—had preliminary plans to visit Mount Rushmore. She concentrated to make her next breath even. "I agree."

"I do, however, often plan more than the twelve hours or so notice of today's breakfast meeting." He bit off a portion of bagel.

Meeting. She considered his descriptor and decided she preferred the word to date. What were the dating rules in this century? Did they even use the term anymore? And no, she was not about to ask her daughter for advice. "How do you want to continue? Do we ask questions or just spout biographies?"

"I'll defer to the lady."

She sipped coffee and assessed him. Too long looking at his face, with its intriguing character lines and easy smile, caused a tingle in her stomach. The sensation was totally unrelated to breakfast. She'd describe the feeling more like something long dormant stirring to life. "In case you had doubts, I enjoy my job. Mechanical malfunctions have specific solutions. Follow the logic and solve the problem. Unlike..."

"People?" He broke the silence after a few seconds.

She nodded.

"Most of us are harmless."

"I've heard rumors supporting your view." Janet banished a memory of a forward former neighbor. A woman needed to be careful when assessing customers and new acquaintances.

"You don't sound convinced." He darted his tongue to the corner of his lips, and a stray speck of cream cheese vanished.

Janet swallowed and blinked, but the delay didn't quench her desire to touch him. She wanted to test if the heat and tingle from their brief handshakes would repeat. "Between the Navy, co-workers, and customers, I've met samples from all portions of the human spectrum—from kind to creepy."

He laughed and set down his coffee. "I like your description. Do you mind if I borrow it the next time I orient a new officer?"

"I don't object at all. Let me guess—you interact with more from the devilish side than the angelic." She shifted her gaze to the tabletop. To her surprise, his laugh crumbled a portion of the shield around her heart. Unpredictable words tumbled out of her mouth when she looked at his face. "Please don't get the wrong impression. I don't often feel in physical danger."

"Neither do I. Movies and TV shows emphasize all the wrong parts of my job."

"A day in the life of an HVAC tech would cause an audience to snore." She heard his laugh and lifted her gaze to his face.

"I'll bet you've had some moments. The film director would compact the time frame and pick the right person to follow. Could you imagine yourself being a role model for girls who enjoy tinkering?" He pushed aside his empty plate and leaned toward her. "Speaking of movies—what are some of your favorites?"

"Are we talking current or classics?" She stacked the empty dishes and slid them to the edge of the tabletop.

"Either."

"Anything with Pierce Bronson." She blinked and sighed. Unattainable actors were safe.

"He seems to be a popular choice."

She detected an undertone to his words, evidently her screen idol didn't surprise him. "What was her name?"

****

"Mary." The word slipped out before Rich engaged his brain fully. He glanced at his left hand. The sight of his bare finger reminded him she was gone, and his ring was stored in a box beside Grandfather's pocket watch. He lifted his gaze to meet Janet's. He detected expectation in her pretty blue eyes.

"Let me guess…Mary had a thing for Pierce Bronson."

"She did. We…our…DVD collection includes all of his Bond movies." He lapsed into silence, thoughts of the hundreds, perhaps thousands, of times he'd shared a café breakfast table with his first love swirled in the background. How many times had they traded opinions of movies and TV shows in a setting fragrant with coffee and pastries? With his next sip, a realization clarified. The memory didn't hurt. Speaking her name and thinking of happy times didn't put a stone in his chest. "I suppose you want to hear more."

"I'll listen." She set one forearm along the edge of the table. "Would you like to tell me about the family portrait in your living room?"

Leaning back, he searched for a starting point. "Mary insisted on a professional sitting before her first chemo treatment. At the time, I considered the idea foolish. Later, I appreciated her thoughtfulness." He rubbed a hand across his short, silver flattop. "She lost her hair. Mine lost its color."

"Sympathetic hair response?" She lifted her coffee and one eyebrow.

"Are you composing the headline for a medical article?"

Janet flattened her lips. "I'm sorry if I sounded flippant. I like your hair. It gives you a certain aura of authority."

"Remind me to point out hair color as an authority feature the next time a rookie balks at an order." He leaned forward and laced his hands on the table. "Our son is Brian. He's in his final year of dental school in Kansas City. The daughter is Rachel, Ashley's long-ago teammate. Last year, she took her marketing degree and followed a young man to Atlanta. Currently, she's a little cog in a big corporate wheel."

"The young man—is he still in her life?"

Rich nodded. "He's decent and intelligent. I'll be disappointed if there's not a wedding after he finishes grad school at Emory."

"I understand."

Do you? He knew Ashley and Daniel maintained separate apartments. From his perspective, Janet was more skilled in getting her daughter to view a wedding as the start of a new life chapter, rather than a mere punctuation mark in a relationship.

He looked into her eyes and felt a magnetic pull. Deliberately, he glanced out the window. Yes, her eyes matched today's sky. "We've talked enough of children for the moment. Should I ask the traditional St. Louis question?"

"You want to know where I attended high school?" She looked out the large window for a long moment. "Consider me a reluctant graduate of Lambert High. I hated most of my time in the classroom. The brightest spot of any school day was shop. Science labs were tolerable." She lifted her coffee to her lips.

"I believe you've explained your decision to join the military." *Hands on training.* He recalled the concise enlistment explanation given by the handful of women veterans at work.

"My parents were disappointed. My brother, Jeremy, thrived in college, and Mother had dreams of me following. But my brother and I are very different. He can handle theories and visualize all sorts of things by studying formulas and descriptions. I do better when I can see or feel results." She shrugged before leaning back. "College and I would have been disastrous right after high school."

Rich held back the questions rising in his throat. *Let her tell the story.* Similar to a witness interview, he'd learn more if he let her direct the conversation.

"I met with the recruiter several times during my senior year. After my eighteenth birthday, I signed the paperwork to make my decision a done deal before I told my family."

He filed the information about a brainy older brother for a future conversation. Wait—he tightened his hold on his coffee. Okay, he'd consider her a friend. She was easy to talk with and appeared to have a sense of humor. "How long did you stay?"

"Four years—I took a discharge after one enlistment. I'd found my career and made some fantastic friends."

Rich glimpsed a shadow cross her eyes at the mention of the friends. *She's not a witness.* Pressing the point today would be out of place.

"After my discharge, I returned home, earned a technical school certificate, and started a full-time job. I decided to live where I could keep an eye on my parents. I married Greg and had Ashley. A decade later, we divorced. I've concentrated on parenting and survival—nothing exceptional."

Before he blurted a contradiction, he stilled his tongue. From where he sat, she faced life with confidence, making forward progress rather than wallowing in the past. He blinked away memories of retreating to murky, numb grief day after day. Thankfully, the worst of the smothering thoughts eased when he moved out of the other house. "I'd say you thrived. And you are exceptional. I've met your ex."

She laughed for a moment before she lifted her coffee cup lid and frowned.

"Empty? Allow me to get refills. Then we can compare notes on something other than high school."

When his second cup of coffee was almost gone, he glanced at the wall clock and hid surprise. For an entire half hour they'd exchanged stories of their former neighborhood and a few selected tales of raising teenagers. Standing and gathering their table trash, he brushed her hand. The brief contact sent a tingle up his arm. He drew a quick breath, his professional armor against showing emotions and surprise suffering a dent. "I've got an errand list to tackle. Want to share a table again? I could give you a call in a day or two to set the details."

She toyed with the straps of her tote. "My week's uncertain."

"I understand irregular schedules. I'll call. We can see what happens." Rich held his breath until she responded.

Chapter Seven

Thursday afternoon, Janet followed the real estate agent's crossover SUV off the freeway. She was on her way to inspect the Butler Creek warehouse before she went further into the Comfort On Call financial reports. In less than a quarter mile, the cluster of businesses at the exit faded from view and the road narrowed.

The road, two-lane asphalt with narrow gravel shoulders, hugged a hill during a descent to an elderly bridge over Butler Creek. The scene gave the illusion of rural with shrubs and stunted trees covering the slope.

Gentle curve. Scarred guardrail. She cataloged driving features by picturing herself in a large box van, carrying a load of new furnaces. The route was manageable. Sparse traffic flow eased a multitude of infrastructure faults.

On her next glance to the left, she spotted the vacant warehouse. The first descriptive words which popped into her mind included large, utilitarian, and abandoned. The dark gray building with a flat roof and five roll-up doors impressed with size, not beauty. Painted concrete block reminded her of the older, practical structures on military bases. The warehouse certainly failed any standard of fancy, perhaps even attractive. Then again, she needed to assess the site as a location for Comfort On Call, not her personal residence.

Janet pulled to a stop beside the realtor's vehicle outside the facility gate. The moment she exited her truck, a yellow flutter in the dark bushes caught her attention. *Is that construction tape?* She took a few steps toward the snagged plastic and read black words on yellow. *Wait. Police tape.* She waved for the realtor's attention and pointed toward the plastic ribbon. "What's the story?"

The stout man in a cheap suit turned from the lock box and looked where she gestured. "I don't know. I haven't been here for two weeks."

Two weeks. Unless another agent at the firm showed the property recently, the information didn't agree with Mike's urgent words. She expected a serious buyer would inspect the property. Wasn't an on-site viewing standard procedure? She filed the information with a mental question mark before pulling out her phone and tapping the note-taking application.

A few birds called to each other from the brush and scrubby trees on the steep slope behind the building. A peaceful atmosphere, complete with an insect drone background, currently filled the tiny valley. She focused on the scene before her.

A large graveled lot with a few patches of asphalt stretched from two sides of the building. The graded area stopped only a few yards from the creek. Across the stream, the hill rose a good sixty feet to the main road.

"I think you'll like what you see inside." The agent unlocked the gate and swung it open wide enough for pedestrians.

"What was here before?" She followed at his heels.

"Tony's Discount Carpets. This building served all

six retail outlets. The founder died last year. The heirs closed up shop and moved out six, maybe eight, months ago."

"I remember some of their closing sales TV commercials." She frowned. Non-cheerful memories of the business came forward. Apartment management, during the time she and Ashley lived in the mid-century complex, often purchased from them. One day, she happened to observe one of their installation crews in action and crossed them off her list of places to patronize. "Has the site gotten much interest—aside from Comfort On Call?"

"Mr. Maguire's the most serious. This place needs the right client. A heating and cooling business sounds like a good fit." He led her to a platform with a steel door marked Office. The area, a small extension of a loading dock wide enough for one truck, bore an edging of chipped yellow and silver paint. "I think you'll like the interior."

Half an hour later, Janet agreed the office, storage, and garage areas were close to ideal for their purposes. The space was triple the square footage of their current building. The walls, windows, and doors looked sound, and the concrete floor appeared devoid of all except minor cracking. The vans would benefit by being under cover at night. She walked out of the large door farthest from the office. Continuing in a straight line toward the creek, she counted her paces to the edge of the gravel.

Pausing, she studied the slope the final yards to the water. Today, the creek ran at a trickle. Shallow water, less than three feet across, rippled over a rocky bottom. She thought back to the weather over the last two months. St. Louis was having a typical, dry end to summer. Turning, she scanned the outside of the building. After a full minute, she spotted a stain, a high-water mark on the loading dock. She tapped another question into her phone app.

"Where are you going?" The real estate agent called from beside the second large door.

"Around the back—do you care to join me?" She crossed two fingers on her right hand in a silent wish he would decline. Terrain hazards were certain. Wildlife at this time of day should be minimal. Keeping track of another person, even an ethical real estate agent, on the windowless side of an isolated building would be an additional task.

"Go ahead. I'll meet you at the other end."

She raised a hand at him in a thumbs-up signal before pushing aside a honeysuckle bush. Stepping deeper into the unknown, she shifted her phone back and forth between apps for photos and notes. She found the sort of beer can and plastic bag debris common to all vacant spaces. Downspouts, water stains, and the packed earth against the outside wall she considered important enough to photograph in several areas. Once, she scrambled up on an old metal drum and peered at the roof. The view from the slightly higher vantage point revealed at least two trees in need of trimming.

"Did you find anything interesting back there?" The agent greeted her at the foot of the office steps.

Janet brushed a few flakes of dead leaves and dirt off her long, uniform sleeves. "I didn't find anything unexpected. I do have one important question. When did the creek last flood?"

****

"And now you know my history with mantel

77

clocks." Janet rinsed the plates and set them in the dishwasher. Summer twilight lingered outside the window, casting a peaceful, timeless mood over the neighborhood this Thursday evening. Inside her home, she fought off the sweet scent of blackberry pie tempting her to indulge in a second serving.

Rich, a personification of a different temptation, sat at her dining table.

"You should take the last piece of dessert home for Henry."

"His appetite is already taken care of. If you recall, a large wedge was missing when I walked in." He fingered the edge of a red-and-white cloth placemat.

She brought a roll of clear plastic wrap to the table and covered the remaining generous piece of blackberry pie. Rich's visit, with dessert, turned out to be the exact distraction she needed after inspecting the Butler Creek warehouse. "I thought a mouse named Rich attacked dessert during the drive. Guess it's a good thing I'm not the detective."

"I could never have eaten so neatly in the car." He spun his hand from chin to waist. "You would have seen berry stains around my lips, not to mention pastry crumbs on my clothes."

"Thanks for telling me what to look for next time." *Next time.* At her own words, she swallowed back surprise. She caught a glimpse of herself in the patio slider and sighed. Her reflection showed the need for more gym sessions. Nothing could be done about the hips; they were inherited, along with the rest of her larger-than-average bone structure. But she could tone her arms to last year's standard. "Do you need a keeper around baked goods?"

He patted his stomach. "I'll admit to a sweet tooth. Tonight's dessert means an extra-long workout tomorrow."

"You're lucky. The gym doesn't make the numbers budge a bit for me."

"Muscle weighs more than flab."

"Thank you, Mr. Fitness." She flashed him a smile and noted a slight curve to his mouth. "Actually, I use the gym machines to maintain upper body strength. The only solution I've ever found for my waistline is diet." She paused for a moment, questioning why sharing personal information, such as gym and eating habits, felt comfortable, rather than awkward, with Rich.

For years, she'd put primary importance on the ability to do her job effectively rather than the raw number on the scale. Could she still lift and hold a wall-mounted evaporator? Could she wriggle in and out of crawl spaces? Lifting her glass of ice tea from the table, she led him into the living room.

"For the record, muscles look good on you. Only men with the brain of a dinosaur think strong and pretty can't share a package."

His words struck deep and curled into a warm spot in her chest. She couldn't recall the last time a man called her pretty. She'd worn a dress to the last Comfort On Call holiday party, but the few comments she remembered ranged from "looking good, Zwingel" to Mike's careful smile and nod of approval. "Why does that comment make me think you've worked with a woman partner?"

"Because I did?" A laugh invaded his smile. "She was, still is, a smart officer. Don't see her much after she transferred to another precinct and got promoted."

"Smart to transfer away from you? Or do you mean 'good at her work' sort of smart?" Settling on the couch, she patted the cushion beside her.

"She's an excellent police officer and deserved the promotion. The transfer became a good career move."

"And now…do you have a regular partner?" She tried and failed to imagine him in any of the popular detective pairs on TV.

Rich shrugged, eased down, and left a generous hand width between them. "Assignments vary by the case. Currently, I'm getting used to a new partner. For the record…I avoid shop talk. Leaving my work at the precinct was a rule between Mary and me."

"Okay—thanks for the information." She brushed an invisible crumb off her jeans before crossing her legs. "Are you familiar with Butler Creek—the area where Old Cabin Road crosses?" If not focused on his face, she would have missed his double blink. Was it surprise, or something deeper, in response to her question?

"I have a pretty good recollection of the area. Which side of the freeway are you referring to?"

"South—maybe southeast." She waited an instant for his nod before continuing. "I went over and looked at a potential new building for Comfort On Call. An old carpet warehouse is available. The building is the only one in the valley. Would you know about flooding?"

Rich leaned back against the throw pillow and tipped his head. "I know the place. Yes, the creek floods. I'm not sure how often, but I remember the bridge being closed at least once when I wanted to cross."

"I suspected a problem. You've just reinforced my

plan to check the highway department records."

"Good idea." He leaned forward and reached for a photo album lying on the coffee table. "May I?"

"Go ahead. You might get a laugh or two out of my wedding pictures." She ignored a ripple of uncertainty skimming her shoulders. She didn't show photos to new male acquaintances. Then again, didn't his profession imply a certain level of confidentiality? She uncrossed her legs and sipped her drink.

He stilled. His hands hovered for two ticks of the nearest clock before he pulled the book to the near edge of the table.

She chuckled and set her drink on a coaster. "The photos won't bite. Before you ask, no, I don't usually have them out. Ashley wanted to look at them for ideas. She'll probably find more things to avoid than to copy."

"I expect you were a beautiful bride."

"All brides are beautiful—and optimistic. Cheerful smiles are front and center in the code." She edged forward until their shoulders were even.

"A code?" He glanced from the album's cream, embossed cover and raised his eyebrows.

"Absolutely. The bride's portion is extensive." One glimpse at his face and she felt a pleasant warmth spread under her ribs. She directed her attention to the hand touching the album. *No. Keep the mood light.* She forced her mind from the silent invitation to touch and returned to the current topic. "The code for the groom is simple. He needs to arrive where and when requested dressed as instructed."

"I remember that part." He flipped the book to a random page. "Hats?"

"A style which died a quick, merciful death." Janet

studied the photo of her with three bridesmaids. Beside her, Sims wore a pale blue dress and held three, long-stemmed pink roses in a death grip. Blinking back an unexpected tear, she glanced over to the walnut steeple clock on the bookcase. The familiar, steady beat offered reassurance.

We looked... Young, she decided. Each of them wore expressions beyond optimistic. She saw eagerness and enough confidence to change the world—without assistance.

Now...the world's the same and Sims is gone. My friend's earthly remains are packed into some sort of temporary container under the care of Paul, her widower. Janet lifted a hand to her cheek and blinked her tears into containment. These moments of grieving surfaced at the most inconvenient times.

"Nice sanctuary." Rich skimmed a finger across the photo of the decorated church interior.

"My parents attend there. Ashley's not an official member, but the current pastor agreed to perform her wedding." She eased closer, reached to turn the page, and brushed his arm.

"Hi, Mom and—. Oops." Ashley burst into the room, wearing a bright white T-shirt with the St. Louis Public Schools logo emblazed in navy. "Should I go out and give a warning knock?"

Heat flooded her face, and Janet half-expected to scorch her finger when she touched her neck. The sight could not be unseen. Would the cozy scene give her daughter too many ideas? She straightened. "Too late. Why don't you get some tea from the fridge? And you're welcome to the pie on the table. Tonight's dessert is courtesy of Rich."

"I ate a late supper." Ashley dropped her purse on the floor and disappeared into the kitchen. "Oh, blackberry. Is it homemade?"

"Anna's Bakery." Rich tossed words in her general direction. "I know better than to attempt a pie."

"I thought your generation learned to cook." Ashley leaned back into view with an empty glass in her hand.

Janet rested her elbows on her knees and tapped her fingers together.

"My mother made a few attempts to teach me. I found more interesting things to do."

"Cooking's such a basic skill, not knowing sounds inconvenient—at the least. I'm glad Daniel knows what to do in a kitchen. Sharing food prep makes life easier."

Janet listened to the familiar sounds of the ice dispenser and the fridge door replace her daughter's voice. "You'll need to forgive her. Greg is a capable chef. She developed the notion all men his age and younger can cook. Her grandfather, by contrast, struggles to use a can opener."

"Mark me down as a throwback to your father's generation. The microwave is my friend—followed by the freezer." He replied in a soft, private voice.

Adding his name to a mental list of people who might appreciate a home-cooked meal, Janet increased the space between her and Rich on the couch. A few moments later, she sipped her tea.

Ashley returned, set her drink on a coaster, and sank to the carpet in a cross-legged position. She reached over and rotated the photo album. "I see you found the pictures."

"I knew exactly where they were all the time."

Her daughter glanced at her. "So did I."

Janet froze in the middle of a breath. *How?* An instant later, logic returned. The album wasn't exactly hidden. Pre-digital camera photos and vacation memorabilia filled half a dozen boxes stacked in her closet. Ashley lived here during college summers. Depending on what sort of hours her daughter's temporary job required, she'd had all sorts of time to explore storage places.

"Earth to Mom." Ashley waved an extended arm.

"Just startled." She blinked and forced a smile. Present company prevented her from asking what other items her daughter stumbled across. One packet of letters remained in the box she'd delayed destroying for too long. "I'm glad you had the manners to ask."

****

For an instant, while Rich moved his gaze from Janet to Ashley and back again, he detected a flash of unpleasant undercurrent, he took a mental step away and kept his mouth shut.

In his experience, the silent, or heavily coded, conversations between women required a special set of skills to untangle. He'd run into some difficult ones on the job—and one memorable one at home. Evidently, fathers were not welcome, even as observers, in mother- daughter discussions involving boyfriends and house party weekends.

Ashley shrugged before flipping the album to the final page.

He risked a glance at Janet, surprised to find a neutral shape to her mouth. *Situation defused?* Tension slid off his shoulders.

"Baker." Ashley pointed to a blonde bridesmaid

dancing in a reception photo. "I'd forgotten she was in your wedding."

Janet uttered a soft sigh. "Baker and Sims."

Rich picked out a sad note in the way Janet said the second name. If she were a witness, or a suspect, he'd dig deeper. Reminding himself she was a friend, he discarded the first question in his mind. "Are they some of your Navy buddies?"

"From day one of boot camp—five of us," Janet lifted her glass. An instant later, she returned the empty container to the coaster. "We enjoyed some good times."

Ashley leaned forward and directed her words to Rich before silence could settle. "Bright ladies—every one of them. I think of them as a tribe of friendly aunts. They'll all be invited to the wedding. We won't know until close to the caterer's deadline how many will attend—with all the travel involved."

"Not enough." Janet's voice trembled above a whisper.

Aware he was the outsider without a need-to-know, Rich held back questions of where these special friends lived. He studied Janet for a long moment. She fascinated him with her small easy smiles which widened or vanished in the blink of an eye. He wanted to learn what brought her joy and present her with a steady supply.

Ashley flipped to another photo from the reception and pointed. "Here—I found a good photo of your cake. I want this classic design."

Rich looked at the simple, three-tiered centerpiece. Flowers, rather than a plastic statuette, adorned the top. He supposed the frosting swags around the edge of each layer had a name reserved for celebration cakes.

"Instead of spring flowers, I'll ask the bakery to do holly." Ashley lingered a finger along the bottom margin of the photo.

"Holly's fitting for the season." Janet leaned forward, her attention on her daughter and the photos.

Rich pushed to his feet. If he didn't get away from wedding photos and discussion soon, he'd brood about a different album all night. He'd packed the book with other photos in the office closet. Months ago, he'd gone looking for a different memento in the same box and the photo set into the cover evoked unwelcome memories. The happy times in his wedding album lacked the possibility of shared laughter while reviewing the pictures. Could he ever face his loss head on?

Daily, he felt a dull ache when he looked at the family portrait in the living room. The photo stayed on the wall because of Brian. On moving day, while most things remained in boxes, his son searched out and hung the familiar photograph. Rich followed the path of least resistance and stayed quiet on the issue. Glancing at one of the several clocks in the room, he cleared his throat. "I'll leave you ladies to your discussion."

"Nice to see you again, Mr. Taylor." Ashley glanced at him before flipping the page to another photo.

"Why don't you call me Rich? We'll be semi-related after Christmas."

"I'll do my best to remember." She paused on a photo of the groomsmen surrounding her father and shook her head. "Nope—no black. I want the occasion to look like a wedding, not a funeral."

"Have you talked to Daniel about tuxes?" Janet stood and walked around the coffee table, pausing to look over her daughter's shoulder.

"He favors gray. Like"—Ashley looked around the room and pointed to a steel gray and red pillow—"that. In fact, may I borrow the cushion? We're going to the tux place on Saturday."

"A dark, rich gray will be perfect with Daniel's fair coloring." Janet tucked in her lower lip.

Rich noted Janet's body language and labeled it as her "thinking" pose.

"I don't have a problem loaning the pillow," Janet continued. "But remember, your grandfather's only suit is black. I think he'll fight the idea of renting a tux."

"Hmmm." Ashley leaned away from the album and focused her gaze on him. "What do you think, Mr...Rich? Should grandfathers be exempt from the wedding party dress code?"

"I think the effort necessary to get Henry into a tux would be exhausting. He wore a regular suit to his own wedding—and mine." He mentally slapped away another image, Mary in her family's white, lacy wide-skirted, wedding dress. *Please, Rachel. Choose a different dress.*

"Talk men's dress code with Daniel. But if I have a vote, I'd let Joe wear his regular suit."

Janet's voice placed a gentle period to the topic. He extended a hand. "Will you walk with me to the car?"

She blinked and contracted her brow for an instant before her lips curved into a tiny smile. "I'll be back in a minute."

Circling a hand in the air, Ashley flipped to another photo. "Don't do anything weird. Neighbors keep an eye on your place."

Weird. He'd asked the question to obtain enough privacy to issue an invitation. If he could steal a kiss, or even a substantial hug, well, he'd consider it a bonus. Walking across the lawn, he matched Janet's steps and offered his hand. "Do you have plans for Saturday—mid-morning and after?"

Clasping her hands behind her, she matched his steady pace across the lawn. "Saturday…I need to grocery shop…after I check out a few yard sales. Why do you ask?"

"Would you like to go to the zoo?"

She paused and turned toward him. "Are you asking me for a date?"

"Henry will be with us." He stopped beside his car and weighed her word choice. "Does a third person make you feel better…or worse?"

"I like Henry. A trip to the zoo sounds lovely. I've not visited for a couple of years now."

"Good—I'm glad you agreed. My father gets a late start some mornings. How about if I call you before we leave my house, probably after ten?"

"Sounds good—gives me time to spend money at the supermarket."

He reached out with his left hand, touched her chin, and caressed her smooth skin with a thumb. He wanted to linger touching her. Her soft skin warmed his sensitive pad. Interpreting the look in her eyes as more curiosity than either welcome or fear, he steadied his trembling fingers.

She licked her lips. "Saturday…"

"…At the zoo." He leaned closer and kept his touch on her chin light. "You…and I…"

"…And Henry," she whispered.

He closed the fingerbreadth between them and brushed a chaste kiss against her mouth. He wanted more…the brief sample stirred desire rather than giving satisfaction. Before he had time to expand and repeat the gesture, she turned her head. "Did I overstep?"

"Too much temptation."

He hid a joyful, double heart thump behind a calm exterior. "Temptation. I'm familiar with the feeling, but usually the object is dessert." He smiled from the safe distance of six inches. If forced to describe his inner turmoil, he'd start with a stick prodding something deep inside of him out of hibernation and continue by comparing it to the first breath of fresh air on a spring morning. "Saturday—after ten—I'll call."

Chapter Eight

In response to the buzz, Janet swatted at the air. The annoying sound continued. She moved her hand again and brushed her ear. Startling to a higher level of consciousness, she listened. The tone repeated. Was this a dream—about bees—with audio? Did the blackberry pie not mix well with white zinfandel? The late treat tasted fine Friday night.

She rolled over. The sound repeated. An instant later, after groping on the nightstand, she gripped the phone. "Johnson-Zwingel here." Blinking, she brought the digits on her alarm clock into focus. Zero three thirty—no one called at such an early hour. Unless— no, she couldn't afford to lose another friend.

"Janet. Let me in."

Greg's voice jarred the remaining thin blanket of sleep from her mind. "Where are you?"

"Outside…front door…please."

"I should call the police." She exhaled and pushed her free hand through her hair. In a fair world, ex-husbands would be penalized for disturbing people before sunrise.

"No. I came to talk. It's important."

She sighed. If she hung up, he'd call back. Greg could be persistent and thick-headed. He was just the sort to make enough fuss for the neighbors to call the police. For all of their sakes, she'd go and talk to the man. But she'd not let him set one foot inside the house. "Sit and wait. Normal people are asleep."

"Please, Janet—hurry, I wouldn't be here if the topic could wait."

Nodding even though he couldn't see her, she got out of bed. Important—he favored the word, often without pausing to think of the effect on others. In her world, the only things urgent enough to wake others in the pre-dawn hours involved blood or flames. By the glow of the tiny light outside the bathroom door, she located jeans and a T-shirt on the top of the laundry stack. Fumbling around for sneakers, she muttered. "Impulsive—inconsiderate—you never pay attention to basic manners."

"Cut the commentary, Janet."

"You better be right about the emergency part of this conversation." She disconnected the call, sighed, and stepped into the bathroom.

A couple minutes later, she checked her pockets for keys and turned the deadbolt. She slipped out to the concrete porch and tugged the door, not releasing the knob until she heard the "click" of the latch. She shivered for a few seconds until her skin adjusted to the pre-dawn cool air. Street and porch lights punctuating quiet darkness indicated a neighborhood at rest.

Greg, hands clasped behind his back and face tipped to the ground, paced a small oval on her lawn. At the edge of the street, his car stood as a darker shape within deep shadow.

She moistened her lips and sought a conversational volume. "Did you bother to check the time before you called? Three-thirty in the morning is outrageous. What can't wait until daylight?"

"I need your help."

Remaining on the porch, within the semicircle of yellow light from a single porch lamp, she crossed her arms. Moving a hand, she made sure her phone was visible. She didn't request this conversation and intended to keep it short. "Do I need to repeat my question?"

"I heard your question plain and clear the first time. It's…you see…well…Pam kicked me out."

"One point for her." Janet gave a mental thumbs-up to wife number three. A moment later, she turned her building laugh into a cough. The man in front of her, even flabby, could physically overpower her in an instant. If he charged her, she wouldn't have time to dial the final one for help. "I'm figuring Pam didn't lock you out on a whim. How long have you been gambling this time?"

"How typical of you to blame me for everything. I didn't give her cause." He stopped pacing and mirrored her stance. "You've always been quick to criticize me."

"You make an inviting target. Now answer my first question. Why are you here?" With each blink, her eyes adjusted better to the subdued light. She silently disapproved of his clothing choice—a cartoon T-shirt and tight shorts.

"I need to be at work by five."

She shrugged. "So?"

"I can't go dressed like…" He gestured to his casual wear.

"Don't you keep an emergency set in your car—or at work?" She thought back to a hard lesson she'd learned on her first civilian job. An unsecured water pipe gave way during a furnace installation. Drenched, she completed the task but lost valuable work hours during the drive home for fresh clothes before the next call. Since then, she kept an emergency bag behind the truck seat. "Nothing in this house would fit you."

"I know."

"There's a twenty-four-hour big box store three miles west. They should have something in your size." She re-crossed her arms. Talking with Greg in the middle of the night reminded her of reasoning with a four-year-old.

"Money…please…fifty bucks should be enough."

Janet closed her eyes for a moment and tucked her lip, searching for polite words to replace the curses lining her throat. "Let me guess what happened. Your wife locked you out. Did you go to the casino?" She waited for his nod. "You lost everything in your pockets, and now you want me to buy you a set of work clothes. Did I miss much?"

"I can pay you back. I'll stop at the bank after work." He drew small air circles with his hands.

She glanced up at the fading stars. How many times would he force her into a variation of the same conversation? "My memory's still intact, Greg. You'll forget. First, you'll delay the errand a day—then a week—and then forever. I've been down this road before." She paused and carefully chose her next words. "Ten years ago, I caved to your pleas and loaned you cash for Ashley's birthday present. You've paid back exactly zero."

"I've changed. I've even taken some of your advice." He reached into his pocket and displayed a worn, slim wallet. "I don't have a credit card. I pay strictly cash for gas and incidentals. Following your financial preaching is why I can't go to an ATM and had to come here. I promise I'll go to the bank today." He tapped his chest with one finger. "You won't even notice a blip in your own pocketbook."

"No." She pointed toward his car. "Go and humble yourself to Pam. Beg and plead with wife number three to toss a set of clothes out the window or something. I'm done with you." She drew a deep breath and counted to three. "I'm finished with your foolishness on the topic of money."

"Janet." He stepped forward with his hands open.

She reached behind and paused with a hand on the knob. "Why don't you just leave? You could accept the consequences at work. Maybe your co-workers will take up a collection."

"Where's your compassion? You've always had a good heart."

Compassion? Was he referring to her actions the day she filed for divorce, changed the locks, and left half a dozen boxes of his clothes and personal items in the driveway? Her supply of sympathy and patience scampered off to hide when Greg mentioned money. "Flattery will get you nothing—go away."

She opened the door enough to ease inside. With quick, sure motions, she secured both locks. Leaning her back against the smooth wood, she listened to the clocks tick and her heart pound. By the time she'd counted a full minute another sound reached her—a car starting and pulling away.

A quarter of an hour later, realizing an attempt at sleep was futile, she stood in the shower. Her thoughts circled around Greg's words quicker than the water slid off her body and swirled into the drain. Did her kind and generous actions match her beliefs? Had all the striving for independence and security since the divorce tilted her moral base?

She shook her head and reviewed her half of this morning's encounter. Toweling off, she tallied recent charitable actions. She contributed money to a variety of non-profits and mentored students from a local vocational school one month a year.

Experience made her attitude toward her ex unique. The accumulation of sleights reached some sort of tipping point a few years ago. Civility when speaking to him required an effort.

After drinking one cup of coffee, Janet studied a street department report. The little bridge across Butler Creek closed for a day or two during the spring rains in four of the last five years. A bridge closure limited access to the warehouse. Did critical portions of the lot itself remained unflooded? She removed the drugstore reader glasses and set them on the reports. Glancing at the nearest mantel clock, she spoke to the empty house. "We're working around a leaky roof, steadily getting worse. Do we want to exchange the current problems for a flooded floor? The numbers aren't helping. Where did the money for building maintenance go?

Standing, she opened the slider and stepped on the deck. She breathed in cool, dawn air and imagined the extent of Mike's anger at a refusal. Would he fire her on the spot?

****

Early Saturday afternoon, Janet eased to the side and allowed several children to get closer to the glass in the zoo viewing area. The youngsters wore matching orange shirts emblazed with a church logo. Two adults, wearing similar tops, answered a jumble of questions.

Releasing a contented little sigh, she shifted her weight. Bright sunshine cast short shadows at the feet of all the creatures, visitors and residents, of the St. Louis Zoo. Beyond the glass and a steep, deep ditch, a mother and child elephant dipped trunks into the quiet pool and drank. The animals looked placid, almost bored, with the babble of humans.

Henry stirred in the rented wheelchair two steps away.

"Water?" She reached into her tote and pulled out a dark blue water bottle.

"No. I'm fine." He laced swollen, arthritic fingers. "Have you ever ridden an elephant?"

"I've never had the opportunity." She smiled at one of the children a moment before a chaperon gestured the group to move on. In a blink, she returned her attention to Henry. Elephants, at least of the animals seen so far today, were clearly Henry's favorite.

"Back in the day...when I was young, poor, and energetic." He laughed. "A long time ago."

"I've a decent imagination." Her mind rolled years off the elderly man in front of her and found an image resembling his son. Her mental portraits of the Taylor men were under constant revision and expansion today.

Henry tipped his face toward her and half-closed his eyes. "They gave rides here—at the zoo. You paid a fee, and Miss Jim carried you and oh, a dozen others, not sure of the number. I came out here with some buddies the week before I reported for the army. We had a grand time."

"Did you only have the one ride?"

He nodded. "I think they took us twice around the

yard. It was a wonderful view. On my next visit, a ride didn't work out. And then…the world changes, life happens. I've looked back many times and felt grateful I took the opportunity."

"Live with gusto," Janet whispered while watching the elephants.

"What did you say?"

"I was just repeating something a friend used to say." Janet turned her attention to a second young animal shaking a bundle of hay into mouthful portions.

"Like I meant to say a minute ago. You get an opportunity. You take it."

"Opportunity for what?" Rich strolled up and paused behind the wheelchair.

"To ride an elephant. I think your father was giving a sales pitch." She skimmed her gaze over Rich. She admired the ease he exhibited while wearing a thin, nylon jacket over a golf shirt on a warm day. His simple explanation when they'd gotten out of the car returned. *No sense in advertising my handgun.* In a blink, she told her imagination to erase a few years. By the time she opened her eyes two breaths later, the image of Rich with dark hair and holding a clipboard—like a coach, vanished.

"Prepare yourself to hear all his best stories. You're a new audience." Rich pulled a water bottle out of a jacket pocket.

Henry harrumphed. "Nothing is wrong with my elephant stories."

"I didn't say there was. I'm merely stating facts. I've heard them all—multiple times." Rich took a large swallow and snapped the lid back into place. "Speaking of opportunities, a moment after you left the other area,

Raja came into view. Then the docent arrived and answered questions."

"Raja." Janet repeated the name of St. Louis' favorite zoo son. "Did you ever go to his birthday parties?"

"Once—I think he was three. Or maybe Rachel was three. Either way, the scene at the elephant yard was pure madness. I grabbed the first opportunity and took the kids to see the bears."

She laughed at the image his words prompted. "I agree with your description. I braved the happy hoard twice with Ashley. My parents brought her other times."

"Knew there was a reason I liked your girl." Henry clapped his hands.

"Is that your test for new friends—must enjoy elephants?" Rich leaned close and whispered to Henry.

Janet savored the interplay between the two men. In another thirty years would Rich have the deep smile creases on his face? Would the twinkle still be in his eye the instant before he laughed? Her stomach rumbled, and she pressed a hand flat against the lower portion of her shirt, failing to silence the soft growl. "Sorry, my lunch alarm is ringing."

"I could do with a bite," Henry commented.

"Two votes for lunch. I'll make it unanimous." Rich released the wheelchair brake and grasped the handles. "Do I hear any objections to eating by the lake? We'll have fries with a view of flamingos. Speak up if you want to stop between here and there."

Janet walked beside Rich, stepping behind when traffic on the paved path required. Memories of previous trips to the zoo jostled each other when their trio passed signs to the various groups of animals. She opened the colorful map and located her favorite area, Big Cat Country. Henry favored time with the elephants, but before leaving the grounds today, she wanted a moment watching the tiger.

A young couple holding hands slowed in front of a concession stand and shared a quick kiss.

She closed her eyes for a moment while her lips and skin re-lived the brief, light kiss from Thursday. *Did I miss a chance for gusto?*

****

A short time later, a babble of voices bounced around the large, quick serve, dining area. Rich backed away from the cashier and lifted the tray high. Skirting around parked strollers and free-ranging children, he sighted his goal. The moment the tray containing three chicken sandwich meals was secure on the condiment station, he reached for two small paper cups.

"Big appetite today?"

Glancing up, he widened his smile at the tall, lean, young man with a black, short trimmed goatee. "Hi, Adam. I haven't seen you for a long time. How are things?"

Adam, Brian's best buddy since junior high, pulled a few napkins from a dispenser and added them to Rich's tray. "I'm keeping busy with work. Is Brian with you?"

Rich shook his head. "Not today." Adam and his son continued their friendship through high school, when they often arrived as a pair for meals. Their bond survived college at different schools, and Brian often arranged to see his friend during visits to St. Louis. "Dental school and his part-time job keep him on a short leash. I do expect him to come home over Labor Day. You're welcome to drop over."

"I might stop in—or at least give him a call." Adam took one step back and extended a hand toward a young lady wearing a red, floppy brimmed hat. "I want you to meet someone."

A few moments later, introductions complete, Rich pointed to the deck dining area. Janet stood like a beacon beside Henry. She moved her hands in circles and swirls while she talked. The arm motions set the hem of her loose, gauzy shirt swaying over a clingy tank top. "Enjoy the sea lion show, and don't worry. I'm not eating alone—Dad and a friend."

Adam turned to look out the generous window wall. "Good deal. Greet your dad for me."

Aware of the younger man's gaze, Rich lifted the tray and weaved his way toward the shaded table.

Janet met him part way and picked up two of the drinks. "We were almost ready to send out a search party."

"I ran into a friend, or more precisely, my son's best buddy." He set the tray on the table and unloaded the meals. The shade, fresh air, and the sound of splashing water combined to send thoughts of active cases into the shadows. He sharpened the line dividing his personal and professional lives.

"Adam?" Henry took a sip of soda. "What's he doing these days?"

"Courting." Rich froze his lips.

Henry laughed. "Smart lad. Zoo's a good place for young love—or old."

Yes, wait. Rich narrowed his eyes at Henry but stayed silent. The older man's expression held a spark of mischief. The brief, frequent smiles reminded Rich of a man enjoying the role of puppeteer—or matchmaker. He'd be better off not analyzing Henry's motives and simply enjoy a pleasant lunch in cheerful company.

He chewed a bite of chicken flavored with sweet BBQ sauce and watched Janet bring a ketchup-dipped french fry to her lips. Kissable lips—sweet and soft according to the brief touch the other night. *Forgive me, Mary.*

"What's on the after-lunch agenda?" Janet lifted her sandwich.

"Lady's choice. How are you holding up, Dad?"

"I'm doing fine. Janet keeps reminding me to drink."

"Water's a good thing. The day's getting warmer. What are some of the shady attractions?" She curled a hand around her drink, sipped, and swallowed.

Rich glanced in her direction in time to watch the mouthful of soda travel down her throat. His body mimicked the action. A desire for a repeat test of her lips, with multiple chapters following the introduction, stirred a portion of him out of dormancy. He pulled moisture into his mouth. "Penguins."

"Of course." She lowered her drink. "Do you want to get downright chilly for a bit, Henry?"

"Polar bear's over there, too. What's your favorite, Janet? I took a lot of time with my elephant friends."

"Tiger." She released the word without hesitation.

Rich nodded and hid a portion of his smile behind his sandwich. "Tiger" from her lips evoked an image of the animal—sleek, strong, and watchful. He unfolded the zoo map and anchored a corner with his diet cola. "I think we have a plan. We'll spend some time with the cold weather animals, then we can walk up the hill through the antelope before finishing our visit with the big cats."

"What about you? Do you have a 'must see' before the day is over?" She dipped another fry.

Raising his gaze over the deck rail, he took in the placid scene. Flamingos stood on one leg, each dozing in the shade. Pelicans, ducks, and swans floated closer to the shore, alert for humans ignoring the signs not to feed the birds. His favorite zoo animal? He couldn't recall the question being asked before. Every trip here was with others: his parents, Mary, the kids. He enjoyed every visit and each section of the grounds. Well, most—trips without a visit to the reptile house rated above the others. Shrugging, he glanced at the map again. "I'm not fussy. It would be nice to see the prairie dogs or zebras."

"Good choices." She dabbed her lips.

Tiger. He studied Janet while taking final bites of his smoky spiced chicken sandwich.

She ate her meal neat and precise. Reaching for a fry at the same time her hand darted into the basket of potatoes, he confirmed one other feline quality. She was protective. No doubt, her company made today his best zoo visit in years.

He tuned in to the music from the carousel behind them. Should he? Would she accept another invitation?

Chapter Nine

Rich propped the putter on his shoulder and walked beside Janet. This Friday evening, the popular mini-golf attraction catered to a young crowd. *Younger than us.* He scanned the groups of teens and families with young children. He didn't see another head of gray hair in the place. Maybe he should have suggested a movie instead of an outside activity before dinner.

Claiming a spot on the wooden bench, Janet stretched out her legs and sighed.

"Good week?" He focused on her profile and admired the delicacy of small, gold hoop earrings. Temptation to reach out and hook a stray lock of hair into place swirled in floral-scented air—either from her shampoo or the potted plants at the check-in booth.

"Today ended well. I had some doubts earlier."

"Care to talk?" He glanced over and silently encouraged the two adults and three children at the first hole not to hurry. A slow round equaled more time with Janet. He hoped conversation with her meant less time to puzzle over a current case, one which showed all the signs of a serious money laundering scheme in the county.

She shrugged. "Today's primary accomplishment was staying coherent and firm when I gave final refusal to my boss' investment option."

He fumbled the neon green golf ball he'd been idly

tossing a few inches and catching over and over. "An investment? He must pay you better than I assumed."

"Union scale."

"A thrifty person can build a reserve." He understood exactly how far middle-class wages went with careful planning. Until Mary's illness, the two of them consistently increased the retirement account and paid a portion of Brian and Rachel's college expenses. But their savings had been far from enough to start a business, or purchase a share of an existing one. Investing didn't square with the scraps of information surrounding her divorce. "However—"

"I don't care to discuss finances. I'm just glad the discussion is all over, and I still have a job on Monday." She pushed against the bench and stood.

He experienced an unfamiliar urge to make her concerns his own. Listening to her doubts and fears and triumphs grew from politeness to genuine desire. How had she gone from turning down a business proposal to being grateful for a job in one leap? But he'd drop the topic, at least for now. "How long since you've played this game?"

"Putt-putt golf?" She caught her lower lip in her thinking pose for a moment. "We came here for a fiftieth birthday. Not mine, so…two years ago."

He exhaled relief. "Thank you. After you agreed to golf, I started to wonder if you'd be some sort of super player who practiced multiple times a week."

"You must have me confused with someone else. I'm the woman who repairs clocks, remember?" She smiled brief but wide.

Nodding, he avoided saying how strong the results of her hobby impressed him. The first time he'd been in her house and all the clocks chimed the hour, he'd held his breath until they stopped. The various bells and tones brought back stories of a European monarch going mad trying to get all the palace clocks in synchrony. "Sounds like we might be even on tonight's challenge. Care to make a little wager?"

"I don't bet money." She dusted off the seat of her dark capris before leading him to the starting mat.

"I wasn't thinking of cash stakes. More like…oh…winner of each hole gets to ask the other a question—no money involved. Are those terms agreeable?" He stepped back to give her ample room at the first hole.

"Anything?" She glanced with wide eyes.

"We could establish a limit. How about we allow one 'no comment' if the topic gets too personal?" He gripped his pimpled golf ball tight before he looked at the sky for an instant. *Please avoid cancer and Mary questions.*

"I'm good with a quiz. Prepare to give answers, Mr. Detective." She turned her attention to her ball. In one solid hit, she sent it rolling into the road construction motif of the first hole.

Rich concentrated on his game and won the hole by one stroke. "Are you ready for your question?"

She smiled enough to reveal even teeth. "First, I'll give you a word of warning. I give honest answers."

"Truth should be a pleasant change of pace." Out of habit, he checked the area for possible eavesdroppers while she placed her ball. "If you didn't live in St. Louis, where in the US would you pick? And why?"

"You've asked two questions." One quick swish of her club, and the bright pink ball rolled past a fiberglass hay bale and lightly tapped the foot of a cow. She stepped away from the starting position and adjusted her pink purse on its cross-body strap before speaking. "The answer to the first part is New England. Do I need to get more specific?"

"I'll accept a region." He placed his ball and lined up his shot.

"I've good memories of my time there. My friends and I experimented with a variety of water sports in the summer. The area has a real winter, the sort where you can plan snowshoeing or other outdoor winter activities more than a day in advance."

He glanced at her an instant before his club contacted the ball. *Snowshoes.* He couldn't stop his mind from replacing the pink T-shirt, denim capris, and silver tennis shoes with a parka, thick pants, and boots. All her enticing curves would vanish. "Winter hiking?"

"I found tramping across an open field or along a stream bank exhilarating. Of course, I was a few years younger the last time I went snowshoeing." She pointed toward his ball and shook her head. "I think you have a problem."

Removing his gaze from her, he discovered his ball had gone too far left and stopped in the plowed field trap. "One non-winter outdoor enthusiast reporting." He concentrated on the game obstacle and his next stroke put the ball one foot from the cup. He tempered a voice which wanted to shout. "Much better."

She studied her own golf situation for a long moment, tapped her ball, and jabbed a fist into the air as the ball dropped into the hole.

Sighing with acceptance of a minor defeat, he sank his ball on the next stroke. "Your turn."

Placing his ball on the starting marker a moment later, he listened for her question.

"Why does Henry live with you?"

"Do you want the long or short version of events?" He watched his ball climb near the apex of the arched bridge, lose momentum, and return to the bottom. He stared at the uncooperative ball, shifted the club to his other hand, and exhaled.

"Either."

"After Mother died, Henry got caught in a scam and lost most of his savings. His finances went from bad to worse. The real estate market was in a slump, which didn't help. He sold the house for a pittance and moved into a small apartment." He glanced at her eyes, detected interest, and continued. "A year or so later, Henry was in a car accident and experienced some health problems. My sister and I took away his keys. He moved in with me. The arrangement's been good for both of us."

He avoided specifics in the timeline on purpose. Six months after Mary died, he'd been so mentally dysfunctional that the necessity of watching out for his dad served as a thread to reality. "Henry needed hip surgery back in March. He went to Chicago and lived with my sister, Betty, during surgery and rehab. He returned in time for the party at your place."

"How thoughtful of him."

Rich shrugged to prevent chuckling at the mixture of sweet and sarcasm in her voice. "What can I say? Taylor men try." He reached out and laced his fingers with hers while they waited for the larger group to clear the next hole. A pleasant warm smoothness seeped into his hand, like a greeting from a friend after a long absence.

The questions and mood remained light and cheerful for the rest of the round. She answered one question with a description of her first car, a vehicle she and her father kept running until she left for the Navy. He confessed that his degree was in business, not criminal justice.

"Let's see…" He tallied the final score as they walked toward the counter to turn in their clubs. "I won overall by one point. I get to ask one final question."

"No outstanding parking tickets." She propped a foot on a decorative stone and re-tied her sneaker.

Cute. He allowed the banter she slipped into their time together to warm his mind with affection. He resisted the urge to wrap his arms around her in a public setting. Instead, he extended his hand and wished for her warm, comforting touch. "Where do you want to go for supper?"

****

"Every bite was delicious." Janet popped the last of a butter-and-garlic-basted breadstick into her mouth. Leaning against the faux leather in the booth, she surveyed other diners in the popular restaurant. During the drive from the mini-golf venue to supper, a calm settled around her. A cozy feeling of comfort and protection slid into the bench with Rich and lasted the entire meal. She lifted her wine glass and tipped it to capture the final sweet drops.

"More?" He extended one finger toward her glass while his other arm rested on the padding behind her.

"I'm good." She felt better, more relaxed than at any time in recent weeks. She minimized a sigh as the restaurant's sound system played a familiar violin classic. The tension from this afternoon's conversation with Mike vanished somewhere between Rich's call confirming the time of their date and the last sip of wine.

She sneaked a peek at his profile. He was more complex and interesting than she'd imagined. The layers to his personality revealed in his replies during their golf challenge increased her curiosity. If she moved into his side, would he drop his arm around her shoulders? Or was he concerned with appearances in view of other patrons? She pressed her lips and stayed still. Conversation between friends stood a great distance from cozy embraces. Exchanging words on a variety of topics—from first cars to baseball to most memorable vacation—left her both satisfied and hungry for more.

Touching him brought a different, unfamiliar sensation. Even brief contact revived thoughts of high school experiences. Waves of exotic hormones made seventeen memorable and packed with life lessons. She reminded her present self to pay attention to her practical education and stay wary of the internal candle lit by a casual touch.

The server stepped to the end of the table and stacked their dinner plates. "Did you save room for dessert? Our specials tonight are raspberry cheesecake and chocolate molten lava cake."

Janet shook her head. "No thanks. I'm pleasantly stuffed."

"I'll take a refill on my coffee and the check." Rich turned his attention to Janet after the server stepped away. "Stuffed? Like the Thanksgiving turkey?"

"Or a new pillow. I really need to hit the gym

tomorrow—early." She did a mental re-organization of her Saturday. She didn't see much room for a visit to the gym. Tomorrow was a scheduled mother-daughter day. Also known as find-the-wedding-dress day. What if she moved the alarm half an hour? She closed her eyes for a moment and recalculated the time necessary for workout, stop for gas, and getting the most vital groceries. *Not enough hours in a morning.* She pushed grocery shopping to what she hoped would be a decent gap after tomorrow's late lunch.

"Quill Plaza?"

"What?" Pulling her mind back to the present time and place, she faced Rich. "Sorry, you caught me thinking about something else."

"Do you go to the gym at Quill Plaza?" he asked.

"I average three times a week, but four visits would be better." She made a mental note to speak to the trainer about changing her routine. Recently, her workout felt stale. In addition, she was falling victim to the desserts Rich brought over or the ice cream he suggested. "While you're enjoying your coffee, may I ask a bonus question?"

"As in?" He tipped his head and kept his mouth in a neutral line.

"The one I would have asked if I'd not botched the last hole of our golf game."

"Go ahead." He took a sip.

"You've been to my house. You're aware of my fascination with clocks. Do you have a hobby unrelated to police work?"

"Word puzzles."

She traced a tiny circle on the table at the boundary of smooth wood and inlaid tile. "Do you mean you enjoy working the daily crossword?"

"No. My hobby is creating the 'find the hidden word' variety. Did you know there's a small publisher in the area? My puzzles are included in workbooks for home schooling and the occasional magazine." He scooted away a few inches and retrieved his wallet.

She tipped her head and focused on his face. In a short paragraph, he'd shattered her assumption of published material being created by language experts ensconced in drafty East Coast apartments. "I'm not very good at those. I always miss the words going from right to left."

He smiled for a moment. "Ever think all you need is practice?"

Word puzzles. Word games. She shook her head. Most of the time she avoided them. When trapped in waiting rooms, she tended to read outdated magazines or a book if she remembered to bring one. "I'll stick with mechanical puzzles. Thank you."

"Won't hurt my feelings."

"What's on your agenda for tomorrow?" She startled herself with the topic change.

"Work. Criminals always seem to have someone on duty, so it follows for the police to do the same."

She curved her lips into a smile to acknowledge the half-laugh tucked beside his words. Glancing at his hand curled protectively around the clear glass cup, she cataloged another instance of soft and strong in her intriguing companion. "Do you work a lot of weekends?"

"Enough. Our schedules are mapped out months ahead. Of course, they remain subject to last-minute revisions and overtime when pursuing an active case."

"I get the impression they work you hard." She could count on weekends and holidays off except in times of summer heat waves and winter cold snaps. Emergency call didn't roll around often enough to count—several of the other techs developed an informal pool over recent years.

"I'm used to the flexible hours and enjoy my job— for the most part. The work suits me and keeps the bills paid."

"That last bit is a very important point." She drew a quick breath at a mental image of her recent inheritance swirling around a drain shaped like the Butler Creek property. *It won't happen.* In a flash, she replayed this afternoon's meeting with Mike, Pat, and Al. Introduced only as a friend of Mike, the tall, balding man sat off to the side and said not a word during the entire time. She was uneasy to begin with, and the presence of a stranger heightened her tension.

In clear, simple language, she told the Maguire brothers she declined the opportunity to invest. She expressed a sincere desire for Comfort On Call to find a different source of funds or a better property. When Mike's entire face blushed to match the company logo, she steadied her breathing and stance to hide her fear of being fired on the spot. Standing in front of the antique desk at parade rest, waiting to be dismissed, had been the longest two minutes of her life.

"Are you ready to go?" Rich reached over and caged her wrist.

She nodded and continued collecting her thoughts during the walk out of the restaurant. "On the way home, could we take a small detour?"

"We could even take a long one. I started the

evening with a full tank of gas."

She laughed, the stress of the memory in Mike's office draining away. "I'm not asking to go on a road trip. My request will only add a mile, two at the most, from a direct route home."

"Where did you have in mind?"

"Sleep E-Z Motel." She pressed her lips tight the instant the locally infamous no-tell-motel's name emerged. What will he think?

He froze with his hand on the car door handle and narrowed his eyes.

Hot embarrassment climbed her neck. "No. Not for…not what it sounded like." Drawing a noisy breath, she followed with a sigh. One glass of wine seldom caused such impulsive words. She forced herself to connect with his gaze. "We're installing their new heating and cooling units soon. I want to get an idea of the building and lot layout."

"I'm torn between relief and disappointment." He formed a small smile and opened the passenger door.

She reached for the seat belt. "I should have kept my mouth shut and driven over on my own time."

"A side trip is not a problem. The location took me by surprise." He hurried around to the driver's seat. "I've never had a date request a motel before."

During the three-mile drive to the motel, Janet reviewed what she knew of the business's history. The building was constructed in the middle of the twentieth century as roads improved for easier travel. Over the years, the business shared both the boom and bust economic cycles. For the first decade or more, the motel was family friendly. Then the building fell into poor repair when corporate chains became serious competition. After several years, the location acquired the reputation of serving the questionable and neglected. Last year, new owners aired a series of radio spots to give the motel a fresh start at respectability.

Janet resisted asking how often police were called to the establishment. Rich didn't encourage shop talk. Stories surrounding the business could be—probably were—exaggerated.

"I'd forgotten the office is a separate building," she remarked the moment Rich turned into the property. Moving her gaze to him, she continued. "I've driven past on the street plenty of times. I've never stayed here."

"I didn't say a thing." He stopped in the wide space between office and main building.

"Two story with rooms opening direct to the outside." She nodded while confirming her memory. "Let's do a slow circle around the building." She alternated her attention between the actual building and the cars parked in front of the pale doors. Many of the vehicles were older, but a few, newer ones were scattered along the row. As they started the curve around the far end of the building, she saw a small, faded red sedan. Before risking a glance at Rich, she swallowed hard.

"Did you see something?"

"Nothing important." She blinked an attempt to forget Greg's car, distinctive by the bumper stickers, sitting beside a black SUV in the extra parking along the fence.

"Everything's important." Rich studied the gray building.

"But not everything is our business." Where her ex

went wasn't her concern. She remembered the agitated man on her porch nearly a week ago. Had he moved here? Unlikely. If Pam still had him locked out, he would have convinced a friend to let him stay. Odds, if she wanted to think in those terms, favored him being inside playing poker and losing another pocketful of money. Rubbing her palms down her thighs, she banished sudden, cold sweat.

"Did you see what you intended? Should I drive another circuit?"

Rich's voice pulled her thoughts back to the scene before her. "No need. I got the building in my mind now."

And more questions. The SUV beside Greg's car looked familiar. She shook her head to delete the thought. Hundreds of vehicles in the metro area fit the same description.

"Any more requests?" He stopped and signaled to make a right turn at the busy street.

"I'm good." She pulled out her phone, tapped the baseball app, and announced a new topic. "Cardinals lost." She sent the sight of Greg's car skittering off to a dark corner of her mind with sports—the safest topic in St. Louis.

"Don't rush. Let me get your door." Rich parked in her driveway and exited the car.

She took her time unbuckling her seat belt and gathering her purse from the floor. The hours tonight floated away. Holding hands with Rich sent pleasurable tingles through her arm. She savored the feel of his skin against her palm. Extracting her keys, she turned to him on the porch. "I had fun tonight. Thank you."

"May I?" He took the keys and undid both locks.

Pushing open the door an inch, he turned back, dropped the keys into her open hand, and placed his palms flat against the brick siding on either side of her head, forming a loose cage. He studied her face for a long moment. "May I?"

"Yes," she breathed. The seconds hung meaningless between them before his mouth dipped close.

He touched her lips.

Soft, warm, weightless contact started a tremble. She closed her eyes, exhaled, and relaxed her jaw in silent invitation.

He pressed against her mouth.

As the pressure became firmer and more urgent, she responded to his kiss. After a blink, she played the invader and plundered with her tongue.

He retreated an inch.

Through her hand flat on his chest, she felt a strong, rapid heartbeat in sync with her own. "I…have…no…words."

He kissed her again.

The kiss started short and firm. In an instant, he changed the pressure to sweet and lingering.

"Speech is overrated," he whispered against her cheek.

She opened her mouth and startled when a quick laugh escaped. Strength returned to her legs, and she laced her fingers behind his neck. The pleasurable carousel sensation in her mind tapered from whirlwind to walk. Leaning forward, she brushed her lips in a light kiss at the open throat of his shirt.

With one finger, he raised her chin.

She blinked once before she drowned in the twin

whirlpools of his sparkling, hazel eyes. Closing the distance, she stamped a kiss on his lips.

The neighbor's dog barked.

Janet's breath stuttered as she retreated half a step. *What am I doing?*

"Thank you…for the evening…for everything."

She imagined his words wrapping around her like a soft, comforting blanket. Easing thorough the door, she hesitated with one hand trembling in mid-air. "I…I…call me…not tomorrow."

"Stay safe."

She nodded and dug within swirling emotions to find a smile before closing the door.

For long moments, she leaned against the panel. Waiting, she listened to the ordinary sounds of car door, engine starting, and fading into the distance. With each tick of the nearest clock, she sensed her defenses, carefully built to protect her independence, develop fine cracks.

Chapter Ten

Glancing at the sky, Janet locked her truck. Fair weather clouds drifted on a robin's egg blue background and tempted her to linger and hunt for fanciful animals. But today was Saturday and she had plans. The most immediate task was wedding dress shopping with Ashley.

She walked toward the strip mall's bridal shop and rapped her knuckles against the trunk of a bright yellow compact without breaking stride. Ashley's car, in honor of the color, wore a row of banana and lemon stickers along the top trunk edge. The hue remained a source of humor among Ashley and her friends. They exchanged good-natured teasing about the number of trips to the repair shop. So far, so good—and her daughter had owned the car for three years.

Two steps inside the bridal shop door, Janet intercepted a young clerk carrying an electronic tablet. She interrupted before the employee completed the scripted greeting. "Good morning. I'm meeting Ashley Zwingel. She has a ten-thirty appointment."

"Over here, Mom." Ashley stepped from behind a rack of long, formal gowns. Her cargo shorts and knit, striped top made a stark contrast to the bridesmaids' dresses.

"I expected you'd be looking at the white gowns." She glanced toward the other side of the store where satin, lace, and tulle skirts bulged from several racks.

"We'll go over in a moment. I wanted to show you what my attendants picked. They went with the red." Ashley moved down the rack, pushing hangers holding long, slender dresses to one end of the dividers.

Janet watched light blue, deep purple, and black garments wave in gentle motion. She shook her head as the final black dress, edged in a wide satin band, settled. She agreed with her daughter. Weddings should be full of bright, happy colors.

"What do you think?" Ashley lifted a hanger from the rack and draped a scarlet gown over her arm.

For a long moment, Janet inspected the dress in silence. She reached out and rubbed a portion of crepe skirt between her fingers. Soft pleats fell from a high waist marked with a wide, white ribbon. A scoop neckline and cap sleeves with a narrow white binding completed the dress. "I love the color. The short sleeves look cold for December. Did you ask about a matching shawl?"

"Both the chapel and the reception hall have heat." Ashley tucked in her lower lip for an instant, a mimic of her mother's body language. "Freezing temperatures were not front and center in our minds when we shopped during the middle of a heat wave. I'll run the idea of a wrap past my attendants. Tiffany's mother makes the most gorgeous lacy shawls."

"I can see either white or red lace supplying just enough to ward off a chill."

Ashley sighed and returned the dress to the rack. "Not all of us shiver below seventy degrees. Now tell me, how was last night?"

"Last night?" Janet held her breath until a cold

ripple passed completely through her stomach. She'd expected the topic to pop up between them today, but she'd imagined a brief mention during lunch, not an interrogation before the shopping started.

"You told me you were going out. Did you?"

Janet moistened her lips and took a moment to sift her words. "Yes, I went out. Rich and I played mini-golf. I lost by one stroke. The evening finished with a delicious dinner at a charming local Italian place in Manchester."

"And…?" Ashley raised one corner of her mouth.

"Miss Zwingel." A petite, middle-aged woman with blonde hair in a perfect French twist approached. "I'm Gina, and I'll be your assistant today."

At the interruption, Janet concealed her relief. Her private life was her business, not Ashley's. Nothing beyond a casual, edge-of-extended-family relationship would come of her contact with Rich. She had neither the need nor desire for a man. Males complicated everything in an already complex life.

After a quick round of introductions and brief discussion of Ashley's dress size, Gina led them across the display area to the racks of wedding gowns.

"I prefer to avoid strapless. I'm fond of sheer sleeves and full skirts." Ashley gave the assistant additional basic criteria.

"And she's on a budget." Janet stepped around a mannequin holding a short train.

"I want to avoid a special order. The wedding's December twenty-sixth, and I don't want to worry about a dress being shipped from New York or beyond." Ashley checked the pink price tag on a gown and lifted the ivory garment off the rack. "I found the first one to try on. How many should I start with?"

The assistant went to the far end of the row and pulled out a gown fit for a princess. "Did you remember to bring shoes the same height you'll be wearing?"

"Absolutely." Ashley tapped her tote. "I'll be wearing white ballet flats—for comfort." She reached for the price tag on the dress Gina held. An instant later, she winced and shook her head. "I need to stay three hundred less."

Later, while Ashley and Gina were in the dressing room, Janet settled on a gold brocade chair and opened a bottle of water. Overwhelmed with the elegance of the store, she glanced around, her senses on alert to the contrasts with the discount chains she usually favored. She became aware of soft music, a classic movie soundtrack, drifting from ceiling speakers.

Lifting the water to her lips, she frowned. This moment marked only the beginning of the main event. Thank goodness her daughter spoke her mind and culled the worst of the suggestions. Several times Ashley reminded the employee they sought traditional, not trendy.

Janet exhaled and closed her eyes for a moment. The action failed to stop the heat climbing her neck. "No. Not here," she whispered the command toward the ceiling. A bridal shop was neither the time nor the place to remember last night's kiss. She'd already relived the sensation over and over during the night. She brought one finger to her lips, as if to prevent them from telling the world. And just what would they say? *I've kissed a man.* For the first time in forever. Okay, not her entire life, but long enough. The kiss was marvelous and powerful. She pressed her tingling lips. Shaking her head, she failed to banish vivid memories of the moments outside her door.

"Ta da!" Ashley emerged from the dressing room and stepped toward the triple mirror. "What do you think?"

No. Janet drew in a breath and sealed her lips. How did that dress make the cut? What happened to the full skirt criteria? The form-fitting, mermaid gown emphasized every inch of the ample Zwingel family hips. "Ummm. The skirt doesn't flatter."

"Oh, I'm not getting this one. I wanted to see how the neckline looked." Ashley turned to gaze at her image and skimmed her fingertips across a narrow ruffle blending into off-the-shoulder sleeves.

"The...neck is fine. The Southern Belle look flatters your shoulders." Janet found her normal voice the instant initial tension vanished. The dress looked lovely on her daughter—above the waist.

"Okay." Ashley pivoted toward the dressing room. "Prepare for number two on the fashion show."

Janet settled back in the upholstered chair and pulled a small notebook from her purse. "Bridal shop and lunch with A" printed in purple ink filled today's square. Tomorrow's entry said simply, "see list." She reviewed the weekend errands jotted on a page at the back of the booklet and made a neat "x" beside the top item.

"Do you like this one better?" Ashley entered from behind the simple white door in a swirl of satin.

Blinking her attention back to the present, Janet curved her mouth into a smile. "Much better. The skirt is generous without looking heavy."

Ashley preened in front of the mirrors. Smoothing

her hands across the front of the finely gathered material, she leaned forward. "I was afraid of that."

"Problem?"

"Bodice." Ashley pinched the material to shorten the deep V neck and frowned. An instant later, she bent as if to look at her hidden shoes. "I'd need to borrow a brooch from Grandma. Or get better endowed before December."

"Marie would loan you anything from her jewelry box. But a brooch isn't what either of us had in mind." Zwingel brides wore pearls. Specifically, each bride used the same single strand of natural pearls handed down within the family since the first years of the twentieth century.

Ashley shook her head and sighed. "Gown number three coming soon."

The modeling of the next two dresses went quickly. While they looked lovely on the hanger, and met the basic criteria, their faults exceeded the scope of simple alterations.

"Two more to go. Hang in there, Mom." Ashley lifted the full, cream skirt a few inches above the carpet.

Checking her watch, Janet sank back into the chair. She'd not expected bridal gown shopping to be this time consuming. Thank goodness, she only had one daughter. Never again would she need to be deeply involved in planning a wedding.

She leaned back and closed her eyes. Rich's image drifted into her mind. She recalled his laugh when he missed a six-inch putt and the time he glanced at the sky, as if requesting divine help at one of her questions. Mostly, she remembered firm lips against hers. In silence, he'd asked permission to explore her mouth.

"First reaction." Ashley stepped into view and paused before turning to the mirror.

Janet opened her mouth wide and blinked twice. Her daughter resembled a fairy princess, movie star, and fashion model all rolled into one. She closed her jaw and hunted for moisture. "Stunning."

Ashley moved to the mirror and lifted her arms to dance with an invisible groom.

The gown's sheer over-bodice, decorated with quarter-sized medallions, responded without binding across her shoulders. Gathered lace at the end of the elbow length sleeves swayed. Stepping behind her daughter, Janet admired the classic line of the white, strapless bodice beneath the layer of loose, sheer fabric. She skimmed her gaze past the dropped waist to the full skirt and all the way to a row of lace medallions four inches from the floor. "You're beautiful. The gown's gorgeous."

"I want it." Ashley traced an index finger along the modest, scooped neckline. "This dress makes my budget—by pennies. To be honest, I'd eat peanut butter and walk to work for months to get it. The Zwingel pearls will go perfectly."

"Priceless," Janet whispered from an unexpectedly dry throat. The joyful glow on her daughter's face surpassed the expression at either high school or college graduation.

"They're not that expensive."

"I didn't mean the pearls." Precious because they symbolized more than money, the necklace would tie Ashley to her ancestors. Greg's mother had two sons, and only one granddaughter. When her health began to fail, she gave the heirloom to Janet to hold in trust for

Ashley.

Janet eased back a step. "Turn for me—nice and slow."

Reaching up, Ashley removed the plastic clip from her hair and gave her head a gentle shake. Chestnut waves settled on her shoulders. "I want to wear my hair down. I think it will be long enough for sausage curls by December. I'll skip a veil and go with silk flowers. Can you imagine white rosebuds?"

"Yes, flowers instead of a veil." She raised her phone. "Turn...just a little more...stop."

"No pictures." Ashley waved both hands in sign language to cancel the shot.

"Not even for Grams?" Janet held her mouth in a small circle. Superstitions, even the ones about grooms and wedding dresses, collected more chuckles than serious looks in their family.

"I don't want any photos of this gown near the Internet."

Janet laughed. "Then you have nothing to fear if they're on my phone. The last time I tried to post a picture to social media the process went all wrong."

"I'm hesitant. But you have a point. I'll delete it after you show Grams."

"When did you get superstitious?" Janet turned her mouth into a mock frown.

"I want to enjoy Daniel's expression the first time he sees me wearing it."

Janet nodded. "Good plan."

"Your turn to become the model, Mom. You need to pick out your dress. I want you to think elegant. Find the sort of gown you'd wear for a second wedding." Ashley gestured to the other side of the store.

Opening her eyes wide and raising both brows, she regarded her daughter. "Second wedding. Where did you get such an idea?"

"Oh, here and there." Ashley's smile was small, but her eyes sparkled.

"You and I need to talk." How much was Ashley extrapolating from one unchaperoned date? Her daughter didn't have a clue about the kiss. Did she? Janet wavered drawing her next breath.

Gina, the assistant, cleared her throat. "The mother's dresses are on the racks at a right angle to the bridesmaids. For a Christmas wedding, I'd suggest something from our champagne or bronze lines to flatter your complexion."

"Don't rush off." Janet tossed out the comment as Ashley stepped toward the dressing room for a final time.

"Don't worry—I've got an alteration schedule to work out."

Nodding satisfaction, Janet collected her purse and headed toward the racks of long, modest dresses. She refused to think about the time span since she last purchased anything formal. Aside from her one "little black dress" the clothes in her closet were casual, suitable for family gatherings and the rare church service. Ashley was right to prod her into selecting an outfit today. Without outside motivation, she'd wait until two weeks before the wedding and end up with something which satisfied neither of them. *Elegant.* Excitement sparked in her core. Only once in her life would she be the mother-of-the-bride. She best give this shopping assignment her full attention. With a little luck, she'd find a gown which would both surprise and please Rich.

How did he get into her thoughts? Again.

****

Late Saturday afternoon, Janet pressed the garage door opener and glanced at the wooden steps to her deck. The view didn't feel right. The atmosphere gave her an unsettled, rather than welcoming, vibe. She spared another glance before she eased her truck inside. A shiver sped across her shoulders.

A few moments later, keys tucked into the front pocket of beige Capris, she approached the collection of potted plants clustered at the foot of the stairs. She inventoried and counted the correct number and type. But…not all of them were in the right positions. She lifted a clay pot of geraniums and moved the container back to the end of the second riser. "What's this?" She closed her mouth, surprised by her own voice.

Squatting, she inspected the rubber tree plant. The black and brown pot sat uneven in the saucer. Had she bumped the container when she watered flowers last night? She shook her head and gazed toward her neighbor's fence. Once or twice in the last year, their dog escaped the yard and had a grand time exploring. But the animal would have tipped over the container completely, not left it looking as if the pot was replaced in a hurry. She struggled for her next breath. "No."

She dashed up the steps and ducked under the round, metal, patio table. Checking at the junction of each leg with the top, she found the small metal box secured to the bracing. She slid the cover with shaky fingers. She felt the extra key for the front door. Relief rushed out of her lungs. *What if?* She walked over to the glass slider. The security bar was in the clip, not snug at waist level. She always checked the deck door before leaving. She froze with a stone expanding in her chest.

A moment later, she hurried into the garage. She grabbed a clean rag from the top of the supply for shop use and took the inside steps at a rush. The kitchen and dining area looked exactly as she'd left them this morning. She stepped into the living room and did a quick visual inspection. The electronics sat in their usual positions on the entertainment center. She counted each of the five, restored mantel clocks in their usual places, and her heart tapered toward normal. She grabbed a little comfort from the steady rhythm of the timepieces and walked to the front door. Both the chain and deadbolt were secure. She retraced her steps to the hallway and halted. *I know I closed the bedroom door.*

She spread the rag across her fingers and pushed the door wide. "How dare he?" As if an internal firecracker exploded, hot anger radiated from her core. Strength evaporated, and she crumpled in the doorway before attempting the next step. "Drowning would be too good for him."

In a few heartbeats, she recovered her senses, checked for tears with the back of one hand, and surveyed the room. Bras, panties, and socks were flung in all directions. One bright green cotton bikini dangled from a dresser knob. The small jewelry box was in similar disarray with necklaces and earrings reflecting colored light into the mirror.

"My clock—where is my clock?" She stalled her gaze where her first restoration, a 1910 Seth Thomas in a walnut case, belonged on the dresser top. A cold shiver radiated out from her chest. "Who would take my favorite?"

With a surge of anger, she stood and stepped into the room. A moment later, she paused her hand an inch from a bra hooked over a corner of the mirror and yielded to practical concerns. She returned to the kitchen, pulled her phone from her purse, and dialed 9-1-1. Janet paced a tight circle in the living room until she couldn't bear the sight of her other clocks. Moving to the front yard, she enlarged the loop and frequently checked the street in both directions for an approaching police car.

The patrol car was still rolling to a halt when she rushed toward the pavement.

"You reported a burglary, ma'am?"

"Yes—from my bedroom—an antique clock." She wiped away another group of tears and led the petite, auburn-haired officer into the house. Then she remained on the threshold to her bedroom, watching the officer make a quick survey.

"Appears they used the window to enter." The patrolwoman pointed out the broken screen and partially raised window. "Please wait in the living room. I'll call the others."

"Others?" Who was she inviting to inspect the humiliation of her scattered underwear?

"I'm requesting a detective and crime scene technician. Is it correct you told the dispatcher the thief left via the dining area slider?"

She nodded and studied the face of the serious young woman. "I always lock the deck access and put the security bar in place."

"When did you last use the door?"

"This morning…before eight." She plucked a fresh

tissue from the box on the kitchen counter. Her day started early and well, with a few extra minutes after her shower. While the coffee brewed, she'd stepped outside to enjoy the still-comfortable morning. "I'm sure I locked it. I'm a creature of habit."

An hour later, under the watchful eye of Detective Randolph, Janet sat on the bedroom floor. She flexed her fingers in unfamiliar latex gloves and peered into one of the boxes the thief removed from the closet. The lid and a portion of the contents lay scattered on her navy-and-white striped comforter. Her task at the moment was to determine what, if anything, was missing from the boxes. She refused to look toward the dresser. The empty space where her clock belonged unlocked an unfamiliar anger. The urge to snatch her rainbow-colored and lace-trimmed underwear out of the sight of strange men was both strong and inappropriate. She swallowed her emotions and focused on the box.

Fanning out several black-and-white photos, she counted them twice. "One of these is missing."

"Who are the people?" Detective Randolph pushed one hand through thick, light brown hair.

"These are the wedding photos of my in-laws…late in-laws…parents of my ex." She evened the edges against the box's rim.

"What's his name?" The detective touched his pen to his notebook.

"The ex?" She waited for a nod. "Greg Zwingel. He lives in South County…Candlestick Lane with his third wife." She steadied her gaze on the officer's face.

Greg stayed at the top of her very short, internal suspect list. Who else would take the first clock she restored? He and Ashley were the only people in the world who witnessed her joy when it chimed the correct hour the first time. "We've been divorced fourteen years. We're not friends. We share a daughter."

Nodding, he wrote a note.

Janet lifted a thick handful of photos, certificates, and letters. Setting them on the floor, she encouraged them to slide apart with one hand. She caught sight of the important church and school certificates—none appeared missing. Returning her attention to the box, she lifted out the remaining papers. "They're gone."

"Description?"

She tipped the box so he could see she'd removed everything except one small, framed photo and two square envelopes. "Jewelry is gone—family heirlooms. The brooch is a gold peacock with real jewels in the tail. The necklace"—she swallowed twice before again finding her voice—"is a single strand of pearls— antique—early twentieth century."

"Is anything else missing?"

Shaking her head, she searched for helpful words. "The jewelry was boxed. The brooch stays in dark blue cardboard. The pearls are kept in hinged, white leather, rose velvet lining." *How do I tell Ashley her wedding pearls were stolen?*

"So…the thief took a clock and two pieces of jewelry—plus one photo. Have I got the list right?"

Janet nodded and fisted her hands. What was Greg trying to prove by stealing Ashley's heirloom? "My ex took them. No one else would know the sentimental value is greater than monetary."

"We need proof of guilt. The law requires good evidence before we can write a warrant or make an arrest."

"I know." She blew out a large breath. In her head, she understood hunches and gut feelings from victims didn't solve cases.

"Do you have pictures of the missing items?"

"I took photos for insurance purposes years ago." She looked at the remaining stack of boxes at the end of the closet shelf. Pointing, she turned to the detective. "May I pull out the bottom two?" *Greg Zwingel—if you gamble away your daughter's inheritance—I'll be guilty of your murder.*

Chapter Eleven

Ignoring a burst of gasoline and old lawn clipping scents released when her foot bumped against the mower deck, Janet pulled her mind back to the Monday evening task at hand. Her father was here to borrow a few tools. "Allow me." She grabbed the bucket an instant before Joe's hand touched the handle. The stump grinder and extra blades gave a substantial, but not difficult, weight to the container. "You said your knee was bothering you today."

"I'm not helpless."

She glanced at him through the deep shade. "Never said you were, but my muscles are younger."

"Are you taking lessons from your mother?" He lifted his arm, swiped sweat off his forehead, and settled his lucky Cardinals cap back on thinning, faded brown hair.

"We want you to stick around." She flashed a grin and gave his face a quick inspection. He dripped sweat like a construction worker in the middle of a heat wave. True, the evening was warm. According to her glance at the thermometer when they'd entered the garage, it remained in the high eighties. Late August appeared determined to live up to its reputation of hot and humid. But the two of them had been in her basement garage, the coolest shade available, while they packed the tools and discussed a tree damaged in a recent storm. "You remember the conditions of this loan?"

He kept pace beside her on the sloped driveway toward his truck. "I need to stay the supervisor and let my neighbor do the actual grinding."

She nodded. Every year the conversations with a reversal of the parent and child roles became more frequent. Joe often forgot his age when he noticed home or yard maintenance undone. He was honorable and stubborn. Taking orders—even simple ones like drinking more water—didn't come easy. Only two years ago, she'd talked him into letting her do the gutter cleaning and other ladder work at his house. Keeping him on the ground eased her mind about falls. Today, her concern was a case of heat stroke.

"I've got tickets for Friday night's game. Do you want to come?" He stopped and mopped his forehead again.

"I thought Jerome, your neighbor across the street, was your baseball buddy this year."

"He's got some big family thing. I think his son arranged a weekend at the lake."

"Baseball sounds good. I'll try my best to get off early." Cheering for the home team would be a wonderful way to start the Labor Day weekend. *Looking for tickets to the final Cubs and Cards game.* A smile tugged at her mouth when a snippet of a recent conversation with Rich returned.

"You work too hard."

"I'm following your example." She opened his truck door and set the bucket of tools in front of the passenger seat. "As I remember, you worked overtime at the factory whenever you could. Then you spent hours repairing cars for the neighbors."

"Your memory's good." He touched a hand to the truck fender. "Doesn't mean you need to do the same. Take some time to enjoy life before the years spin out of control and vanish."

"Don't worry about me. I've got plans. Come inside for a bit. I'll give you water or tea for the road. You can relax and look over what I brought home the other day."

Joe frowned and examined her from pale blue eyes. "I don't want to see any dress or wedding stuff."

"I promise not to show you wedding things today." She hooked an arm through his and guided him into the house. Snatching bright brochures from an end table, she waved them. "I stopped by a travel agency last Wednesday."

"Are those your tickets to San Francisco?"

She shook her head, attempting to banish the gloomy reason for her next trip to California. "I'll book those online after I get a definite date for the memorial service. I'm exploring taking a trip for fun."

Joe claimed a seat at the table and opened the first folder. "Adventure vacation?"

"It's time to put a little gusto on my agenda." She set a pair of tumblers on the counter. "Do you prefer water or raspberry tea?"

"Either." Joe turned his attention to the single large window facing the quiet street. "Are you expecting company?"

What's the time? She glanced at the nearest clock. "Not exactly company, closer to a special delivery dessert." She laced a laugh between her words. "Don't fret, he typically brings enough to share."

"Your detective?"

"He's not mine. Don't believe everything Ashley says." Against her wishes, Janet's Friday night date claimed a large portion of Sunday's lunch conversation with Joe and Marie. On purpose, Janet presented the events as casual. Now she touched a finger to her lips and remembered the kiss.

"Good men are rare these days." Joe studied the photo of three ocean kayaks off the California coast.

She stopped a wise crack reply in the back of her throat. Changing her father's opinion of anything was beyond her power. The problem, from her point of view, was his habit of being correct in the long run. She hurried across the living room and opened the door as the first note of the chimes rang out. "My lookout spotted you. Come in. You remember my father."

"I came to borrow from her tool bank." Joe stood and offered a hand. After a quick shake, he excused himself and walked down the hall toward the bathroom.

Janet curved her mouth into a smile, and her spirits lifted like a bright helium balloon. "The question of the moment is water or tea."

"Either." Rich set a pastry box on the table and glanced at the scattered brochures. "Are you planning a trip?"

"I think I deserve a treat."

He stepped over and captured her hands before she could object. "I missed you." He brushed a kiss over one cheek before tipping his head and giving her a slow inspection. "I need a repeat."

She mirrored the tilt of his head. Suddenly, she heard her heart beating fast and a pleasant warmth lingered where his lips grazed her skin. Leaning forward, she rested her brow against his. "About dates…and other things. We need to talk."

"My pleasure. Does he know?" He gestured down the hall.

"Well, I told my parents the basics." She eased away but kept her fingers enclosed in his hands. She ignored mention of Friday evening and skipped straight to Saturday afternoon. "I clued them into when and what is missing. They both know who I suspect."

"Missing?" Rich's eyes widened, and his mouth flattened.

Janet sighed. This was not the way she'd planned to introduce the burglary topic. Yesterday, during lunch with her parents, she related events much better. Gesturing for him to sit, she added ice to three large glasses. "Saturday, when I got home from my day with Ashley, I discovered a break-in."

He straightened and stared into her face.

"Now don't go all caveman." She slipped in the words the instant his posture stiffened. The wooden mask set to his mouth and the silent questions leaking from his eyes made her hesitate. She drew moisture into her mouth. "I promptly reported the burglary to the police. I met a nice Detective Randolph."

"And?" He blinked.

The silence stretched while she searched for words containing neither false optimism nor defeat. She didn't want Joe to overhear too much worry in her words. "I had photos. Your department will check local pawn shops. I called my insurance agent and started the paperwork."

"What's missing?"

"A clock…antique jewelry…all sentimental pieces. The thief left my electronics undisturbed." She spoke soft, her heart sinking a little each time she mentioned the missing items.

"Entry?" He gestured toward the front door.

"He removed the screen and climbed in my bedroom window—left via the slider." She pointed toward the deck entrance. Before she could add another word, a noise, a mixture of word and groan, came from the hall. Breaking away, she stepped around the corner. "Dad, are you sick?"

Joe leaned against the wall. "Weak…all…of…"

"Let me help you. We'll get you into a chair." Her heart pounded louder with each beat. Less than five minutes ago her dad's only physical problem was a worn knee. She hurried to him and draped his left arm over her shoulders.

"Allow me." Rich stepped forward and took Joe's other side. "We'll get you on the couch."

"I…I…"

Janet noted the droop to Joe's mouth, and her stomach turned to ice. Dad suffered from more than too much sun.

"I'll move him. You call 911." Rich maneuvered Joe toward the sofa. "Now."

Call 911. Now. The command echoed in her brain for a second. She stared for another moment, blinked, and rushed for the phone. She pulled the cord out of the charger on the kitchen counter and tapped the numbers. "My name is Janet Zwingel, and we need an ambulance for my father. The address is…" She spoke over the operator's scripted lines.

"Please repeat the address."

The dispatcher's clear, calm voice eased Janet's panic. Drawing a deep breath, she answered questions.

She repeated the address and concentrated on the operator's words. "His name is Joe Johnson. He's seventy-nine. Medications?" Recalling an image of her parents' kitchen cabinet with prescription bottles, she shook her head. "He takes something for high blood pressure. One pill for cholesterol—one of the statins, I think. Over-the-counter pain killers."

"Joe, what day is it?" Rich asked.

Following directions from the operator, she crossed the room and opened the front door. At the edge of her awareness, she realized Rich asked Joe a list of scripted questions. She shifted her focus back to the voice on the phone. "Yes. The front door is unlocked. No…I'm not sure…one moment."

She held the phone away from her ear and turned to Rich. "They're asking about oriented to time and place?"

"May I?" Rich lifted the phone from her hand and pointed for her to sit beside Joe.

Janet adjusted the woven throw hastily tucked around Joe's legs and then enclosed his left hand. Sitting on the coffee table, she moved her thumbs in slow circles on his cool skin. "Daddy. What happened?" She drew a quiet breath and forbid panic to surface. "Did you get too much heat? The medics are coming. I'll have to call Mom. She won't be happy. We're interrupting her weekly pinochle game with the neighborhood gang."

Joe mumbled two words.

Leaning forward, she cupped his chin with one hand. "You don't need to talk. I'm just prattling away. We'll both be fine in a little while." A glance at his pale face sent a shiver down her back. The illness, or attack, or episode was serious. She wasn't ready for Dad to be an invalid. Or… She shook away the worst-case scenario. "You'll get through this. We both will."

Childhood memories rushed in and overwhelmed the present.

Too sleepy to walk, she rode draped over her father's shoulder from the car to the house after a late movie.

Father and daughter played catch in the back yard—beanbags, softballs, baseballs. At least twice, they tossed a football.

She caressed his flaccid hand, a hand which less than an hour ago picked out the grinder blades and reached for the tool bucket. "I love you, Daddy." *Don't die.*

****

Two hours after the ambulance arrived at Janet's house, Rich set a final cup into the cardboard drink carrier. He skimmed his gaze around the emergency department waiting room and ignored the concrete block inside his chest.

Low conversations rumbled from men, women, and children in various stages of worry. Two teens attempted a card game across a low table. A housekeeper pushed a cart with a squeaky wheel out of the elevator. A moment later, the automatic doors swished open to admit a couple with a crying child.

He rolled his shoulders in a futile attempt to dispel a shiver. He hated hospitals, especially emergency departments, and Meramec in particular. For too many hours of his life, he'd been banished to one of the lightly padded chairs while the professionals prodded and tested Mary. *Keep the past in the past.* He forced his thoughts into the present and increased his pace toward the small group waiting for Joe to complete radiology testing.

"I could have helped with coffee." Janet met him three steps away from the others.

"No problem. Do you think I brought enough sweeteners?" He glanced at Marie, Janet's mother, twisting her hands in her lap as she whispered to her friend, Grace.

"Mom, Rich brought us coffees." Janet set one cup on the tiny table beside Marie's chair.

"Why is it taking so long?" Marie tore open two pink packets and dumped them in her drink. The small actions caused her tight, short curls to quiver.

"It's only been twenty minutes."

Rich glanced at his watch and confirmed Janet's reply.

"An x-ray takes a minute. It's like posing for a photo." Marie sipped coffee, frowned, and reached for more sweetener.

"Relax, Marie." Grace placed a hand with elegantly manicured nails on her friend's arm. "They're doing more than a simple chest x-ray."

Janet removed the lid and blew across the dark, steaming beverage. "Thank you, Grace. I want them to get the diagnosis right, Mom. If they require a little more time…so be it."

Rich studied Janet perched on a large rectangular stool beside him. The calm words came from a person with a death grip on her coffee cup.

The contradiction was familiar. He'd practiced and grown a stiff, calm shell over inner turmoil. Only once, early in Mary's cancer war, did anger over-ride good manners. He stood in the fourth-floor waiting room and told the hospital staff his exact opinion of the delays, bland statements, and pleas for patience. The other times he behaved like a gentleman in public. Later, with Mary settled either here or at home, he took out his frustration at the firing range.

"Did you call Henry?"

Janet's soft question brought his thoughts back to the present. "I did. He's fine. He agreed not to wait up." A tiny, brief smile crossed her mouth. He savored a burst of warmth in his chest and kept his expression neutral. "Did you talk to Ashley?"

"Affirmative." Janet brushed one hand across worn jeans. "With much persuading, she agreed not to come immediately. I placated her with the promise of frequent updates."

"You've got a level-headed daughter." *Similar to her mother.* He remembered the one, brief moment of panic at the house. Joe moving in the hallway dragging his left foot and losing the ability to speak in front of them was a scary scene. However, Janet followed his command to call for help. Her voice wavered a few times, betraying her confusion, but she'd retrieved the necessary insurance cards from Joe's wallet and responded sensibly to the paramedics' questions.

Currently, he felt like an intruder in a tight group. Grace, the kindly pinochle player who'd driven Marie, was a long-time acquaintance to the other women. Once the ambulance arrived at the house, his job was over. No, he reminded himself, Janet was in no mental condition to drive.

Grace leaned toward Janet. "I understand Ashley found a dress."

"We went shopping Saturday. It turned into a very successful outing."

"Why don't you give us a detailed account?" Grace prompted.

Rich looked at Janet over the rim of his cup. "You want to talk about wedding dresses?"

Lowering her coffee, she smiled small and shook her head once.

What did I miss? He swallowed and understood a comment would be a waste of air.

"Gowns and weddings beat other topics which come to mind." Janet looked toward her mother.

Grace gave him a wide-eyed look.

He resisted reaching up to check if horns had sprouted on his forehead. He shrugged defeat and sighed. If wedding fluff kept their minds from exploring more dark alleys than necessary, he wouldn't interfere.

"Do you own a red tie?" Janet touched the back of his hand.

"I'm not sure. I'd have to paw through my collection." *What does a red tie have to do with anything? Did they expect him to participate in this conversation?* He sipped coffee and waited.

She widened her eyes and regarded him for a long moment. "The bridesmaids picked red dresses—sleek, pretty gowns with cap sleeves and white ribbon trim. You might want to coordinate."

"Red, a perfect choice for the season." Grace smiled and laced fingers with Marie.

"I'll ask Santa for a red tie. Maybe he'll add one of those pocket squares to match."

Janet rolled her shoulders and relaxed a few

degrees. She directed her next words to the other women. "The colors will be red and white—with green for accent. Holly seems to be the default answer for all the decorating decisions up to this point."

Rich allowed the conversation to flow between the three ladies. He grasped the concepts of "lace" and "neckline" but let the specific descriptions pass through his brain. Keeping an eye on Marie, who let the others do most of the talking, he tried to recall her image from Janet's wedding album. *Mother and daughter smile alike.*

"Johnson family." A clerk dressed in black scrubs approached.

Janet jumped to her feet. "Joseph Johnson."

Standing a step behind Janet, Rich watched the clerk give their little gathering a smile worthy of a toothpaste commercial.

"He's being admitted. He's in good hands. Follow me, I'll show you to the sixth floor."

Rich trailed behind Janet and Marie, matching his step to Grace's. "Thank you again for driving her here."

"She'd do the same for me. Actually"—Grace stepped close as the group waited for the elevator— "she already has. Last year, my George had a heart attack. He required an emergency stent. Joe and Marie…well, true friends."

"Good to know."

"Kindness runs in the Johnson family." Grace jabbed a finger in the general direction of Janet's back. "She, for example, is top quality. She keeps her word and looks after her parents more than they want to admit."

He nodded and followed the others into the

elevator. A non-solicited compliment—always the best kind. He studied Janet's posture after they exited on the sixth floor. She walked with her head tipped a few degrees to better hear her mother, a woman six inches shorter.

Life's temporary. An ache formed in his arms as his muscles begged to hold and comfort her. He longed to give her a safe place to spill her tension in the coming days. Would she allow him?

Chapter Twelve

Thursday afternoon, Rich left the station and detoured from his usual route. He needed to run a special errand today—one which caused anger and grief to wrestle in his gut.

A short time later, he squatted and pushed a bouquet of multi-colored iris into the permanent holder beside a gravestone. Resting one wrist on his knee, he studied the gray, polished granite. In the center, the single name "Taylor" was carved in a large, plain font. In an instant, his gaze moved lower. He traced the smaller letters forming a name above a pair of dates on the lower left. "Mary Louise. Happy Birthday. I love you. I miss you."

Pouring bottled water into the flowers, he pictured another bouquet. He remembered a mass of pink and white roses sitting in the master bedroom at their old house. The blooms, crowded into a green glass vase, numbered one blossom for each year of marriage. The roses were the last meaningful flowers he gave her. He steadied his breathing. "Sorry, at times the past wants to drown me."

He stood, scanned the area, and relaxed his shoulders. One couple walked within sight, a dozen rows off to his left, intent on their own visit. The tall, slender cypress trees cast exaggerated shadows across the uneven stones. A bold robin fluttered out of a tree and eyed him from the neighboring plot.

Assured no one in the cemetery would hear his words, Rich cleared his throat. "Henry's moved in. He plans to stay at least until spring. The new hip and he appear to get along well. He registered for a basic cooking class at the supermarket. Mostly, he's the same slightly frustrating old man to live with."

He paused the family report and scanned his surroundings. "The kids are fine. Rachel sounds happy every time she calls. I'm hopeful she and her man will make their relationship official with a wedding. You know my opinion. I'm determined to grab hold of a good thing and formalize it promptly. Our little girl grew up, Mary. I turned my back, and she went from learning to put on socks to earning her own living."

Shifting his weight, he listened to the distant hum of freeway traffic. "Brian's coming home over Labor Day. He started his final semester last week. Going to his graduation will be…strange. I've never attended any of his graduations without you. We'll have a dentist in the family. Who would have suspected it? The little boy who panicked when we said the word will make a career of dentistry." Rich swallowed, sending a quick gaze in most of a circle. He paused his scan on a mound covered with green carpet. *A new grave.* He pushed back at a sudden realization. One day, he would rest under a similar covering in front of this stone. Blinking his attention back to Mary's engraved name, he continued condensing events since his previous visit.

"I expect Brian will make the time to come and pay his respects. He's…the change has been the most difficult for him. I don't think he understands my move, even all these months later. I needed to escape. The memories were too thick in the other house. I looked into any room or out any window and all I saw was you." He clasped his hands behind his back.

"Do you know what I miss the most? Our conversations—you made me laugh—or think. Toward the end, I considered you the philosopher of the family. Maybe you got some sort of special insight from all those serious books you read."

Rich looked down the row of uneven stones. In a few minutes, at official sunset, the caretaker would come and lock the gates. "Daniel made his engagement official. Wedding's set for the day after Christmas.

"Life's temporary. Remember how you reminded us near the end? Well, life's changing. I mean in more ways than relocating to a different house or Henry moving in. I met a woman. Janet—she's near our age and tends to speak her mind. I think you'd like her." He rubbed the back of his neck in reaction to warm embarrassment.

"Remember how we talked about the future near the end? I tried to promise not to look at another woman after you were gone. You laughed and told me to be happy.

"Life's lonely without you. I look at Henry and wonder if I can stay sane another twenty years or more. Will I be satisfied playing dominos and cards with the guys for entertainment? I miss having one person to spill my thoughts to—or get advice from."

He closed his eyes for a moment and listened to the soft sound of leaves in a gust of wind. A memory from Monday evening eased forward. He re-played Janet welcoming him into her home and giving a casual re-introduction to her father. *Temporary.* Less than half an hour later, Joe Johnson suffered his stroke and priorities changed. Trouble didn't play favorites.

Opening his eyes, he read both inscriptions, one date missing below his name. "Janet, the woman I mentioned, makes me smile. Can my heart hold both of you?"

****

"Thanks for offering to stay." Janet pushed the elevator button and glanced to her left. Beyond her daughter, three employees in apricot scrubs clustered around a computer at the nurses' station as they worked the Thursday evening shift.

"Your attention please." A smooth female voice flooded from the overhead speakers. "Visiting hours will end in ten minutes. Thank you for complying with the rules and giving our patients a time for quiet rest."

Janet sighed. While she and Ashley willingly left Joe in the care of professionals for the overnight hours, Marie insisted on staying. With stubbornness worthy of the stereotypical Missouri mule, she remained at her husband's side.

Ashley shrugged. "Grams looks exhausted. My best guess is she's getting less than an hour sleep per night on the little cot in the room."

"I think your estimate is high. Yesterday, I offered to check her into a motel half a mile away."

After a quick laugh, Ashley again called the elevator. "I don't need to be a psychic to know Grams' answer."

"Absolutely. I didn't know she had some of those words in her vocabulary. For an instant, I was back in boot camp. Her tirade was worthy of a failed bunk inspection." Janet stepped into the elevator and cut off the conversation. Life got complicated with one sick parent. Three days after Joe's stroke, she worried about Marie collapsing from fatigue. At least, her father was improving. The doctors planned his discharge to a rehab facility this Saturday.

"Daniel and I drove out to Oak Leaf Center last night." Ashley resumed their conversation three steps after their exit from the elevator. "From the outside, the facility looks nice and well maintained."

"The inside passed my inspection. The transfer is all set." Janet glanced at her daughter, smiled, and increased the pace. "Please ignore your grandmother's first reaction. She refused to go with me when I visited and picked up the paperwork packet. While the center is nice, it's not perfect. You know how she is."

"The bathroom floor must be sterile." Ashley followed the slight exaggeration of her grandmother's immaculate standards with a sigh.

"Good. I've got both of you."

Janet snapped her attention to the speaker and pressed tight her lips. What was Greg doing at the hospital? She blinked and searched for polite words. "You've surprised me."

"A pleasant one, I hope." He crowded the rim of her personal space.

I didn't say that. She adjusted the pink purse on her hip and crossed her arms. "What brings you here?"

"I came to visit the sick. The gatekeepers over there"—he waved a hand in the direction of the information desk—"wouldn't give me a room number. The taller one said I was on some sort of not-allowed-to-visit list."

"Joe Johnson is improving. He does not want to see

you." She glared at Greg. Her ex-husband didn't do well with direct eye contact, but tonight, she was not in the mood to cater to his ego.

"You don't need to be hostile. I was being polite."

Janet drew a deep breath and counted silently for patience. Part of her wanted to accuse him here and now of the burglary. She won the internal tussle and held the words at the back of her throat.

"Chill out, Dad. I've been giving you information on the phone." Ashley, the family peacemaker, walked to a seating arrangement and set her tote on a cube-shaped chair.

"Secondhand information isn't the same." He alternated his gaze between them.

Janet placed her hands behind her back and rubbed them to relieve building tension before taking one step toward the entrance. "I think we should each go to our respective homes. We all have work in the morning."

"You don't give the orders, Janet."

"Going home makes sense, Dad. Didn't you say you were doing the breakfast shift all this week? I know I want to be rested and sharp for twenty, lively, five-year-old students."

"Then you go ahead. Your mother and I have business to discuss."

"Business with you involves money." Janet contained a frustrated sigh. "I'm not loaning, gifting, or investing in your idea. I've learned a few things from past mistakes." An instant later, she turned on her heel and marched toward the automatic door.

"Janet." Greg's voice and quick, heavy steps followed. "I've got a good idea—a food truck. I've got a partner. We just need a little more cash to get started."

She continued at a brisk pace until they were away from the entrance canopy. Halting under one of the parking lot lights, she turned and faced him. A sweet scent from the strips of prairie grasses planted between the rows of cars wafted in the early night air.

Evidence. In silence, she reviewed Detective Randolph's brief description of the procedure for a search warrant. Moistening her lips to delay her words, she glanced to her left and sighted Ashley watching from a few paces away. "It's okay. We don't need a referee. Your father will put any serious request in a letter."

Greg shook his head. "I don't have the time to jump through your series of hoops. In case you haven't noticed, the world moves fast."

"One rotation every twenty-four hours, same as always." She raised an index finger and traced a small circle in the air. In conversation with any other person, she'd admit that events of all sorts moved faster and spun out of control.

"Listen. I want to apologize for the other morning. I wasn't thinking clearly. And…and…you're the best, Janet. You're dependable…and level-headed. I'm in a bit of a spot with the food truck deal and really need your help."

"You want to waste my money." Mirroring the rerun of the verbal exchange, the flavor of a molasses cookie she ate an hour ago returned to the back of her throat all soured. She pulled her keys from her jeans pocket and ran her thumb over the flat, decorative fob.

"My problem's not gambling. I swear. I'm going to the meetings. I'm staying out of the casinos."

"No." Janet leaned an inch toward him. "What part

of that simple word bounces off your solid bone brain?"

He cupped his hands into a bowl for a moment. "We'll be selling comfort food—mashed potatoes and noodles with sauces. This idea's solid."

She watched a sparkle build in his eyes as he talked. The man did a good job of cooking. Unfortunately, his planning and business skills stalled out at the level of a first-grader. "I'm sure the food would taste delicious. You need to find a different investor." She turned away and walked past Ashley. Scanning the parking lot, she hurried along the row toward her truck.

"Desperate men do desperate things," he called to her back.

Halting for a moment, she looked over her shoulder and tossed her next words directly toward him. "Are you threatening me, Mr. Zwingel?"

"I'm stating a fact. I would never hurt you." He placed a hand over his heart.

Except for the time you... Greg physically threatened her only once. He specialized in inflicting emotional and psychological damage. During and after their marriage, he exhibited a talent for getting on her last nerve. Currently, with Joe's illness and Marie's exhaustion, she didn't have many in reserve.

She slipped into her truck, pulled out her phone, and smiled. A text waited for her reply.

—Dessert and chat Friday???—

Lifting her gaze, she confirmed Greg remained standing beside the light pole. In the next instant, she tapped her response.

Chapter Thirteen

The next evening, Janet stood at her dining table and smoothed a sticky note into a thick cookbook. Similar volumes formed multiple low stacks from one end of the table to the other.

Why did professional chefs make mixing a cake sound like one of her brother's chemical engineering projects? Did people actually taste a difference if liquids were added in three portions rather than four? She closed the library cookbook and added the hardcover to two others with bright flags. She opened the next book to the index.

The doorbell chimed.

"In a minute."

"Take three." Rich responded.

She curved her lips into a genuine smile and hurried across the living room. His words, a variation of a standard reply, lightened both her feet and spirit. She opened the door and patterned her gaze from silver hair to his black oxfords and back to his hazel eyes. "Welcome…come in…pardon the clutter."

"I bring supper." He lifted a yellow-and-white restaurant take-out sack. "I settled on Asian chicken salads. I hope my choice meets with your approval."

"As I said earlier, I'm not a fussy eater. I'm sure anything on their menu beats the leftover leftovers in my fridge." During a mid-day text exchange, the offer of dessert and coffee changed to a substitute she couldn't refuse—a carry-out supper. Since Joe's hospital admission, contact with Rich had been limited to brief emails, two phone calls, and half a dozen text exchanges. She looked forward to being face-to-face.

Arriving at the table, she moved several cookbooks to the far end. "I got a little carried away at the library."

He leaned over, lifted one slender hardback, and met her gaze. "Are you opening a catering service?"

"The world is safe from that disaster. I'm baking Mom a birthday cake."

"I can give you the names and addresses of some good bakeries."

She added a volume covered with bright photos of ethnic desserts to the top of the last pile. "A bakery purchase is out of the question."

"Have you considered a cake mix? It would be fresh from your oven. If that's what you're aiming for."

"No short cuts allowed for this birthday. Don't misunderstand. Lots of baked goods in this house start with a box, but for this occasion, I'm going for special." She pushed a pad of bright sticky notes and a pen against the book collection.

"Does this birthday end in zero?" He tipped his head a few degrees and raised an eyebrow.

Shaking her head, she moved into the kitchen and opened a cupboard. "I've never seen a mix for mother's favorite, Black Forest Cake. I've decided this is the year to actually carry through with an idea that's been brewing for a long time. Now, what do you want to drink? I'm offering water, ice tea, and a cranberry with tropical fruit."

"I'll be adventurous and try the juice."

While preparing the drinks, she sent frequent glances in his direction. He moved unhurried, yet with purpose, setting their meals on the table and opening the drawer to find silverware. His presence calmed the air around her. The silent moments between them trembled with both comfort and anticipation. She disturbed the quiet when placing their drinks beside the salads. "Did you have a busy day?"

"I made progress on the chore list—haircuts for both Dad and me." He skimmed one hand over his silver bristles. "How was your day?"

Sighing, she popped the plastic lid off her meal. Re-capping her day could have a variety of starting points. "I guess you'd call my day full. I intended to take a half day of vacation. The time turned out to be closer to two hours after I finished the paperwork from my last call. Then I stopped at the hospital before going to the library. As you can see, I had a grand time."

"Measured by the number of items checked out, I'd say you were one of their better adult patrons today. How's Joe doing?"

"He's making progress." She picked a crisp noodle from her salad and savored the crunch. "Tomorrow, he moves to Oak Leaf Center for three weeks of rehab. Do you know the place?"

He drizzled dressing over half of his salad and nodded. "I'm familiar with it by reputation—a positive one."

"The location was a large favorable point. It's a scant two miles from my parent's house. Mom will have one less excuse to stay with him overnight."

"Has she gone home at all?"

"Twice, but only long enough to shower and repack her bag." She cut a piece of deep-fried chicken into small bites. "Mom turned me down the night I volunteered to stay. She brushed off Ashley's offer, too. She can be a determined woman."

"I think the entire generation drank stubborn juice instead of water. I need to get myself into a different sort of mindset, heavy on the patience, when I interview them." He pushed his fork under a snow pea and grated carrot.

"A statement like that makes a person wonder what our children will call us."

"Perfect."

Glancing across the place settings, she saw a serious set to his mouth. His eyes, in contrast, sparkled with mischief. A giggle bubbled up all the way from her toes and turned into a real laugh on the way. "Please. We won't hear 'perfect' if we live to be a million."

"I enjoy hearing your laugh."

"Gusto." She wiped stray droplets of drink off her mouth. "Sims would call my response gusto."

"What about you—have you been sleeping since Joe's stroke?" Serious replaced the trace of humor on his face.

She looked at her meal to avoid direct exposure to hazel eyes connected to a sharp brain. "Some—I lay in bed with my eyes closed. Does staying quiet count?"

"It's a start."

I miss... She put a morsel of chicken in her mouth and chewed slowly. Every night she lay awake, listening for the missing sound of her favorite, faithful Seth Thomas. The silence, added to thoughts of Joe, Marie, Sims, and work, filled her nights. "I'm open to sleep tips which don't involve prescription drugs."

"Sorry—I don't have a cure in my pocket. Time is the only thing which worked for me." He reached for his drink.

She minimized a sigh. "I rather suspected you'd say that."

"Why don't you tell me about the cake? I think you said this isn't the first time you've thought of making one from scratch."

"True." She stabbed a piece of *bok choy*. "After Sims…and Dad, I decided I'd delayed long enough. I need to carry though before…well… before it's too late."

"Life's temporary," he whispered.

"Do you care to repeat?"

"No thanks." He didn't look away when their gazes met. "After the chemo stopped working, Mary reminded us how temporary life is."

She filed the comment beside proverbs obtained from other sources. "I've found three possible cake recipes so far. When I decide which one to try, I'll make a test cake. Do you want to be a taster?"

"Eating cake sounds like my sort of test." He smiled before taking another bite of shredded purple cabbage.

"Henry's invited, too. Two sets of taste buds should be better than one." She performed a silent summary of the various steps involved. "I'll call your place when the cake's in the oven, and we can make plans from there."

"Any idea which day you'll be baking?"

Janet turned and checked the calendar held to her fridge by half a dozen state-shaped magnets. "Mom's birthday party is always on a Sunday. This year the closest will be the fifteenth. So—maybe a week before. I want to give myself a chance to figure out any changes necessary."

"I'll look forward to it." He reached for his drink. "I'd like to hear about Sims and her gusto. If I remember correctly, she's a Navy buddy?"

"One of…was." She swallowed an invisible lump. The past tense didn't seem right. "Our group was five recruits who bonded while surviving boot camp." She remembered the first morning. Recorded reveille, then, an instant later, shouts from the drill instructor. She popped open her eyes and discovered she stared directly at the equally startled Sims in the lower bunk eighteen inches away. She knew before she blinked that the two of them would look out for each other. However, she didn't realize the strength of the bond until much later.

"And after?"

"After boot?" She waited for his nod. "Sims was slotted into shore patrol. Our schools were on the same base so we crossed paths for a few months. After we were sent to our duty stations, contact within our entire group became snail mail and the occasional expensive phone call."

"Am I right in recalling you got out after four? How long did Sims serve?"

She nodded. "I took a discharge after my initial enlistment, and Sims stayed for eight years. She and Paul were married and ready to put down roots. She soon joined the San Francisco police force and her husband…er, widower, finished his degree and started teaching in one of the high schools."

She listened to her clocks chime nine. Images of

Sims exhibiting behavior from serious to hilarious passed like a slide show with the hour markers. "Her death is a stupid waste. She was killed by a drunk driver while crossing the street after her shift." She turned her napkin into a handkerchief. "Paul is planning a memorial service near the end of September. I don't want her death to be real."

He reached across and encased her free hand in both of his.

Swallowing hard, she blinked away a memory of Sims lifting an empty margarita pitcher to get service at their boisterous table. "I miss her. I want to call and hear her voice. Am I over-reacting?"

"Sounds normal."

Comforting warmth spread from her hand all the way to her chest. "Sorry. I didn't mean to complain. The last couple of weeks…they've been rough."

"Life happens in batches. I think it's some sort of test."

She focused on his face. He appeared a little blurry from her unshed tears but also solid and trustworthy. She needed to remember he survived his own bundle of tragedies.

"Do you have plans for Sunday? I'm referring to the afternoon—three o'clock and following." He eased away one hand.

"Nothing specific. But the laundry is threatening to crawl out of the hamper and attack soon." Surprised at the light tone of her words, she nudged her lips into a smile.

"Come over to my place. I've invited some of the friendly relatives to share brisket from Smokey's. We make the gathering casual and tell each other lies."

Brushing her cheek with the back of her hand she checked for tears. *Good, none escaped.* "Tell lies to each other—you word a tempting invitation."

"Free beer is included." He stood and signaled her to do likewise.

She complied. When he stepped closer, she caught a whiff of cedar and soap. Blinking, she gazed at their feet, uncertain of her voice if she looked at his eyes.

He slid his hands along her arms. "Food. Beer. A change in your routine. What do you say?"

At his touch on her shoulders, she shivered.

An instant later, he skimmed his fingers down her arms and grasped both her hands.

A cloud lifted from her heart. She leaned against his chest and sighed. *It's safe here.* Listening to his heartbeat, she gathered confidence with each steady thump. She closed her eyes and savored her personal comfort zone. *Stay. Hold me.*

****

Rich released one of her hands and caressed her back. The gentle pressure of her against his chest awakened long-dormant sensations. *Protect. Cherish.* He buried his nose in her hair, closed his eyes, and surrendered to the light floral scent. He feathered his lips along the soft skin behind her ear. "Relax. Trust me."

She trembled within his arms.

"Cold?" He raised his eyelids and backed until he brought her ear into focus.

"Warm…very warm," she murmured.

"Me, too." He abandoned speech for a further exploration of her neck. Smooth, soft skin invited him to get lost in her. He wished to caress her and fill his lungs with her delicate, unique scent.

Keeping his lips gentle on her sensitive skin, he investigated from her hairline to the edge of her knit top. He closed his eyes, sighed, and held her tight against his chest. Memories of last week's kiss swirled in his brain. *Slow down.* He fought the urge to break unspoken boundaries.

"Mmmmm." Janet shifted.

Relaxing his hold, he smiled.

She straightened, blinked, and looked at him with moist eyes.

Swiftly moving his hands, he cradled her chin and smoothed her cheeks with his thumbs. "Shhh." He pressed his lips against hers. Prompted by the softness of her mouth, he lingered. His heart pounded with anticipation. Tempted by her taste, he coaxed her lips apart with the tip of his tongue. He savored the mixture of tang and sweet. He desired her.

A moment, or an hour, passed before she drew away. She paused with an inch of air between them. Somewhere during the kiss, she'd laced her hands behind his neck. Now she studied his face.

He became aware of a pulse in his lips, an echo of his excited heart. "Are you okay?"

"I'm surprised."

Me, too. Traces of hormone-powered teen urged him to complete the conquest. The responsible adult swallowed and leaned until their foreheads touched. "You are amazing. May I have more? Please."

She smiled.

He kissed her again. Instinct and desire smothered logic while he thanked, urged, and promised without uttering a word. Magic touched his heart and stirred a shriveled plant to life. Pausing for breath, he traced a path from her neck to the delicate hollow above her breastbone. He reached and fumbled with the hem of her shirt. Warm, smooth skin rewarded his palm.

She purred.

A moment later, she gasped.

He froze. "Did I hurt you?"

Shaking her head, she skimmed her hands across his jaw until she cradled his chin.

Reading doubt in her eyes, Rich dragged in a deep breath, took control of his hands, and tugged her shirt over her shorts. "I'll mind my manners."

"Slower...I'm spinning...out of...control."

The whisper prompted him to find her gentle lips again. She opened at his light touch and took him on the first step to paradise.

A bit later, he threaded his hands in her soft, fine hair and studied the delicate arch of dark eyebrows.

"You're beeping," she whispered an inch from his lips.

Beeping? In a heartbeat, he gathered enough brain cells to understand. Rich stepped back and reached for the phone at his waist. He took one glance at the screen and frowned. "An urgent message from work. I need to go."

****

Fifteen minutes after leaving Janet's house, Rich drove into an office building parking lot. Pulling to a stop beside an unmarked police sedan, he blinked and banished memories of Janet. Before both feet were out of the car, he grabbed the camera and started an inventory of vehicles and personnel on the scene. Four patrol cruisers and one ambulance sent flashing red, blue, and white light beams bouncing off the building windows on one side and into an undeveloped space on the other.

He raised his hand the moment Cal turned in his direction. Displaying his badge to one of the uniformed officers stringing crime scene tape, he approached his fellow detective. "Situation?"

Cal gestured to the scene at large. "Building security discovered a car he couldn't account for. One occupant...adult white male...alive...extent of injuries unknown. Medics are preparing for transport to Meramec. I retrieved his ID, but I'm still waiting for background check."

Snapping on a latex glove, he accepted the wallet. Flipping the dark, scuffed leather open, he focused on the Missouri license. An instant later, he shifted his attention to the patient on the gurney. "Greg Zwingel?"

"Do you know him?"

"I met him once...socially." Rich cataloged the prominent facts from the engagement party, Janet's hesitant comments since, and the information in the wallet. The available facts defined Mr. Zwingel as a restaurant shift manager with a gambling problem, two ex-wives, and one daughter. The address on the license indicated an older, well-maintained sub-division of the county. He remembered comments from the party which indicated his current wife was an office manager.

Rich quickened his steps toward the mound of a man under the emergency services blankets. "One moment. Please." He signaled the medics to pause. "Who did this?" Rich studied Greg's injured face under the pulsing, colored light. Ripped flesh and fresh bruising indicated a beating. At first glance, the injuries appeared consistent with either brass knuckles or weighted gloves. The victim definitely had a broken nose. Blankets and clothing covered any other damage.

Greg struggled with his next breath. "Accident"—his eyes drifted closed—"all an accident."

"Tell me the truth, Mr. Zwingel. Now is better than later." Rich shook his head and refrained from voicing his disbelief in the victim's words.

"Accident…"

"I'll be speaking to you later. Expect visitors after the docs work a little magic."

Greg coughed and turned his head to the side an instant before expelling a wad of thick, blood-tinged fluid.

"We need to get going." One of the medics pointed toward a ragged line on a portable monitor.

"One thing first." Rich photographed the driver's license before setting the wallet on the gurney.

Cal joined the group and faced the medics. "Let us know who you hand him off to at the hospital. We'll be by with questions after we finish here."

In silence, Rich waited until the ambulance doors were closed. An instant later, he uttered a single word. "Accident."

"Same sort of accident Robard claimed back on August seven." Cal led Rich toward the car where the security guard discovered Greg.

"How did the conversation with building security go?" Rich snapped a photo of the rear license plate. *Expired.*

"Helpful. Mr. Rent-A-Cop didn't have the plate on his list of people staying late in the building. He noticed the victim slumped in the passenger seat, tried to rouse him, and called for assistance."

"Our victim"—Rich squatted and opened the compact sedan's glove box—"has a history of gambling problems." He imagined one of Janet's deep sighs if she learned this incident related to betting.

"Do I want to know how you learned this information?"

Rich glanced at his partner. "The background's a story for the station. I'll save the details until during the check for a connection between Robard and Zwingel."

"Discussion over computers and coffee works for me." Cal steadied a flashlight beam over the registration papers in Rich's hand.

Robard. Zwingel. Rich compared the initial findings in the two cases. Neither incident was an accident. Mr. Robard remained uncooperative and refused to press charges. Therefore, his case file moved to the bottom of the stack.

Rich played his light around the driver's side. Pushed back almost to the limit of the rails, the seat would accommodate a much taller person than Greg Zwingel. "Move 'who was the driver' to the top of our interview questions."

Chapter Fourteen

While Janet waited for the traffic light to change, she exhaled a mixture of exhaustion and frustration. Accepting Rich's invitation was a mistake. Sunday afternoon would be more productive if she returned home. She estimated two or three days to work through her chore list.

Yesterday, she spent every minute occupied with transferring Joe from hospital to rehab center. Completing all the paperwork, reassuring Marie, and attempting to understand Joe's slurred comments used all her Saturday time and energy. She needed a nap—not a party.

"Rich Taylor, you complicate my life." She muttered the complaint an instant before her gaze paused on the passenger seat. A plastic container dominated the space. Drawing in a steadying breath, she talked to the empty truck cab. "A promise is a promise—and I'm not in the mood for an overdose on deviled eggs."

She flicked the turn signal and committed to attending the party. Rich and Henry were good people. She would be sociable and give the benefit of the doubt to their friends and relatives. Then she would do the sensible thing—end the budding relationship with Rich.

She imagined an old-fashioned balance. Placing her current independence against a future containing

Rich, the independent life won.

What about gusto? The word dropped into the scene and disrupted the balance. She shook her head to banish the idea. Life tossed her enough activity to juggle. She didn't need to go looking for additional problems to solve.

A few minutes later, she eased into a parking space in front of a silver mini-van. Smoothing her hands over tan slacks, she glanced at her red, scoop neck top. Her clothing suited the occasion, neither too tight nor too low. "Time to make my entrance."

"Welcome. Welcome." Henry pushed up from a lawn chair inside the open garage and limped toward her.

She put urgency in her step and met him at the edge of the asphalt. "Good to see you." She shifted the container of deviled eggs to her other hand and accepted his hug. "You're looking fine today."

"I dressed up for the women." He patted a pale blue shirt worn with charcoal dress pants.

"Who did you find, Gramps?" A young man, notable for abundant light brown hair threatening to brush the collar on his yellow golf shirt, stepped forward.

"The jackpot." Henry laughed and parked both hands on his cane. "Janet, meet Brian. He's home from dental school for the holiday."

Before she approached, Janet studied Rich's son for a moment. Brian stood a good inch taller and appeared a tad slighter than his father. He held his mouth in a straight, firm line and inspected her through dark honey eyes.

Henry thumped his cane once and addressed his

grandson. "She prefers tigers to elephants. I expect you to act appropriately."

"I'm also Ashley's mother." She smiled small and extended her hand.

After an instant of hesitation, Brian responded with a brief handshake.

"I understand you live in Kansas City." She started with one of the few items Rich mentioned about his son.

"For one more semester."

"And then?" She tilted her head a few degrees and hoped her stance broadcast friendly curiosity.

He narrowed his eyes. "I'll need to find a job. It's time to start paying off student loans."

I didn't ask for a deep, dark secret. "Of course—student debt is the burden of your generation." She forced her gaze to remain level. He looked like Rich's son on the outside, but he emitted more suspicion than warranted for an initial meeting.

"The others are inside—in the kitchen." Brian jerked a thumb toward the closed door.

"Thanks. By the way, I don't bite young men." She broadened her smile before she stepped past. Conscious of his stare, she opened the door and entered the back foyer. *Protective? Or more serious?* She walked toward the hum of female voices. "Good afternoon, I'm Janet."

"Welcome, I'm Sue, Rich's cousin." A round-faced brunette wiped her hands on a towel before extending one for a shake. "Rich said he'd invited a new friend. The family considers a new friendship a good thing—and younger than Henry is a bonus point."

The two other ladies quickly introduced themselves as Barb, a neighbor, and Lisa, the wife of a police officer.

"Oh, you brought deviled eggs. I'll pop them into the fridge for a bit. Now tell us all about how you and Rich met?" Sue, clearly in charge of the kitchen, accepted the plastic container.

Aware of a warm blush on her neck, Janet hesitated. "You ask a good question. A proper answer gets complicated."

"We've got the time. Men are on a beer run." Barb selected a long, narrow knife from the block and directed Janet to the desserts. "Can you talk and work?"

At ease with the other women, Janet recounted the basic facts of the service call and the subsequent engagement party. "Turns out he coached my daughter in soccer years ago."

"Typical Rich." Sue crimped aluminum foil around a loaf of bread fixed with margarine, garlic powder, and parmesan cheese.

"You should get a lot of mileage from that story." Lisa opened the oven. The scent of warm, sweet, bar-b-que flooded into the kitchen.

"How long have the men been gone? The store's less than a mile." Barb opened a sleeve of plastic cups.

Without moving her attention from cutting a fresh peach pie into equal pieces, Janet caught a note of impatience from the neighbor.

Sue looked toward the digital clock on the stove. "Half an hour. Let's see—four men, three items on their list—I'd expect them most any time now."

"Do you think they'll remember ice and soda to go with their beer?" Barb stood in the opening between kitchen and living room.

Janet wiped off the knife and prepared for the first

cut into a chocolate cake with white icing.

"Oh, good, we've more guests. A handsome young man and girl to match just arrived in a blue compact."

Janet stepped over and glanced out the front window. "You're looking at Daniel and his fiancée, my daughter, Ashley."

Sue nestled the bread beside a ceramic dish of beans in the oven. "Daniel. I haven't seen him in ages. Well, except for Mary's funeral, which I don't want to count."

A minute or two later, Ashley entered the kitchen carrying a clear plastic bowl of pasta salad. "Hi, everyone. You, too, Mom."

Janet smiled at her daughter's casual humor. "I told them about the engagement. Now be a good girl and display your ring."

Ashley gave an exaggerated sigh and shook her head, which sent her pony tail into motion. "Really, Mother, what if they're not interested?"

"We're interested." The three women responded in unison.

Sue stepped in front of Ashley and admired the round-cut solitaire in a simple white gold setting. "Beautiful. Daniel did well."

Quick introductions followed the admiration of Ashley's new jewelry. "Have you set a wedding date?"

"December twenty-sixth."

"The men are back." Janet watched all four doors and the trunk of Rich's car open the instant it came to a stop.

"Mom." Ashley touched Janet's elbow and pointed to an empty portion of the living room.

"What's up?" Janet followed her daughter. Neither

were in the habit of sharing confidences in semi-public settings but Ashley's tone implied a serious, private topic.

Before speaking, Ashley shifted her gaze to the view of the street. "Have you heard from Dad?"

"Greg? Why would he call me? We're not on the best of terms." She recalled the brief encounter outside the hospital as their last contact.

"Friday night he was in an accident of some sort. He called early yesterday and asked Daniel and I to drive him from the hospital to get his car out of police impound."

Janet covered her surprise with several blinks and scanned the sparsely decorated room until she trusted her voice. "Why you? Where was his wife?"

"He didn't say a word about Pam. Actually, he avoided answering my direct questions on the topic. He's hurt, Mom. I saw bruises all over his face, a black eye, and stitches beside his lip. He moved like his ribs hurt." Frowning, Ashley gripped her hands in front of her waist. "The whole situation…felt upside down. I played the role of adult and he the child."

Pressing her lips, Janet concealed her sigh. In one sentence, her daughter summarized a good portion of life with Greg. She remembered incidents before the divorce where he behaved more childish than his young daughter. "Did he request money to get his car released?"

"He asked us to stop at a bank and went in alone."

"Good." She shed relief with her next breath. Perhaps Greg actually took a little responsibility. Then again, the injuries sounded like he'd been in a fight, not exactly mature behavior.

"Hey. Are the Zwingel ladies going to stand in the corner all day?"

"Absolutely not." Janet moved her gaze and smiled for Rich. Why did her heart give that odd little double thump and feel lighter when he grinned in her direction?

****

Late in the afternoon, Rich jiggled a small, bright blue, cloth bag in his hand. The dry corn inside shifted into the shape of his palm. The stakes were high for his next toss. The men's team trailed by two points in the cornhole game. A clean drop into the target would give them the win.

"Imagine a fleeing thief or drug dealer," Daniel encouraged.

"No pressure—just the entire game on the line," Sue remarked from his left.

He glanced between the target and the ammunition in his hand. The game board, one of Brian's shop projects, sloped at a shallow angle. A colorful cartoon bear—dressed in overalls, paws raised, and mouth open—decorated the plywood.

"Don't take all day," Henry, the designated scorekeeper, prompted from his lawn chair.

Rich inhaled, held his breath, and released the corn bag on the exhale. The pouch thumped on the bear's forehead and slid. For a moment, the small sack covered the character's left eye. An instant later, it corrected course and dropped from the figure's black nose into the round hole of the mouth. He raised a fist into the air. "Three points—for the win."

"You won us bragging rights. Talk quick—they're a fleeting thing." Tom, Sue's husband, clapped Rich on the shoulder.

"Victors claim first in line at the dessert table." Rich named a prize consistent with the easy, light conversation of the entire party. A moment later, he joined Brian collecting the red and blue corn bags.

"Good toss, Dad."

"Thanks for bringing out the board. The game was exactly what we needed." He appreciated the activity which prevented the after-meal conversations from circling over the same four or five topics.

"I'm surprised you kept game equipment."

Rich straightened and studied his son. "I saved a lot of things." Boxes of memories filled the deep shelves in the garage and the closet in the bedroom office. He didn't want to look at many of the items. But he understood the importance of photos and trinkets for his children. "I probably kept too much."

"I doubt that." Brian folded in the flaps on the cardboard box marked "games."

Not now. Not here. Rich shrugged. Conversations with his son frequently included differing opinions concerning the changes he made or the things he disposed of during last year's move. He'd been unable to proceed forward with all of Mary's possessions within sight. The overwhelming number of memory-evoking furnishings in their home of nineteen years prompted his move. Decisions made thinning and packing photos and fancy dishes proved to be the major source of friction with his son.

"The Taylor men and their sweets." Sue removed plastic covers from the assortment of desserts. "It's a wonder they don't all have the physiques of Sumo wrestlers."

"I heard you." Rich took a paper plate and plastic fork from the supply at the end of the picnic table. "Have you ever considered the amount of energy necessary to plot and stay ahead of the women?"

"Ha."

"I'll take one of those if you're serving." Rich pointed toward the piece of cake Janet loosened in the pan.

"Only one?" She raised an eyebrow.

"I'm saving room for a lemon bar." He widened his smile to match hers. "Join me in a minute?"

"After all the victors are fed." She lifted a second piece of cake and added the rectangle to Tom's plate.

A few minutes later, Rich stood next to Janet under the only shade tree in the yard. He glanced toward the other guests chatting in pairs and trios. "I've been thinking."

"Should I be worried?"

"No need to over-react." He paused a forkful of cake and appreciated the rich chocolate scent. "Do you still plan on making a special cake for your mother's birthday?" He lingered his gaze on her lively blue eyes. He appreciated every glimpse her eyes allowed into the depths of her mind. She intrigued him like no other woman since…well…since he'd been a young man.

"Absolutely. The party's two weeks from today. I plan to make the test cake toward the end of this week. Are you and Henry agreeable to critique?" She closed her mouth around a bite of peach pie.

"Do you have one of those big mixers—on a stand?" He drew a circle in the air with his fork.

"I've never been able to justify the cost."

"Would a large mixer be helpful? I've got one

sitting in a box I'm willing to loan. You could return it after your mother's party." He lifted a forkful of lemon bar. The mixture of sweet and tart refreshed his palate after the super sweet icing.

"Are you sure?"

He read hesitation in her eyes. "I'm sure I won't be making any cakes."

"Henry's not learning to bake desserts? I'm sure he mentioned registering for a cooking class."

Rich shook his head. "He signed up for kitchen basics. I'm hoping they cover how to fry an egg without setting off the smoke alarm and other first steps."

She quirked her mouth higher on one side than the other. "Sounds intriguing. Do you want to say more?"

"Ask Henry for details. He claims I exaggerate." He didn't want to share how often he tested every smoke alarm in the house since the burned potatoes and sausage incident.

Janet laughed. "With such a charming offer, I accept the mixer on loan."

"Good." He glanced toward the others and realized his neighbors were getting ready to leave. "Now excuse me while I go act the gracious host."

About twenty minutes later, Rich carried a lawn chair as he walked beside Sue and Tom to their van. The majority of his host duties were over. In another few minutes, or however long his cousin took with parting comments, the only guest left would be Janet. At the moment, he half-listened to Sue, aware she rambled on about the flowers along the back of his house. She called them a name, familiar in a vague sort of way, which confirmed his late spring decision to keep them. He glanced back to the garage and saw

Janet talking to Henry. "Thanks again for coming."

"You should invite guests more often, Rich. Why, you didn't even give us a chance to organize a proper housewarming when you moved." Sue formed her mouth into an exaggerated pout.

I didn't need a party. He kept his commentary silent. Closing on the houses and organizing the move came during the same week he gave testimony for a difficult case. At the end of it all, he craved quiet rather than people. "I gave you my new address."

"You sent an email the next week." Sue stood outside the open passenger door and gave him a peck on the cheek. "Now keep in touch. I'll email you the date for our Halloween bash."

"Last Saturday in October." Tom winked at Rich and stowed chairs and a cooler in the back of their van. "Bring Janet."

Rich held in a sigh. The end of October was almost two months away. A lot could happen between now and then. "No promises." After Sue and Tom drove away, Rich returned to the garage. One glimpse of Janet's smile and his chest lightened.

"I'm sitting. Are you satisfied?" Henry thumped his cane on the concrete floor and glared at his son.

I didn't say a thing. By the set of Henry's shoulders, Rich suspected the older man neared exhaustion.

Janet stood in front of Henry and toyed with her purse strap. "Let younger men move the picnic table. Rest a bit. I left the last deviled egg in the fridge."

"Bless you. The egg won't last long." Henry burped and rubbed a tiny circle on his chest. "Soon as the bar-b-que and chocolate cake settle, the egg's a goner."

"Slow down, Dad. I'll warn off Brian. You can enjoy your treat tomorrow."

"Good idea, all your education is paying off."

"Glad you share my opinion." He turned his attention to Janet. "Give me a couple minutes and I'll find the mixer."

"Are you certain you want to loan a kitchen appliance?" She adjusted her grip on an empty plastic container.

"Absolutely. It's been sitting in a box taking up space since before I moved. Consider it advance payment for the tasting party." He walked over to the shelves and removed a pair of totes labeled "Christmas." A moment later, he set a box of books at his feet and peered into the second row on the deep shelf. He recognized the box immediately, one stand mixer in a faded, red-and-white box.

"What are you looking for, Dad?" Brian stepped out of the house.

"I found it." Rich tugged the box forward before studying his son's uneasy posture. "I'm lending the mixer to Janet for a couple of weeks. Henry and I won't be using it."

"Giving away mother's things?" Brian crossed his arms.

Rich shrugged. "She won't object. If you want to get technical, it's mine to do with as I please." He snapped his mouth. Brian's stance was defiant, but his eyes revealed a weariness. Some days his son wished too hard for the days before Mary's illness. "I'm sending a mixer on loan, son. Janet will treat it with care."

"I heard your words." Brian lifted one of the totes and shoved the plastic cube to the back of the shelf.

"Ready?" Rich asked Janet a moment later.

She nodded before leaning down and giving Henry an awkward hug. "Take care of yourself. Let Joe settle in for a day or two before you call."

"Yes, ma'am." Henry tossed off a sloppy salute.

Halfway to her truck, Rich glanced back toward Henry before speaking. "Are you sure you want Henry and Joe to put their heads together?"

"They formed an instant bond at my place. I'm thinking an auto assembly worker and a brewery warehouseman should have a few things in common."

"I'm not worried about them talking jobs and unions." He didn't trust Henry to avoid conversations involving the need for companionship. The old man recently showed a meddling streak. Little comments made when Rich returned from an elongated shift or a visit to Janet ventured into new territory for his dad.

"I hope you realize Henry will do most of the talking. Two clear words in a row from Joe are cause for applause these days."

"Is he scheduled for speech therapy?" He recalled portions of casual precinct conversations.

She nodded and opened the passenger door. "Therapy goes into full force the day after tomorrow. The therapists scheduled both speech and physical sessions for Monday through Friday. I told him he should view the situation like starting a new job."

"How was that received?" He glanced toward Henry, aware of the prodding necessary to keep him on track with post-surgery exercise.

"He's become expert at frowning with the good

side of his face."

Rich stashed the mixer on the cab floor and slammed the truck door. "I feel like I owe you an apology."

"For?" She glanced at him with raised eyebrows and led him around to the driver's side.

"Brian's behavior. I noticed he either avoided you or was curt."

"He's an adult, capable of making his own apology. If he sees me as a threat, he's wrong."

"I'd pick a different word." He lifted his gaze and noted Brian squatted, talking to Henry. "Some days I think he's stuck in the angry stage of grief. Mary was his confidante. I'm guessing my irregular hours contributed to the situation. In addition, change has always been difficult for him, much more so than with his sister."

"I'll keep those facts in mind."

Rich reached for Janet's hand. He sighed at the comfort from her touch. He weighed the temporary pleasure from giving her a proper farewell kiss against the almost-certain verbal sparring with his son to follow. *It's my life. Life's temporary.* He leaned closer and gave her a gentle kiss on her mouth. She tasted of sweet peaches and fresh air. He drew her closer and deepened the kiss.

"Mmmmm."

He retreated an inch. A hint of power rolled up his muscles from where his fingers held her upper arms. With her beside him, he could slay dragons—win cornball—or go another verbal round with his son. "Stay safe. I'll give you a call or text tomorrow." He eased back and slid his hands down to her wrists.

"Sounds good."

Life's temporary. He sighed and watched her drive away. What word did she use in reference to her recently deceased friend? Gusto? Did gusto come packaged in brunette hair and blue eyes?

Chapter Fifteen

Tuesday afternoon Janet tucked the needle-nosed pliers into her tool belt. She and Pat were making excellent progress for the first day of the Sleep E-Z Motel installations. If the next two units went without problems, they would finish the even-numbered rooms in this section.

She welcomed today's work as a change of pace from residential clients recovering from the holiday week-end. The minute she walked into the office this morning Pat informed her the project started today. Without delay, she lent a hand to finish packing the van.

"You got everything under control?" Pat set the large black trash bag outside the door.

"Affirmative." She turned the controls to the low and heat settings and listened to the mechanical purr as she gathered bits of debris from the worn brown carpet. Following the steps on the field test, she reached over and turned the fan to high. She listened for a long moment before holding her hand above the vent.

Pat grasped the handles of the two-wheel dolly and bumped the discarded unit over the threshold. "I'll leave you to finish here. Meet me at the next door."

"Works for me." She checked the fan speeds with the unit set in the cooling function. She and Pat worked well together. During their discussion of procedure on the drive over, he treated her as an equal. Conversation during unit removal and installation stayed on the topic at hand.

A few minutes later, Janet stepped outside into bright afternoon sunlight. She pulled the door closed and checked the lock before she lifted her water bottle. Two gulps later, she set the empty container beside the entrance to Room 112.

Stay safe. She paused for a moment and allowed Rich's final words from last night's phone call to drift in a circle before settling. The first time he ended a conversation with them she ignored the phrase. Now, after what…three weeks…the expression returned at odd moments and offered comfort like a blanket on a cold night.

Swiping sweat off her brow and replacing her cap, she checked the list from the office and then her watch. The room in front of her was the only first-floor, even-numbered room occupied last night. Now, more than two hours past check-out time, she expected the room to be empty, though perhaps not cleaned by the maids.

Knocking on the door with one hand, she dug for the master key card with the other. "Maintenance." Silence greeted her statement. She counted to ten under her breath, then pounded harder. Startling a guest could be embarrassing. "Maintenance."

A moment later, she inserted the master key and turned the handle. "Maintenance." Sticking one sturdy work boot toe over the threshold, she called out again while pushing the door wide.

What? When the first breath of still, copper-scented air reached her lungs, she coughed. Who in their right mind soldered in a motel room? She blinked twice to adjust to the dim light behind the closed, heavy drapes. The linen on the lone, queen-sized bed was rumpled—the bed empty. She exhaled a large dose of relief at one good point. An instant later, she spotted a man's worn wallet beside the lamp on the bedside table. She listened for running water. Silence, not even a drip. She glanced at the quiet A/C unit. A little shiver ran along her spine. "Anybody here? Speak up."

Leaving the door wide open, Janet took several steps into the room. Patterning her gaze around the room, she shivered in the heat. *What's off?* She didn't see any figure through the open bathroom door. After taking another step toward the closet, she glanced to her right.

She froze—forced one blink—and then a second. "Oh…my…" Clamping a hand over her mouth, she backed out of the room and pulled the door closed tight. Turning, she stood on the edge of the sidewalk, placed her hands on her knees, and leaned forward. *Breathe in. Breathe out.* She urged her lungs back into a regular rhythm. *No. It can't be.* She dragged in warm, fresh, air and prayed her stomach would keep lunch where it belonged. "One Mississippi, two Mississippi, three Mississippi." She counted seconds which felt like hours.

"Zwingel." Pat approached with the loaded cart. "What happened? You look pale as a ghost."

She shook her head. An explanation drifted in a fog. Straightening, she avoided looking into Pat's face and retrieved her phone. She stared at the numbers for a long moment before her finger touched the nine button. "Dead body."

****

The familiar red logo on the white van caught Rich's attention from half a block away. Comfort On Call, Janet's company, was on site. Before he recalled if she was definitely assigned to this project, Cal turned their black sedan into the Sleep E-Z Motel driveway.

Memories of his most recent visit to the property returned like a punch to the chest. Sitting beside him while he drove around the building, Janet chatted about a contract to install new heating and cooling units with the sort of enthusiasm he reserved for paydays and vacation. Today, his presence was strictly business—homicide.

"I'll take the room. I want you to start with the caller and follow with employees." He glanced at Cal and saw an unasked question on his face. "I've got a possible conflict."

Cal parked between the Comfort On Call van and a patrol car with all its lights flashing. "You're the senior."

A moment later, Rich exited the police sedan with the camera in one hand and confirmed his fears.

Janet came into view from the dumpster area, carrying a bottle of water and wiping at her face. She walked straight toward the unmarked cruiser.

"You." He sealed professional authority into the word and wore another portion in his posture.

"Me." She pointed to her chest.

"Did you call it in?"

"Affirmative."

He glanced toward the sky and dragged in a portion of warm afternoon air. A crime scene wasn't the place he wanted to see Janet. She belonged across a café table…or walking hand-in-hand. He drew on an internal reserve of professionalism and gestured to the front of a patrol car. "Wait over there until Detective Collins can talk to you."

"Will do." She shifted a few degrees, continued walking, and stopped after reaching the shaded walkway.

"Is she your conflict?" Cal came around the nose of the car and looked in her direction for a moment.

Rich remained silent. How was a man to keep his social life private when she pops up on the professional side?

With a shrug, Cal followed him the few steps to the uniformed officer outside Room 112.

"We'll talk later." *Much later. Next century.* Rich sent a final glance toward Janet before he clicked his attention to the task at hand. He paused in front of the young officer at the door. "Were you first on scene?"

"Yes, sir. I confirmed the situation and called the station. You're prompt." He gestured to a fourth marked patrol car now arriving.

Rich scanned the area where uniformed officers took positions to control access to the property. "Medical examiner?"

"Notified—on their way."

"What's inside?" Cal snapped on a glove.

"Adult, white male. Deceased."

"Overdose?" Rich floated the most common cause of death in the motel population.

"Highly doubtful, but nothing's ruled out at this time."

The officer, Lankford, according to his name tag, used carefully chosen words. Rich nodded and displayed his badge. "Until further notice, stay on the door. I'm Taylor."

"Collins." Cal displayed his ID and nodded as the officer jotted a note.

Humid, stale air laced with the metallic tones of blood and a sharper note of urine, greeted Rich's nose. *Smelled worse.* He focused on his work. First, he scanned the bathroom and closet for a hiding witness before standing near the head of the victim. One gunshot entrance wound in the bare chest and a blood pool extending from the body gave a strong indication of cause of death. Open eyes and specks of dried blood around the mouth contributed to the sort of scene civilians should not witness.

Cal squatted and played a flashlight beam at the junction of bed and carpet. "No weapon on the first pass."

"Killer likely took the gun with him." Rich turned his attention to the items on the nightstand. Lifting the camera, he began taking photos. After opening the wallet, he photographed a Missouri driver's license with the name Alan Wilson. The address was in adjacent St. Charles County, and the photo appeared a decent match to the victim. Rich directed his next words to Cal. "Hand me your phone. I'll give you a preliminary for your interviews."

"Thanks." Cal checked the likeness and paused at the door. "I'll start with our reporting party."

Rich nodded. "Send the next detective to the motel office. I want all the surveillance footage from an hour before he checked in until…eleven this morning."

During the next fifteen minutes, the number of law enforcement personnel at the scene mushroomed. Several uniformed officers sealed the entrance and others started going door-to-door in the building. The assistant medical examiner and an evidence collection specialist from the crime lab joined Rich inside Room 112.

Starting with the wallet and eyeglasses on the nightstand, Rich and the crime lab tech described, bagged, and labeled evidence, including the contents of a wastebasket.

Next, Rich turned his attention to the closet. He pulled a black, wheeled, carry-on bag into the main area after the initial photographs. In the second outside pocket, he discovered a passport and airline boarding pass. "Interesting."

"Sir?" The crime lab tech stood beside him with his electronic tablet, ready to record a description.

"I've found a passport issued to Alfred Winston. The address is in the East Metro."

"Not the same…" The tech entered the address into his device.

"Exactly. Passport is not the same name or address as the wallet." Rich stood and flipped through the airline tickets. St. Louis to Chicago, then a change of airline for a flight to Miami and finally to Grand Cayman. According to the papers in hand, the flight from O'Hare would land in Miami within the half hour. He turned to the forty-something female physician squatted beside the body. "Anything to report, Doc?"

"Our man is in full rigor. I've only found one entrance wound. His phone is ringing, or rather vibrating, on his waistband. I'm ready to empty his pockets if you are."

"You've made good progress. Can you delay for one moment?" He handed the boarding passes to the tech and crossed to the door. "Lankford."

"What do you need, sir?"

"I see him." Rich stepped from the shade provided by the second story walkway and hurried to Cal. His partner was testing the doors on a shiny, black hybrid hatchback. "Is this our victim's car?"

Cal shook his head. "According to the HVAC techs and the maids, the vehicle was here early this morning. The plates are registered to a Pamela M. Cork."

"A woman was in the room last night." Rich recalled a condom and wrapper from the trash basket.

"Sounds typical." Cal lined up a photo of the car's console from the driver's window.

"Come with me. I'm giving you a phone assignment." During the short walk to Room 112, he outlined the flight information and conflicting identification.

"I'm sorry about the interruption, Doc." Rich turned his attention once again to the body dressed in jeans.

"Delays happen. Shall we begin? In the right front pocket—one set of keys: Ford auto, two smaller brass, and one chrome.

Rich and the tech received the items and transferred them into evidence bags.

"Clipped to waistband over right hip, one smart phone."

Rich accepted the phone, a model available for the past two years. Tapping the call history icon, he learned a local number called four times since the first officer responded. He pressed for a call back and put the device on speaker. On the third ring, a young, male, semi-panicked voice came on the line.

"This is Charlie…at the motel. We got a problem. Police crawling all over the place."

Rich disconnected the call. "Who went to the motel office?"

"Jones. She obtained the surveillance footage and stationed a uniform in the lobby."

"Get her back in there. Find out who Charlie thought he was calling."

Cal took off at a sprint, his phone at his ear. "Yes, ma'am, I'm waiting to speak with your supervisor."

"Right back pocket. One man's wallet, tri-fold style, black." The doctor handed it to Rich.

Another billfold? Flipping open the wallet, he read highlights from the driver's license. "Albert Williams— address in west county. Cripes, now we have three names and addresses."

"Al W. on the toe tag works for me." The assistant medical examiner pulled a white, cotton handkerchief from the left back pocket, and three dollars and fifty-five cents in assorted coins from the left front. Her immediate task completed, she stood and carefully stretched. "Do you want a few moments before we roll him?"

Rich studied the victim's face for a long moment. *Al W. What's your story?*

****

Janet sat cross-legged on the cement and rested her head against room 108's smooth door. Closing her eyes, she failed to banish the image of a tall, balding man sitting in Mike's office. The voices of police officers and the slap of their shoes against hard surfaces made a swirl of background noise. *His face. His eyes.*

Drawing a breath, she counted three seconds, and

released air through pursed lips.

"Are you doing yoga?"

Snapping open her eyes, she forced a small smile for Pat. "I don't do yoga. But this position feels as comfortable as circumstances allow."

"I brought you something." He bent from the waist and held both hands behind his back.

"Top of my wish list at the moment is a hot shower. I'd settle for a glass of wine." She called on her reserve of humor to prevent a complete emotional collapse.

Pat laughed and extended a large candy bar. "Be careful, Janet. Next thing we know, you'll embarrass me with your secrets."

Tearing off the end of the wrapper, she studied him. "Join me. I promise not to say anything your wife couldn't hear."

"An offer which I find impossible to refuse." He sat beside her with his legs straight across half the shaded walkway. "I called Mike."

She bit off a mouthful of chocolate, peanuts, and caramel. "Did you go into detail?"

"I told him we encountered a problem on the property, and we'd come back to the office when the police gave permission. I didn't tell him...you found a body...or my best guess at the identity of the man. I figure my brother deserves a face-to-face retelling."

Chewing, she tried to imagine Mike's reaction to the truth. From her vantage point, Mike and the dead man, Al, didn't seem close. But she'd only seen them together twice and both times were business situations.

For a long moment, she concentrated on the controlled chaos in front of them. She ceased counting police personnel on the property a few minutes after Detective Collins took her statement. The officers walked with purpose and kept verbal exchanges brief and low. She listened to the voices of the two maids through the open door to the linen room. What if…any other day…she took another bite of candy and pushed away the image of a young housekeeper finding Al.

"Are you coming in to work tomorrow?" Pat opened a bottle of soda.

"Absolutely. Why wouldn't I?" She raised her brows and stared.

He shrugged. "Let's just say I've worked with techs who would take off for a day or two."

"I'm not one of them. I learned early in life to pick myself up and try again." She pressed her lips for a moment before continuing. "Don't get me wrong. I do need a few hours to pull myself together. When I mentioned a hot shower and a glass of wine, I was serious. However, tomorrow morning, I'll get back into uniform and carry on." Her words brought a childhood incident at her grandparent's home to mind.

One day, in the midst of a soccer game with her cousins, she didn't pay attention and collided with a tree—hard. After going to the house, getting her shoulder inspected, and her tears dried—her grandmother told her to do two things. First, go outside and apologize to the tree. Second, rejoin the game.

Pat looked toward the activity on the parking lot. "I'll postpone the balance of this project a few days. Regular service calls and furnace preventative maintenance will keep us busy. Maybe we can reschedule a few things and resume motel work next week."

"I still want to be assigned to the installations." She crumbled the candy wrapper. "I'll simply let you enter any possibly occupied rooms first."

"So generous of you." He reached for his phone on the second ring.

Janet pushed to her feet. She wanted to move. All the waiting after giving her statement gave her mind too much time to spin in circles. Walking to the end of the building, she finished her water.

News vans from three local stations gathered across the street and pointed cameras in her direction. Turning, she glimpsed Rich near the far end of the building.

He held a phone to his ear and beckoned an officer.

He's working. She set one hand over the iceberg forming behind her ribs. Crime scenes and dead bodies weren't new to Rich. His work took him to sites of violence—a world very different from her familiar surroundings of burners, condensers, and motors. He'd seen other murder victims. How many?

We didn't talk shop at home. She swallowed hard. Immediately, she viewed his barrier between work and home in a new light—protection. The concepts of thoughtfulness and concern took on new shapes and melted the edges of dread in her chest.

Janet darted her gaze around the scene and shivered when an officer's holstered weapon came into sharp focus. Blinking, she searched among the personnel and settled her gaze on Rich. Could she accept his partitioned life? Did she want to try?

****

Two and a half hours later, Rich started the car and eased into the quiet subdivision street. Official sunset came and left a deepening dusk while he and Cal turned Mrs. Al Williams' life in a new direction.

Cal tapped the computer screen to action and scrolled through field reports. "I don't mean to jinx us, but today's death notification is near the top of my personal strange list. Until half an hour ago, I never heard a person self-describe as non-grieving widow. Have you?"

"The interview was odd." Rich nodded. "Her demeanor suited a neighbor or business acquaintance instead of close family member. One of the poker buddies she named, Mike Maguire, is already on our interview list. Who has the assignment?"

"Jones and Lopez." Cal switched to another computer screen. "The Maguire interview shows a status of 'in progress.'"

During the following moments of silence in the car, Rich reviewed some of the information from Mrs. Albert Williams. According to the new widow, she and Al were in the middle steps of a divorce. Three weeks from tomorrow they were due to appear for a hearing. She stated his affair with a married woman, recently confirmed by a mutual friend, was the last straw. Mrs. Williams believed the woman to be named Pam. The dry-eyed widow cooperated and gave the detectives copies of credit card and bank statements for the previous three months. She also volunteered several photos taken in January during a trip to Grand Cayman.

"An attempt at reconciliation." The new widow put the phrase in air quotes and laughed. "I shopped and spent afternoons at the beach. Al disappeared for hours at a time on 'business.'"

In addition, Mrs. Williams saved the police a little

effort by confirming the name and address of Al's game and vending machine business. A third pair of detectives was currently on the way to gather information from any employees on site.

Ten minutes later, Rich eased over a speed bump and followed the gentle curves of a subdivision street. Split-level houses with a pair of dormer windows above the garage were silhouetted by the street lights. Mature trees in the front yards hinted at an age in excess of thirty years. Confirming a number on a mailbox, he parked the police sedan to block the driveway.

"Once upon a time, when I was in elementary school, we lived in a house and neighborhood similar to his one." Cal tapped the computer screen to black.

Rich allowed a brief smile to reward Cal's attempt to break the tension. The imminent interview could take a variety of directions. "Do you suppose our subject knows where his wife is?"

"Are you considering using her location as leverage?" Cal closed the car door without a sound.

Coincidences make me suspicious. In recent weeks, an ongoing loan sharking and money laundering investigation showed numerous threads too similar to ignore—including the Robard and Zwingel beatings. Neither man could be persuaded to file a complaint. Now, Rich and Cal prepared to question Zwingel while his wife, a.k.a. Pamela M. Cork, sat under the watchful eye of the Miami police.

A minute later, Rich stood in a pool of light from a single bulb on the semicircular top of three curved steps and rang the bell. He glanced back at Cal.

Detective Collins stood away from a corner of the house where he could catch a view of movement in the back.

Rich calculated how long since he'd last seen the man and estimated the amount of healing to his face. Light flickered from behind the drapes, consistent with a large TV. He pushed the doorbell again.

"In a minute." A male voice was followed by muffled footsteps.

Staying alert, Rich prepared himself to duck, charge, or start a conversation.

Greg opened the door the length of the chain and peered out. Dressed in faded jeans and a gray T-shirt, he kept one hand on the knob. "It's late. Go away."

"Detectives Taylor and Collins. We want to ask you a few questions." Rich displayed his badge and placed his steel toed oxford across the threshold.

"I told you over and over—I'm not pressing charges. Friday night was a misunderstanding."

"Our questions aren't about Friday. May we come in? You might have witnessed an incident and been unaware of the significance." Rich shifted his weight forward. The motel surveillance tape clearly showed Greg's car entering the property at Al's approximate time of death and leaving twenty minutes later.

Greg frowned, shrugged, and fumbled with the chain. "Ask your questions quick. I've got work in the morning."

"I understand." Rich stepped inside and eased past Greg. Keeping his movements deliberate and unhurried, he took a position between Greg and the half flight of steps to the area above the garage. The location also gave him a clear view into the dining area and a glimpse of the kitchen.

"Are you Gregory W. Zwingel?" Cal halted two

steps inside the door and pulled out his notebook.

"You knew my name before you parked your car." Greg grabbed the remote and muted the TV.

Rich patterned his gaze over the clutter on the dining table while listening to his partner confirm background information. Envelopes with prominent return addresses from banks and credit card companies lay in an untidy pile of mail. In a small glass dish, a large red stone on a man's signet ring glinted in the light. He caught a semi-familiar sound, lifted his gaze higher, and noticed a dark, wooden, mantel clock on the china cabinet.

"What was your business at the Sleep E-Z Motel last night?"

Rich switched his attention to Greg's body language the instant Cal's questions entered new territory.

"How?" Greg opened his mouth, closed it without another sound, and swallowed.

"We have your car on surveillance tapes."

Rich watched a drop of sweat form above one of Greg's remaining butterfly bandages.

"While on the property, did you see anyone go in or out of any of the rooms?" Cal moved to the next question without a noticeable pause.

Shaking his head and brushing a finger along the hairline at his temple, Greg mumbled a negative reply.

"Did you see or hear anyone get in or out of a car?"

"Nothing I remember."

"Did you hear anything—a crash—a shout?" Cal touched his pen to paper.

"Normal street traffic—nothing else." Greg pressed his lips for an instant and winced.

"Where's your wife this evening?" Rich slipped in the question.

Greg turned to face him and paused with his mouth open. "I know you...not just from Friday. You were—"

"At the same social gathering." Rich completed the sentence with his prepared response. "Now answer the question. Where is your wife?"

"She's not here." Greg stiffened and crossed his arms.

"When do you expect her home?" Rich held his tone even.

"She's visiting relatives...out of town."

"We want her contact information." Cal turned to a fresh notebook page.

"I'm done with your questions. Go—out of my house—now." Greg strode to the front door and jerked it open.

Cal snapped his notebook closed and shrugged.

Staying in place, Rich hid disappointment at the abrupt end to the interview. He looked at the carpet for a long moment and shook his head.

The mantel clock began to chime the hour.

Exaggerating his turn toward the cabinet, he pretended to have just noticed the antique. "Nice clock...is it a family heirloom?"

"You could say that."

"But it would be a lie." Rich made eye contact with Greg and watched the heavier man's bravado fade. "I'll give you a word of advice, Mr. Zwingel. Be careful during police interviews. Lies and evasions make us suspicious. Truthful answers make life more pleasant for everyone."

Chapter Sixteen

The radio announcer started the top-of-the-hour newscast as Janet pulled away from the drive-thru window and eased toward the busy street. The aroma of hot, salty french fries rose from the bag on the passenger seat. While waiting for a gap in the Wednesday end-of-workday traffic, she slid one hand across her uniform pants, removing a portion of sweat.

What do I say? She knew her mother would remark on last night's absence. The hastily concocted story of a headache was thin. Lying to her parents bothered her—no matter her age or degree of independence. However, telling the truth yesterday felt equally impossible.

"Sorry, Mom. I couldn't visit last night. I needed the evening to recover my nerves after finding a corpse." The words sounded wrong the instant she spoke them to her truck's quiet air. The lie had been kinder—and included portions of truth. She did have a headache last night—not to mention recurring images of the body beside the motel bed.

She glanced toward the red-and-white paper sack leaning against her purse on the passenger seat, and her stomach rumbled. Nervous or not, she craved food. She hoped tonight's supper tasted better than lunch eaten under the awkward gazes of co-workers. With her next breath, the scent of hot fries and grilled chicken sandwich tempted. She eased to a stop at a traffic light and lifted her ice tea for a sip.

"Today was good," she whispered into the cab. Before the first service calls, Pat announced he suspended the motel project until Monday. Part of her wanted to return today. Her fears always shrank when she promptly faced them a second time.

An incident involving crawl spaces surfaced from deep within her memory. Eight years ago, she wriggled under a residence to trace a homeowner installed line. While under the home's addition, she encountered a skunk family. Two days later, after more silent prayers than at a pastoral conference, she took her fears and left them under a different customer's wooden deck. Monday—she would deal with the time lapse.

Today, she discovered no dead bodies. During several routine furnace inspections and preventative maintenance calls, she didn't find even a petrified mouse. The homeowners, except one grumpy lady, were cooperative and on the friendly side. She didn't see Mike. Then again, she spent a minimum of time in the office. Not crossing Mike's path for a day happened frequently. Yes, Wednesday rated good by any standard. Compared to yesterday, today approached paradise in HVAC land.

Fifteen minutes later, Janet walked softly across Oak Leaf Center's community room, signaled her mother to stay quiet, and set a hand on her father's shoulder. "Hi, Dad. May I join you?"

Joe tipped his head and sent her a lopsided smile. "Missshed you."

She translated his slurred speech and kissed his cheek. "You need a shave. Do you have a story?"

"Ssssssupper over. Massshed everything." He

pointed to her bag with his good hand.

"I'm sorry to hear you didn't care for supper. The sandwich is mine. If you don't tell the aide, I'll let you sneak some fries." Janet pulled a chair close and gestured toward a woman in bright scrubs.

"Too much salt." Marie tugged on vivid orange yarn and made another crochet stitch on her current project.

A moment later, Janet ripped open the fast food bag, spread it to shield her lap, and dusted obvious salt off a few fries. "I won't give you all of them." She set the reduced-salt treat on a napkin within Joe's reach. "Consider them dessert."

"I see you came direct from work." Marie looked at her and continued her stitches.

Her uniform, dark blue pants and gray shirt with the Comfort On Call patch above the pocket, made the statement obvious. "Coming from the shop saves a few miles—and minutes. I got off early enough to beat the worst of rush hour today."

"Newsssss. Read to me." Joe gestured to the large screen with the closed caption summary at the bottom.

At conversational volume, Janet relayed the story of a fatal crash on a highway ramp and the continuing traffic difficulties. Next came a summary of a shooting in the city. She reached for her drink an instant before the news anchor began the next segment. She froze. Her throat refused to allow either a swallow or sound for a moment. She couldn't read this news story. She wanted to be anywhere except in front of a TV with her parents. Why was the incident on again? "You take this one, Mom."

"The man found murdered at the Sleep E-Z Motel

yesterday has been identified as Albert Williams, owner of Happy Face Vending. Police are seeking leads in the case and urge citizens to call the crime stoppers hotline with any information." Marie turned her gaze to Janet. "Are you well? Have you gotten too warm?"

"I'll…I'll be fine…in a minute." She sipped her drink and wiped her face with a napkin during the commercial break. At least the station showed a decent, DMV-style photo to the public. Concentrating on steadying her breathing, she focused on several other residents in wheelchairs and sturdy upholstered furniture gathered for the after-supper social hour.

"Ghosssth?" Joe smeared the word in her direction.

"I don't believe in ghosts." She crossed two fingers and made a silent wish for her recent nightmare to skip an encore. During her next blink, Pat's image intruded. Today he looked tired, worn, and every one of his sixty plus years.

Marie looped yarn around her hook. "Dead man discovered in a motel. I pity the poor maid who found him. People have taken to the bottle over less."

"I'm sure they have." Janet visualized the level in the wine bottle she opened last night. She drank two glasses—rather large ones. Supper consisted of crackers and cheese nibbled between sips of alcohol. Twice she went outside and paced large circles in the back yard. The activity failed to destroy memories of her brief time in the motel room. Inside the house, concentration on either a magazine or the TV proved impossible. In bed, she heard every clock strike every hour.

"Did you figure out what made you sick yesterday?" Marie ignored the news when the anchor returned.

She swallowed the tender piece of chicken in her mouth. "Nothing contagious."

"That's a relief. Did you notice the signs at the entrance and front desk? They're urging visitors with a cough to wear a mask."

Janet lifted her chicken sandwich and tried another bite. A flavor burst from the thick, spicy spread coated her palate. She gave silent thanks her mother assumed a maid found the body. If Marie didn't see a Comfort On Call van when news outlets aired file footage, the questions would stop.

"Jeremy called this morning." Marie crocheted a neat row without looking down.

"And how are things going in dear brother's chemical engineering world?"

"He's flying in Tuesday…for two weeks. He mentioned renting a car, but I think I've convinced him to use the truck. Joe won't be driving yet."

She glanced toward her father's weakened hand. It would be months, if ever, before he touched a steering wheel again. "Tuesday…give me his flight details, and I'll meet him at the airport. Two weeks sounds good." She paused for a moment and ran an invisible calendar through her brain. "Jeremy will be here for your birthday party. How long since he's attended?"

Marie's birthday, no matter the year, was one of the larger family celebrations. From the time Janet could remember, the day included cards, small gifts, and a day with Marie banished from her kitchen. Her brother's visits didn't often coincide with the celebration. This year, he and his wife visited for a week in April.

"Five years." Marie sighed. "I'll be glad to see

him, don't get me wrong. I simply hate the reason."

"None of us expected to see him until December." Janet smiled behind her napkin at the memory of a recent three-way call between her brother, her daughter, and herself. In the middle of the conversation, Ashley requested Uncle Jeremy to take over referee duties between her parents during the wedding festivities.

Joe startled out of a light doze at his wife's touch. "Sssshorry. Missshed that."

"Don't worry." Janet tapped salt off the last fry and offered the treat. "You didn't miss anything vital. The world's still here."

Reaching over with his good hand, he snatched the potato piece. He held it away from his mouth while he shaped his lips into an uneven line. "Sssseeen your de…tec." He blinked slow, pressed most of his mouth into a thoughtful position, and began again. "Taylor, sssseen him?"

She drew a deep breath and exhaled slowly. "Rich Taylor is fine…working hard…and he's not my detective."

"I like Henry." Joe chewed on the good side of his mouth.

"So do I." She recalled the older man's enthusiasm while recounting his elephant ride.

Marie tugged another length of yarn, glanced at Joe, and met Janet's gaze. "The son, Rich, is a good age for you. You don't want to be alone as you get older. Bad habits and medical issues included, I'm thankful Joe's around."

I'm surrounded. She rather liked her parents' habit of limiting interference in her personal life. What prompted this interest in Rich? She could manage on her own. Hadn't she established independence during the post-divorce years?

Her daughter grew into a charming, confident, young woman.

She shared ownership of her home with the bank. Every month, she chipped away at the bank's share.

Her profession was stable even if the economy took another dip.

I don't need a man. Then why did Rich's arms make her feel safe? Why did his kisses send her floating like a party balloon?

****

The noises of the police precinct main room in early evening were a constant, like tires against asphalt when driving. Rich shoved the familiar sounds of constant conversations, ringing phones, and intermittent footsteps into the background. Instead, he concentrated on the property records of the Sleep E-Z Motel displayed on the screen. The ownership threads were tangled in holding companies, shell corporations, and individuals dead for years. Somewhere under all the slight-of-hand, an actual owner sat cloaked in the current name of CM&W Enterprises.

"Taylor."

Shifting his gaze from the computer, Rich acknowledged the officer assigned to the front desk. "What's up?"

"You have a visitor who insists on speaking only with you and refuses to give a name."

"Is she a pretty woman with short, brown hair?" Cal deadpanned from the next desk.

Rich sent a frown in Cal's direction. His partner ran on the silent side, seldom making comments on other officer's private lives.

"No, sir. White male, forties, five ten, one fifty." The officer recited a basic description.

"Tell our mystery guest I'll be out directly. Is interview three available if needed?"

A few minutes later, Rich escorted Ken Robard into a small interview room, closed the door, and tapped a wall switch. "This meeting will be recorded."

Ken removed his baseball cap and nodded.

"Have you decided to file charges?" Rich gestured for the other man to sit.

Staring at the orange fiberglass chair, Ken shook his head. "I…I brought a tip. I'd prefer to stand. The shot in my…my…"

"Buttocks," Rich supplied. "Okay. Speak."

"My…assault wasn't an accident." Ken looked down and moved his fingers along his cap's sweatband by millimeters. "I was running away—or rather, trying to."

Rich waited. He sensed today's statement would be closer to the truth than previous interviews.

"I owed money. Did I mention that fact before?" He paused until Rich nodded. "The man in the motel…the dead man…I borrowed from him. I recognized his picture on the news."

"Go on." Rich shifted his weight in anticipation.

"I always talked to Al and received the cash at the motel. I never knew where and when until late in the day." Ken licked his lips. "Payment location changed every time. I…I got a call a few hours before the loan was due. Al would tell me an exact time and place to pay."

"You had a payment due the night of your assault."

Rich waited for Ken's nod. "Tell me the details of your meeting."

Ken stared at his hands. "I went to the meet with only a partial. I planned to talk them into an extension. Guess you can figure things didn't follow my plan."

"Where did you meet?"

"Warehouse…near Butler Creek…first time I'd been there."

Rich pictured the building and grounds where Mr. Robard's blood trail led the detectives. The wooded hillside behind the building offered privacy and the nearest businesses worked daytime hours. The vacant lot was an excellent location for illegal transactions of multiple kinds. He signaled for his guest to continue the story.

"A big man walked out of the shadows behind me…same man who collected before. He's the silent type…only speaks a couple of words per payout." Ken glanced from the floor to Rich's face. "The big man's not Al…never gave his name. I understood the situation well enough to not ask."

"Continue." Rich added another fact to the threads leading from Al Williams to several crimes.

"I gave him my money. He counted it and told me I was short. Before I got half an explanation out of my mouth, two agile guys jumped me. Big man threw the first punch." Ken touched his jaw. "Heavy ring on right hand…smoking a cigar…smelled expensive…it was too dark…and I was too scared…to see more."

Rich made a mental note to check the case file for the type of cigar found below the disabled security light. "Tell me more."

"I lost track of who hit me where. I punched back,

but if my fists connected, they didn't have much effect. I scrambled away but got shot on my way out the gate."

"How many shots were fired?"

"Two. Can I go now?" Ken looked toward the door.

"Tell me more about Al. How many times did you meet him? Did you see him smoke—drink—flash jewelry?"

With the topic changed from his beating and gunshot wound, Ken loosened his tongue. He answered questions about his three visits to the motel room during the past year in detail.

Rich kept Ken facing the camera and listened to every word, confident Cal watched on the video monitor. Was Al shot by a loan seeker balking at the terms? Or was the killer a jealous husband? Al's lover, Pamela, spilled all sorts of interesting information to the Miami police. The police already watched the husband in question, Greg Zwingel, until they collected enough evidence to obtain a search warrant. Or was Al double crossing the collector—the big man with a strong right fist?

Chapter Seventeen

Glancing out the window of the Taylor house, Janet viewed a gray, wet Saturday afternoon. Rain pattered on the roof and gurgled in the nearest downspout. Lawns and gardens, deprived of water for more than a week, received an overdue drink. The sound lulled her sense of timing and gave her a mental excuse to ease her pace.

Henry brought the coffee carafe to the table.

"No more for me." She placed a hand over her mug.

"Lady's choice." He poured half a cup for himself. "You've done a full day's work by mid-afternoon."

"No more than usual. Bank"—she began to tally her errands on her fingers—"supermarket, Oak Leaf Center, and spice shop. The only change in routine was doing laundry around baking the test cake."

"Are you aware you just listed at least three days of work for me?"

She raised her gaze to the wall clock, a sheet of pounded copper shaped like the state of Nevada. "I should go home. My kitchen won't clean itself."

"No hurry." Henry waved a hand in the general direction of the battery-operated timepiece. "In case you wondered, Rich and Mary bought the clock during one of their western trips."

"They made several?" She sifted memories of the

questions traded during the mini-golf game. Rich mentioned road trips as their favorite sort of vacation. He didn't supply many details. By adding together stray comments and doing a little extrapolation, she calculated their family visited close to half of the fifty states.

"At least two—I can't remember which one took them to Nevada."

She filed the additional information beside the childhood stories Henry related over generous slices of cake.

After placing his half-filled mug near the center of the table, he set his hands on the smooth wood. "Where was I? Oh, Rich worked in a department store while getting his business degree. He didn't voice complaints, and the money was enough, but the entire family realized he felt trapped."

"What happened next?" She failed to reconcile the man who loved desserts and word puzzles with a clerk selling furniture, tools, or luggage. After only a few conversations, she understood Rich enjoyed variety and motion in his workday. On the other hand, she found it easy to imagine Rich as a married, part-time student with a full-time job. A sense of responsibility seeped into his actions and conversation.

Henry rubbed at a swollen knuckle. "Rich made friends with the police officer husband of a co-worker. Next semester he added a criminal justice class. He found his profession and never looked back. Mary and the kids experienced some rough times while he finished his degree. The final year and a half, when he increased his class load, was especially rough."

"He mentioned a business degree, but he didn't go

into specifics."

Lacing his fingers, Henry glanced beyond her and leaned back. "Rich figured he'd complete a degree quicker without officially changing majors. Once my son makes a decision, he gives the project his full attention. He took the tests and scheduled entrance to the county police academy weeks before graduation. Then…well, you've a decent imagination. He gave his career full attention…well…he found time for family again, too."

Janet pressed a few cake crumbs together with her fork and licked the sweet chocolate. Today's conversation with Henry hinted at more layers to Rich than she'd imagined from their brief acquaintance. Evidently, he proved modest, also. While no trophies or plaques were on display in the house, Henry mentioned his son earned several. No doubt the awards lurked in boxes, deemed not worthy of unpacking.

"I've been thinking about it, but I can't remember any actual conversations with him when he coached Ashley. I picked her up after practices and games, but I guess I had my own set of concerns."

He smiled and looked straight into her face. "Those were some of his best years. The entire family thrived. Their world didn't go sour until Brian started college and Rachel was in high school."

"Is that when Mary was diagnosed?" She moved her gaze over Henry's features, comparing father and son. She rubbed her arms in response to sudden gooseflesh. What would have happened to Ashley in a similar situation? Live with Greg?

"My wife died first. She passed away a year before Mary's troubles started. Her death…struck a terrible blow. Here we were, five years into my retirement and working our way down a wish list. She started feeling poorly…doctors found one of those aneurysm things." Henry glanced away, removed his glasses, and ran one hand over a cheek. "Before we got all the pre-approvals from the insurance companies, the blood vessel burst. She went from breakfast at our kitchen table to buried in five days."

Janet held her breath and blinked. *Five days?* Less. A normal human lost their balance when events moved so fast. She resumed regular breathing and placed a hand over his holding the eyeglasses. Memories of Joe's recent brush with death invaded her thoughts. What would her mother do? Or Ashley? How would Jeremy take the news? If…the idea of Joe's death ripped her heart. She moistened her lips and focused on Henry's face. "Sounds like a rough time."

"The worst." Henry nodded. "For months, Rich and his sister were each in their own version of shock. I didn't think straight and caused myself more problems. I thought we found a new sort of normal—then Mary got sick. I think you know most of the rest."

"I've enough to create a picture." She refused to press for more details. Rich, or Henry, should pick the time and extent of the conversation on their own.

A memory of Sims in her summer whites intruded. "Live with gusto and soar." Janet filled the soft words with sorrow.

"You want to repeat that?"

"Oh, I didn't intend for you to hear." She pressed her lips and considered her audience. "A dear, recently departed, Navy buddy gave the motto as advice." Janet allowed the sound of the rain outside to blanket the table before she repeated the phrase and gained Henry's nod.

A soft growl from the garage door motor signaled Rich's return. Janet listened to the ordinary sounds, gathered their plates, and took the dishes to the sink.

"Your truck's getting a wash." Rich entered the kitchen while shedding his dark brown nylon windbreaker.

"Only if I go and sprinkle soap." She turned and absorbed the sight of him. Raindrops glistened on his short silver hair and his eyes sparkled as he met her gaze. Little smile lines bracketed his lips. In the next blink, the open neck of his white golf shirt drew her attention. The stories Henry related this afternoon swirled, settled, and added clarity and depth to the man wearing a cool exterior.

"Hi, Dad. Did Janet bring us dessert?" He touched Henry's shoulder and leaned over the table.

"She did…the test cake."

Walking to the nearest cupboard, Janet opened the door and searched for a small plate.

"Skip it…or rather…delay. I'll be home for an entire hour, and I need some real food first." Rich crossed the room to another cabinet and lifted a can of hearty chicken soup.

"Since when do you pass on dessert?" Henry asked.

"Breakfast was a long time ago. Don't worry. I'll eat my share of cake before I go back to work."

Janet turned her attention to finding crackers to go with Rich's late lunch.

"Do we need to fill out a score sheet? Are you looking for a critique of texture, flavor, and appearance?" Rich tipped his head and gave her a long look before clamping the soup can in the electric opener.

A giggle built in Janet's chest. "You don't need to make it complicated. I'll settle for an honest opinion on overall impression."

"I can manage a few kind words."

Pressing her lips, Janet studied him for a long moment. The deepened lines around his eyes hinted at extra hours of work and less sleep. She decided to stay quiet on the topic rather than overstep an invisible boundary line. He worked on a murder case. His waking hours involved following leads to a crime she, and the entire community, wanted solved.

In daylight she comforted herself with the knowledge she acted correctly at the scene. She touched the door—nothing inside the room. She called 9-1-1 promptly and kept Pat outside. Her embarrassing visit to the weeds behind the dumpster occurred after giving the first responding officer a summary.

Yet, in the small hours of the morning, Al's likeness returned. A memory of the victim's open eyes and bloody chest sent a shiver racing across her shoulders. She crossed her fingers. *If Rich makes an arrest, will the haunting stop?*

****

Concentrating on finding his favorite soup bowl, Rich avoided staring at Janet. Her presence lifted his spirit and enabled a portion of the weariness caused by the long hours studying computer screens and interviewing the victim's acquaintances to slide off his shoulders. Touching her would be better. He resisted the urge to step across the tidy kitchen and give her a warm hug.

"I filled in Janet on some family history." Henry wiped his glasses with a white handkerchief.

Rich started the microwave and leaned against the counter. "I'm not surprised." He settled his gaze on Janet and resisted licking his lips. Dark capris and a pink T-shirt looked good on her. He read the single word on her shirt and broadened his smile. "Diva," spelled in sequins across her chest, conflicted with every bit of the self-sufficient, independent woman who fascinated him. Chicken soup, even fresh cake, didn't satisfy the appetite she awakened. "Offer Henry sweets and he loosens his tongue."

"I noticed. What about you? Is there any special food to lower your guard?"

Rich skimmed his gaze over her before shrugging. "Nothing I'll say in this room—with this company."

"Hmmm." Janet worried her lower lip.

She's a civilian—the reporting party. He turned and filled a large glass with ice water. For his own peace of mind, he voiced the ground rules. "Work and private life stay on opposites of the fence."

"Fence? You've built a Kevlar wall and reinforce it from time to time." Henry slapped the table.

"My method works." The microwave beeped, and Rich fussed with his meal.

"Maybe I should go." Janet pushed away from the table. "You can give me a cake report later…by phone or text if you wish."

"Wait…stay…I want your company. Bear with me if I keep certain topics off limits." Rich rubbed a hand across his cheek. If she left, the bubble of invisible sunshine in the room would vanish. His main reason for coming home was to recharge, a task which appeared more likely under the spell of her alto voice. "Tell me news from the outside world."

After settling in her chair, she plucked a napkin from the holder, and laid it at an empty place. "My brother arrives Tuesday. Mother is making a list of enough projects to fill months, not two weeks."

Rich set his glass bowl of soup on the table and adjusted his chair. "Is two weeks your brother's usual visit?"

"It's longer than most. He's staying an extra couple of days to cover until I get back from San Francisco."

"You have exact dates?" He watched her face for the brief shadow which appeared every time her friend was mentioned.

"I leave early a week from next Friday and return late Sunday."

He swallowed a bite of noodle. "Are you okay with the trip?"

"I'm doing okay—better than at first."

Her platitude stated the expected. He sensed the truth lay deeper. If she were a witness he'd probe until she revealed her true feelings. But she was…a friend. The flat description stayed uneasy in his mind. Friend didn't begin to describe what a corner of his heart yearned for. Walking into a house filled with her essence every day might be about right. "And Joe, how's he doing?"

"His complaints against the therapists are getting easier to understand." She sighed and lowered her shoulders. "He's not kind to them."

"Swearing relieves stress." Henry stood and carried his coffee mug to the sink.

"Using your theory, Dad's the least-stressed, living human in St. Louis."

Rich hid his smile behind his spoon. Soup and a glass of cold water calmed his body's demands for fuel. Janet's voice and words soothed the rough edges to his attitude. A conversation about her family improved his general outlook.

"I have a question." She tapped one finger on the table. "Did Ashley email you?"

"She asked for Rachel's contact information. I forwarded the request." He omitted mention of the note he'd added, which urged his daughter to reply.

"Do you think we can trust our daughters together?" She leaned back and tilted her head.

He tipped the bowl to collect the final spoonful of soup. "In case you haven't noticed, our daughters are adults."

"I'm aware. And I'm grateful mine's educated, employed, and not living under my roof."

Dabbing his lips with the napkin, Rich steadied his gaze on her face. He didn't see any problems in encouraging Rachel to get better acquainted with her cousin's future wife.

The child who caused him to worry was Brian. In their one and only phone call since Labor Day, his son warned him off Janet. He hinted she might be after money or at least prestige. Rich laughed at the idea. His bank account bore scars from medical bills, and his employment commanded less respect with each passing year. "Good to know we're both proud of our children."

Henry placed a small, clean plate and a fork within Rich's reach. "I'm going to see if I can find the Cubs game."

Janet toyed with the napkin holder but delayed speaking until Henry was in the next room. "Maybe I'm concerned about the wrong generation."

"He'd love to meddle." Rich switched his gaze from her thick, dark eyelashes to her agile fingers and their short, rounded nails. He became aware of every movement her hands made, and he longed to dance his fingers along her arms. Her posture invited him to smooth tension from her shoulders and explore her hair. He shook his head. Danger lurked if he let his thoughts run free on a street paved with emotion. He, and Janet, would fare better if he installed a few speed bumps of practical concerns. "I'd call him harmless. But I avoid outright lies."

"Is he really a Cubs fan?"

In silence, Rich transferred a large serving of cake to his small plate and put a large bite on his fork. "Henry's conflicted. He raised his children to be loyal Cardinals fans. A few years ago, my sister started working at Wrigley Field—in the ticket office. Do you happen to know any widow ladies willing to help occupy his time—cooking ability preferred?"

"No Cubs fans." She shook her head.

He made a show of shrugging. "I'm guessing he shared all my secrets over your cake." Savoring the trace of cherry in the sweet chocolate, he wiped a crumb from the corner of his mouth. "The dessert is good. I'd call it a winner."

"Thank you." She lowered her gaze for a moment. "We didn't have time for *all* your secrets."

"Good—I want to keep a little air of mystery. Did he mention what happens when I set my mind on a goal?" He lifted another forkful of cake.

"We touched on the topic."

"I want you to remember it's true." He took another bite of dessert, delighting in the texture of the filling between the thin layers. An instant later, temptation of another sort won. Reaching across the table, he gathered one of her hands in his. *Right.* He refused to put words to the warm comfort he felt from her skin. The instant he touched her, he wanted time to be suspended until she filled him with quiet energy.

"I should go. I left hours of housework undone." Janet slowly withdrew her hand and pushed back her chair.

"Wait a minute and I'll walk you to your truck. I told the truth when I said I would only be here a short time." He glanced at the clock. Any moment Cal would notify him the documents were signed. Next came a conference to solidify the final details to serve all the arrest and search warrants simultaneously. He took a final bite of cake, leaving only a swirl of white frosting and a tiny chocolate curl on his plate. "Excellent—your family should be proud of your baking skill."

"I suspect you enjoy all desserts."

"Sweets are the best part of any meal. Cookies were the first thing Mary taught the kids to make."

"Are you saying her cooking and baking lessons were successful for children but not husband?"

He laughed short. "Before the wedding, she learned I was hopeless in the kitchen. She started our kids early. Aside from a few memorable accidents, we ate most of what they cooked." He recalled one day when he found Rachel surrounded by dirty bowls and staring into the microwave. "A few grew into family legend."

"Beyond hope?" She stood a moment after he did.

"You should not turn a child loose with a muffin mix until they've been introduced to fractions."

"Bad?"

"Flour soup—with blueberries." He shook his head. Rachel's big surprise for the family refused to set.

"I think the Navy served that dish once—over biscuits."

"Really? I assumed tales of mess hall fare were exaggerated."

"Some are…others actually turn funny in hindsight…for the survivors."

He turned from washing his hands and looked for mischief in her eyes. How could he label the way she prodded a dormant portion of his mind, and body, back to action? She claimed to be a casual friend. He blinked and remembered the kisses. A kiss, or a touch, with Janet defined excitement. He studied her mouth and the smooth expanse of her cheek. Would more kisses satisfy his swelling desire? Or touch flame to tinder?

Chapter Eighteen

Early the next afternoon, Janet studied the collection of garden tools on the garage shelf and added a hand trowel to the bucket. Pursing her lips, she whistled a popular advertising jingle. Only one item remained on the household portion of her weekend "to do" list. Two pots of bright yellow mums awaited planting. In a short time, she intended to kick back on the couch with a tall, cool drink and a favorite movie. Joe and Marie did not expect her at the rehab center until early evening.

She walked up the driveway with optimism in her steps and heart. One of these years her mums would respond according to the garden books and survive a St. Louis winter—or not. This year marked her sixth autumn in the house, and she had five attempts behind her. She was well past any "third time's a charm" and into the land of family stubbornness.

Kneeling at the edge of the flower bed, she pushed the trowel into the moist soil. Yesterday's rain worked wonders for the marigolds and lilies. The flowers stood a little taller under the living room window today. The moisture also eased the digging for the new arrivals. Breathing in the tang of good, clean dirt, she dug until she estimated the hole larger than the thin plastic pot. Giving in to a distraction, she used the trowel to loosen two weeds near a large, ornamental rock. "Away you go." She released an easy laugh and tossed the unwanted plants on the grass. As she worked, she compared her efforts to her mother, the best gardener in the family.

The twin flower beds in front of the Johnson home looked a little ragged and neglected at the moment. But Marie forbade her children to clean them. Very firmly, she'd announced her intention to do the work herself after Joe moved back home. According to her, garden work furnished a necessary excuse to get away from his constant, mumbled complaints.

"Or not so mumbled." Janet smiled. Joe's speech improved daily. He still smeared a few sounds, but when Janet listened carefully, she understood his meaning. Physically, Joe's progress was slower. He continued to lack strength in his left hand and dragged his foot.

Ignoring the familiar sound of an approaching car, she settled the first pot in the fresh hole. "Hmmm. I need to dig an inch deeper on the right."

A car door opened, and Janet paused with her trowel above the dirt. Rocking back on her heels, she turned toward the driveway and smiled. "This is a surprise. I thought you'd be at the music festival."

"Plans change." Daniel slammed his door and shrugged.

"Oh, Mom—Dad…he's…it's dreadful." Ashley hurried across the lawn before she sank to the damp grass beside Janet and covered her face with her hands.

Janet reached for her daughter's arm and steadied her breath. Greg's antics were one of a very few things which brought out the drama queen in his daughter. By historical standards, the current tone of her voice signaled a major event. Ashley's posture and gulps for breath between each word reminded Janet of the time her daughter came home tearstained and angry because wife number two insisted on being called "Mommy."

Leaning for a better view of Ashley's face, she steadied her voice. "What has Greg done?"

"He…they…he's…"

"He got arrested." Daniel handed his fiancée a packet of tissues. "He called an hour ago from jail."

"What? Greg's arrested?" Janet pushed to her feet. For a long moment, the words hung in her mind without context. Greg's past actions tended to fit under the headings of stupid or childish, but not illegal. The man exhibited no financial sense—ditto for personal relationship skills. But a criminal?

She opened and closed her mouth without speaking. *The burglary.* She shook her head, squatted, and reached for Ashley's hand. The police needed a warrant to search Greg's house for the clock and jewelry. Detective Randolph explained the procedure in clear, concise language. On Friday, when she called for a status update, the officer reported no change.

Ashley blew her nose and wiped at her cheeks. "Dad needs a lawyer…before a hearing…by tomorrow morning."

"What are the charges?" Janet turned her full attention to her daughter.

"Theft…he babbled a mixture of fact and apology about pearls…something about…they needed to be his gift, not yours. Did he mean the Zwingel necklace?" She dabbed at more tears. "Were the pearls…were they stolen with the clock?"

Janet exhaled until she felt deflated. So much for

holding back information in an attempt at kindness. "I'm sorry. I should have given you the entire list of stolen items instead of only the clock and brooch. The pearls were missing—and a photo from your Zwingel grandparents' wedding. The police didn't give much hope of recovering anything. I filed an insurance claim on the Monday after the burglary."

"Who except Dad would steal antique jewelry and your favorite clock?" Ashley's breathing quieted to near normal.

"Exactly my thought…I told the police who I suspected and why. I got a five-minute lecture about evidence, procedure, and warrants."

"Maybe the police found them in a pawn shop." Daniel shifted his gaze to Janet.

Janet nodded. "They promised to check. I gave them photos."

"At the end of the conversation"—Ashley dabbed at another batch of tears—"Dad said something really strange. 'I didn't kill Al.' Who's Al?"

Janet shivered under her T-shirt. She glanced up to the sky to confirm the sudden chill was internal. Sunshine and two small, high clouds filled her view. The man in the motel—the dead man—his name was Al. With each news report, he sounded more and more like the man she'd met briefly in Mike's office. She clicked her mind over to Ashley's statement about a lawyer and a hearing. "You said Greg needs an attorney." She waited for Daniel's nod. "I won't pay a penny toward his fee, but I'll give you a starting place. The deck door is open. Beside the cookbooks, you'll find an old-fashioned paper set of yellow pages."

"You won't need to pay." Ashley reached for

Daniel's hand and stood. "Dad added my name to his bank account."

Janet rocked back and nearly lost her balance. "He did?"

"In March. I think his bout of pneumonia scared sense into him. The balance isn't large, but it will be enough to get started."

"Good." Surprised at the sense of calm Ashley's information granted, Janet pushed to her feet. "I'll join you after I get this first mum in the ground."

"Good idea." Daniel placed an arm around Ashley's shoulders. "Come on, Sweetie. I'll bet your mom has ice tea to go with the phone book."

"Cut lemon's in the blue, square container." She widened her smile for Daniel before she turned to the waiting plant. Did Greg kill Al? Why would he profess innocence unless someone accused him? Why was Greg's car at the Sleep E-Z motel the Friday night she did her reconnaissance? Was Al's SUV parked on site the same night? She shivered from one end of her spine to the other. Never during twelve years of marriage to Greg would she have said he was capable of murder. Did she not know him at all?

****

Rich stood in the video viewing area and tapped one finger against his chin. Under a calm exterior, his mind and body churned in turmoil. Late yesterday, prior to finalizing the plans to serve the arrest and search warrants, he initiated a conversation with his captain. After detailing his possible conflict of interest, he was cautioned not to interrogate these suspects. Fortunately, he was retained on the case.

The left portion of the large, split screen showed

Greg Zwingel in interview room three. He leaned forward with both elbows on the table and his head propped between his hands. He glared at the door and moved his mouth as if speaking in full paragraphs. "How's your lip reading, Jones?" Rich glanced toward the slender, blonde detective the moment she entered.

"Poor to non-existent. Mr. Zwingel contacted his daughter."

"No surprise." Greg's call to Ashley seemed logical. His present wife was currently in no position to receive phone messages. Rich switched his attention to the right side of the screen. "What about our other guest? Who did he call?"

Mike Maguire paced the confines of interview room two while holding a fresh, unlit cigar in one hand. With cuffed wrists, he patted and searched his pockets.

Distracted? Overwhelmed? Rich squinted at the screen and mentally acknowledged Maguire wasn't the first suspect or witness to forget the police confiscated lighters.

"Maguire called an attorney."

Rich focused again on Greg. "The man without a lawyer gets the first interview. Are you ready to go in with Collins? Last moment questions?"

"I plan to start with the burglary. Our best evidence is for possession of the stolen property. Do you have any objections?" Jones tapped a slender pen against the file in her hand.

"Considering what I know of his personality, I think you've made the best choice."

Jones opened the folder containing the arrest report and re-arranged the photos of the stolen goods and the murder scene. "Do you care to say why you're not going in? You're lead detective on the related loan sharking case."

"We both remember meeting at a social event." He sealed his lips. The dry facts of where, when, and under what conditions he initially met the suspect were included in the report from the hospital interview. Greg's injuries, plus his refusal to press charges, prompted the detectives to look for connections to Ken Robard. Thanks to Robard's current cooperation, the police established several lines of evidence between loan sharking and money laundering suspects.

A few minutes into the interview with Greg, Rich heard Jones shift from preliminary, baseline questions to burglary specific.

Greg startled when the photo from his parent's wedding was laid in front of him.

A few moments later, Jones turned the topic to the antique clock.

The instant the photo of the pearl necklace lay in full view, Greg's answers grew clipped and too loud for the small room. He pushed his chair and stood. "No. Not fair." He leaned forward, his soft belly against the table, and yelled. "Those belong to my daughter. They're part of a family wedding tradition."

Collins, using a gentle voice suitable for a church, pointed. "Please sit, Mr. Zwingel."

"The necklace was reported stolen. We found the pearls in your home's guest bedroom. Can you explain?" Jones made a show of being ready to take notes.

"I don't want to talk about it." Greg sat with a rattle of handcuffs against the metal table.

Rich prepared himself for a stronger reaction to the

next photo. Closing his eyes for a moment, he recalled his first sight of the brooch in clear detail. As the assistant medical examiner and aide rolled Al's body to examine his back, a lumpy, fine handkerchief came into view. Using his pen, he'd lifted away the cloth to reveal an antique golden peacock pin. The bird featured a diamond eye. Rubies, sapphires, and emeralds scattered across the tail. Immediately, he'd recognized the jewelry from Janet's description.

The brooch tied Greg to Al and the motel room. Motive and opportunity were established, but the police needed to connect Greg to the murder weapon before pressing additional charges.

Glancing at his notes, Rich refreshed his memory on the highlights of the preliminary timeline. Greg's car arrived at the motel nine minutes before Al's SUV departed. Pamela M. Cork, or Wilson, or Zwingel—depending on which piece of ID she presented—admitted driving the SUV. She insisted Al was alive when she exited the motel room. She told the Miami police she kissed Al farewell in the doorway.

Ignoring Greg's babbling response to the photo of the brooch in relation to Al's body, Rich turned his attention to the other side of the monitor and finished reviewing the timeline. Greg's car left the motel property fifteen minutes after his wife drove away in Al's vehicle. Twenty minutes later, Mike Maguire's luxury sedan arrived and stayed eight minutes.

Mike paced a small oval in the interview room. He avoided touching the small table and three sturdy steel chairs in the space. Tipping his head, he squinted at the ceiling. The unlit cigar settled in the corner of his mouth.

According to the time on the monitor, well over an hour had elapsed since the suspects completed their phone calls. Maguire's lawyer had not reported in. According to body language and frequent glances at his watch, the delay added to Maguire's irritation. Rich made a mental note to get the attorney's name.

"Do you own a hand gun, Mr. Zwingel?" Jones gathered the scattered photos, evened the edges, and placed them in the folder with the necklace visible on top.

"No. Never." Greg added a liberal number of swear words to his quick denial.

Rich held his reaction to a small smile.

"When did you last fire a gun?"

Springing to his feet amidst the jingle of chains, Greg stared at his interrogators. He licked his lips and glanced at the camera. "I'm asking for a lawyer—now."

"Are you certain?" Collins stood.

"I'm done talking to both of you." Greg set his hands on the table, leaned forward, and pressed his lips.

A few moments later, Jones entered the monitoring area. "Your assessment?"

Rich pointed to Greg's image on the split screen. "His lawyer will earn every penny."

****

The moment Janet drove through the gate Monday morning, she sensed a difference. Gooseflesh appeared on her arms, and she couldn't control a shiver across her shoulders. Skimming her gaze across the Comfort On Call property, she confirmed all the early techs and Pat on site. Only two vehicles were missing, equal to the techs with a habit of arriving on-the-dot, not a minute too soon.

A stillness or a pause, similar to the anticipation before a thunderstorm breaks open surrounded her. She opened the truck door and listened. No birdsong greeted her from the hedge. Traffic on the busy street appeared hushed.

Kim, the receptionist and dispatcher, opened her door and exited a silver van.

Slamming her truck door, Janet crossed a few yards of packed gravel to join the other lady. "How was your weekend?"

"Hectic—the in-laws drove in from Des Moines. My boys planned for every minute of the visit. How are you doing?"

"Things are settling down a bit." Janet pushed the topics of dead body, Sims, and her father behind their respective mental doors, and closed each one. Most days she enjoyed an opportunity to chat with Kim. The mother of twin fourteen-year-old boys always had a story to counterbalance the usual work topics. Today, Janet remained silent, tightened her grip on her lunch bag and searched for a visible abnormality during the walk to the building.

She conquered the temptation to break the silence. The morning's mood was all wrong to chatter about preparations for her brother's visit. The test cake, and the people she'd shared her experiment with, remained definitely off limits. The only worse topic would be mention of yesterday's tedious search for a criminal lawyer with both a current license and nearly affordable rates.

"What?" Kim skidded to a halt beside her desk.

One glance down the hall and Janet struggled to keep a prime Navy curse inside her mouth. Why was police tape across Mike's office door?

"Morning, ladies." Pat spoke from beyond her left shoulder.

Janet pivoted and waved an arm in a wild gesture toward the office. "What—?"

"You want an explanation… you'll get one at the same time as everyone else. All employees in the break room in ten." Pat pulled a pack of gum from his shirt pocket before striding toward the warehouse.

Staring at Kim failed to decipher the questions on the other woman's face. Shock and confusion jostled for dominance. Moistening her lips, she prepared to speak. The phone rang, and she closed her mouth.

"Comfort On Call, this is Kim. May I assist you?"

Pieces of Janet's normal world slid into place. She listened to Kim's familiar voice ask for address, contact information, and a description of the problem. One side of a mundane conversation comforted after Pat's brief, atypical greeting and the sight of yellow-and-black ribbon across the office door.

Fifteen minutes later, Janet sat silent between two of her fellow techs.

The men bantered about the prospects for the Kansas City Chiefs.

Don't they feel it? She could hardly breathe under all the gloom and trouble in the air.

"Okay, people." Pat followed Kim into the room, closed the door, and remained standing. "We've got a company problem." He raised his hands, palms displayed, and gestured for the group to settle. "The problems which came to light over the weekend are not the fault of anyone in this room."

A murmur started behind Janet and stopped the

moment Pat rapped twice on the wall.

She counted three seconds, drew a breath, and held it for another three.

"Attention, everyone. Some important changes in our work routine today. Beginning immediately, use only parts already in stock. I don't care if you're one block from a hardware store and need two more quarter-inch sheet metal screws—don't buy anything. I'm not sure I can reimburse you. I'm trusting you followed procedure and fueled the vans Friday afternoon."

"What if a customer needs a part we don't have in stock?"

Tim voiced one of Janet's questions.

"Tell them...no...give them my cell number. I'm in negotiations with Silver Star Enterprises about our next step." Pat pushed one hand through his hair.

Janet allowed the words to sink in. Since the company's founding in the mid-1950s, they were an authorized dealer for the brand. Aside from periodic training, she had little contact with the corporation. Why the sudden need for their permission for day-to-day operations?

"And another thing—you won't be seeing Mike on the property. My brother was arrested early Sunday morning."

Whipping a hand in front of her mouth, Janet succeeded in minimizing her gasp. Wait—

"Damn." Tim ducked his gaze to the floor.

Pat cleared his throat. "The charges are fraud—various descriptions. The police and prosecutors are working on the theory my brother used Comfort On Call funds as his own personal bank. You may accept checks for payment today—or cash. We'll need to go old school and send statements to the others. Kim"—he turned to face the woman—"have you saved the old templates?"

"I'll find something." The receptionist jotted a note on a pad.

"Absolutely no credit cards until I speak with a banker. Understood?" Pat drew a small notepad from a back pocket.

"Question—what happens on payday? I've got direct deposit—and auto pay on my mortgage." One of the newer techs voiced his concern.

"We'll arrange payroll by Friday." Pat moved his wad of gum to the other side of his mouth.

Janet released a small sigh and visualized her current checking account balance versus bills due. Thanks to a delay in the billing cycle, she could postpone payment on her airline tickets to California. This month's mortgage was covered—ditto for utilities. She could drop gas and grocery purchases to the bare basics. Attending estate sales with interesting clocks listed vanished from the near future. If Pat didn't get the payroll problem solved? She blinked and imagined dollars flying out of her modest savings account.

Half a dozen other questions from the techs trotted over the same ground. Janet listened without absorbing the meaning. She remained stuck on the word "fraud." How long? How much? How close had she come to getting entangled via the offer to purchase a percentage of Comfort On Call?

She swallowed and sealed her lips against a groan. How did she end up with an ex and a boss arrested the same day?

Chapter Nineteen

"Janet, this is Rich. We need to talk. I'll be at your house in five." Disconnecting the call, he exited the gas station and merged into Monday evening traffic.

Sleep, meals, and leisure time felt like events of last year. In the eight days since his team served the warrants, he packed all his waking hours with work. The motel murder case, with tentacles into loan sharking and money laundering, furnished plenty to keep his mind busy. Interviews, computer searches, and conference calls with other jurisdictions filled the days and portions of the nights. In addition, yesterday his captain assigned his team a new assault case, which might, or might not, involve some of the same players.

Naps at irregular intervals substituted for regular sleep and included vivid dreams. Janet—instead of Mary, or Henry, or his kids—refused to be ignored. He envisioned blue eyes above the rim of a coffee cup. He remembered how she tucked her lower lip when she was thinking. His skin tingled with excitement and desire an instant before an alarm jarred him awake. He longed to slide his fingers deep into her fine hair and lower his mouth for a kiss. He missed her voice across a table—or on the phone.

Since he walked her from his kitchen to her truck more than a week ago, he'd received no response. She returned zero of his calls, texts, and emails. According to Henry, she hadn't called the landline at the house.

When he retrieved the newspaper this morning, he found the mixer. The sight of the familiar box, with a simple "Thank You" taped to the top, snapped his patience. He would speak to her face-to-face—tonight. A conversation, including her side of the story, in her living room was his first choice. If necessary, he'd tail her and make a scene at the rehab center.

"I'm getting an explanation—now." He pulled to a stop in front of Janet's house and slammed the car door harder than necessary. While pressing the doorbell, he drew a deep breath and slowly exhaled.

"One minute."

"Take two." *Hurry.* He set his hands on his hips and stared at the doorknob.

Janet opened the door shoulder width and stood in the space.

"We need to talk." A wave of relief rolled through his core at the sight of her. Aside from a trace of weary or worry in her eyes, she appeared well. He'd never seen a fitted T-shirt with a print of bright flowers look so appealing over feminine curves. He edged one toe over the threshold. "Why don't you answer my messages?"

Tucking her lower lip, she gazed past him.

He stared into her face, held his breath until he caught the rhythm of her loudest clock, and exhaled through parted lips. To gather her in his arms would be so right—and so wrong.

"If I asked nice, would you leave?"

"No." He shook his head to underline his word before returning his gaze to her face. The flat set of her mouth sent a tremble through his body. Was he responsible for squashing her usual sparkle?

She sighed before stepping back and opening the door wider. "Since you're here, we might as well finish the encounter."

A moment later he stood in the center of her living room, his interior quaking more than the last time he faced an armed drug dealer. He secured a calm mask and ignored the personal risk. Lifting his hands to his waist, he displayed his palms. "Did you get my messages?"

"At least a dozen—I'm ignoring you." She crossed her arms and tapped an index finger. "I worked on the theory you'd go away."

"Notice any results?" He kept eye contact for a long moment.

She broke the stare, glanced toward their feet, and lowered one arm. "Not yet."

He resisted the urge to wipe at the sweat forming above his lips and scanned the room. The cluttered dining table offered a route to the primary topic. He pointed toward a wooden clock case, tools, and a mixture of delicate parts. "Am I looking at mechanical therapy?"

"You arrested my ex." She moistened her lips, straightened her shoulders, and adjusted her arms.

Studying her posture, he subtracted the obvious acting and nodded. Her words and actions in previous weeks negated today's sudden show of concern for Ashley's father. Ignoring his question and diving right to the heart of the matter suited him. "We followed the evidence and arrested multiple suspects—including Greg Zwingel."

"You also detained Michael Maguire, my boss. Did

you do a little happy dance when you threw my professional life into turmoil?"

While one portion of his brain enjoyed her use of air quotes, he held his mouth firm and level. For the moment, listening was more important than speaking.

"Thanks to you and your cohorts, my co-workers and I don't know from one day to the next if we're employed. What about our customers?" She pivoted and moved to put the upholstered chair between them. "Furnace inspections are under contract. Prepaid. Will you tell the elderly widow she can't trust a company that's been in business sixty years?"

"Evidence points to crimes."

"What about the rest of us? Do you sweep us into a garbage can marked collateral damage?"

Silence dropped between them until the five clocks in the room became the only sound. Rich counted the seconds in silence. After twelve, he cleared his throat. "You told the police from the beginning you suspected Greg of the burglary. The theft is solved."

"Did you recover the pearls?" She blinked, and a hint of sparkle shone in her eyes.

"We're holding all the items as evidence." He rested a hand on a hip and made a small, restless circle with the other. Studying her face, he noticed her angry mask shift for an instant to reveal a glimpse of her usual concern for others.

"Will the necklace be returned in time for the wedding?"

Rich hesitated and searched for words weighted toward accurate information rather than false hope. "Much depends on Greg's degree of cooperation. I really can't talk about an active case."

"You're in for a really short conversation then. I went online to find the public information and got lost in a maze. The reports I found are as transparent as sheet metal."

He pulled out his notebook and pen, wrote down a website pathway, and tore off the page. "Try navigating the web site with these keywords. The charges the prosecutor is pursuing will be listed." He shrugged. "I can't address the website clarity."

"How many charges?" She accepted the paper and held it between thumb and forefinger.

"Enough to justify the bail figure."

"About Greg's bail"—she glanced at the words divided by forward slashes—"his employer paid. He's out, working, and refuses to speak to Ashley."

Rich minimized his sigh. Greg's silence toward his daughter appeared out of character. However, family spats weren't his business until a crime was committed.

"If the information's public, you should be able to tell me. What's Greg charged with?"

A glance toward the ceiling bought him an instant of time. Visualizing the prosecutor's most recent filing, he stayed well aware additional charges were under consideration. "Burglary. Weapons violations. Manslaughter."

"Al—the man in the motel?" She pressed her lips tight. A pair of deep breathes and swallows later, she straightened and stared. "Mike Maguire—what are his charges?"

"Fraud—half dozen banking charges—accessory to manslaughter." He skimmed his gaze to her bare feet and back to her face. The prosecutor added the last charge against Maguire early today. The ballistics report confirmed the handgun found in Mike's car matched the single shell casing recovered from the motel room.

"Sit." She pointed to the single upholstered chair, turned away, and disappeared into the front bedroom.

Ignoring her command, he drifted toward the dining area and took a closer look at the work on the table. Grime-coated gears lay in order beside brass shafts. A small jar of clear fluid and a tweezers claimed space beside a folded, clean cloth. The scene indicated a precise and organized mind in charge of the mechanical pieces. Muted sounds consistent with a metal drawer opening and closing reached him.

"I see you follow directions worse than Ashley's kindergarten students." She crossed the room toward him, pressing a manila folder to her chest. "I'll give these to you on one condition."

He tipped his head and waited.

"I expect you found copies in Mike's files. I never signed them—refused his offer. The financial reports provided included too many numbers I didn't understand. I smelled a bad deal but nothing illegal."

"I appreciate your cooperation." He studied her face and silently admired the determination in the stillness at the corners of her mouth.

"Stay away from me—no calls—no emails." She released one hand from the file.

"How long?" He resisted the urge to ignore the necessary professional fence between them and embrace her.

"Forever."

"I didn't hear you," he whispered.

Raising her gaze from their shoes, she blinked. "I

can't continue. My friendships don't work with a reinforced concrete wall down the middle."

He shivered as if dunked in ice water. Her request collided against his unspoken desire to keep her in his life. Until several months ago, he wandered in the cold, stagnant land of grief and depression. He couldn't endure a return. After a taste of sunshine, he wanted more lively banter across a café table—with Janet. She fit in his arms to perfection. He yearned to hold her close. He longed to bury his nose in her hair and refresh his spirit with the scent of her shampoo. "When do you get back from the Sims memorial?"

"The twenty-second. Why?" She widened her eyes.

"Plan for dinner with me on the twenty-third. You pick the place. I won't send an electronic word until you return." He plucked the folder from her hand and took two steps toward the door. He scrambled and clung to the loophole in his promise. Whatever the relationship between them became, he needed more time and contact to explore the potential.

"I…I take Jeremy to the airport that evening."

"Then we'll eat late, after you drop him off." He reached the door in half a dozen large steps and continued without breaking stride. *Another week.*

Chapter Twenty

Lifting her face to the late Saturday morning sun, Janet rested two fingers against the polished metal rail. She blinked against the sunlight and shivered. A pale blue turtleneck and her best navy-blue suit supplied physical warmth. A salted breeze caressed her face and immersed her in old, familiar smells. Seaweed, fish, and a hint of diesel swirled as the boat left the California coast behind. The weather was glorious on the water.

In the next moment, sadness and dread replaced the joy of the setting. Janet imagined a gigantic clock hand dragging her forward into a dim future.

The captain called from his post at the wheel. "We've passed three miles."

"I paid for five." Paul replied from the bow.

Carry us to the end of the earth. Janet surrendered tumbling memories to the scattered, fair-weather clouds doing a slow dance above the private vessel.

The captain shrugged at his passengers and continued on his current heading toward an invisible spot on the horizon.

Janet studied her best friends gathered starboard near the bow. To her left, Carter's long, dark hair rippled in the breeze while she fingered the edge of a bright scarf. Baker also wore a colorful scarf, but her curls were short and blonde. Next to them, Holt maintained parade rest in her service dress whites. One step farther, tucked into the very point of the bow, stood Paul. He wore a dark business suit and stood with his feet the military distance of twelve inches apart. He gripped a wrist behind his back while his fingers pointed down.

Following the direction of Paul's fingers, Janet stalled her gaze on a brass cylinder set in a milk crate on the deck. *Sims. Is that what we all become?* She spun thoughts through her mind of Sims' vibrancy, compassion, and wisdom. The complex, lively images contrasted with the container of bone fragments and dark ash.

The bow sliced into a larger-than-average wave and spewed droplets of water over the mourners.

"Shall we begin?" A chaplain from the San Francisco police department left his position beside the captain. Reaching the bow, he touched Paul on the shoulder and opened a small black book.

While prayers were read, Janet allowed her mind to drift back to the first time their group gathered in Hawaii.

Sims urged her companions to match her pace as they hiked the well-worn, switchback path up Diamond Head. Janet, softened by two plus years of civilian life, dug deep and moved her feet to Sim's melodious cadence. Finding a new reserve of energy and determination, she emerged from the dark, steel stairs and grinned. She immersed herself in memories of the glorious view from the summit. Sims encouraged her with a sparkle in her eye, and she accomplished the goal. Her body survived. Her spirit thrived.

The engine tone shifted, and the boat swung to a new heading. Glancing to the sky, Janet estimated their direction and smiled.

The captain slowed the engine to little more than an idle. "We've reached five miles—steady at heading three five eight."

Half a bubble off true north. Janet exchanged understanding glances with the other three women. She curved her lips into the first genuine smile of the day and laughed short. Sims retained her sense of humor and snail mail letter sign-off to the end.

Paul reached for the cylinder.

Holt placed a hand on his arm. "First, we sing."

An instant later, four female and two male voices lifted the words of the Navy hymn to the breeze. Joining more than a century of sailors' tradition, they released both a statement and plea to the Almighty.

After the final note faded away, Paul picked up the cylinder, unscrewed the brass cover, and extended his arm over the rail. Letting the lid sway by the short chain, he tipped the container until a few ashes dribbled and dropped into the ocean. Adjusting the urn's angle, he cleared his throat. "To the best wife and lover. You will always remain in my heart."

When Paul handed Holt the cremains, she startled back half a step. After a nod from Paul, she returned to the rail and gave the container a gentle shake. "To a traveling companion of excellence."

"Lovely Sims, your laughter sparkled brighter than stars dancing in the night sky." Baker yielded the urn to Carter.

Carter hesitated a moment before holding the container over the rail. "A true friend, Denise Sims always had your back."

The instant smooth metal met her hands, Janet

blinked back unexpected tears. Whole paragraphs of words tumbled out of order in her mind. She forced a breath and banished the ache in her heart. The finality of death threatened to overwhelm. A moment later, she tipped the mouth of the urn until a black clump dropped toward the sea. "Dearest Sims, thank you for showing us how to live with gusto." She blinked too late to stop her tears and surrendered the cylinder to the chaplain.

"Speaking on behalf of countless lives touched—go in peace."

"Taps" drifted out of overhead speakers and blanketed the passengers of the small boat. Janet glanced beyond the stern until the final note faded. Did Sims' ashes linger on the surface? Did her friend cause one smooth spot among the constant chop? She moved her lips in silence. "Live with gusto and soar."

****

Late Saturday afternoon, Rich parked across the street from the ambulance. He skimmed his gaze around the homes adjacent to the Zwingel and Cork residence. Aside from the half dozen emergency vehicles, the immediate area of the subdivision appeared abnormally deserted. No neighbors stood gawking from the small porches or driveways. He figured the residents demonstrated reluctance to become involved and watched from behind sheer curtains.

Exiting the car a few seconds ahead of Cal, he quick-stepped toward medics guiding a gurney across the lawn and signaled them to stop.

"She shot me." Greg spat the information toward the detective.

"Am I to understand you'll be pressing charges?"

Rich sent his gaze into a quick inspection of the patient's visible parts.

Greg winced and lifted a hand to a reddened cheek. "Throw the book at her."

Rich nodded and turned his attention to the nearest medic. "Is the suspect inside?"

"Yes, sir—an officer has her in the kitchen."

"And he's going?" He tipped his head toward Greg.

"Meramec. Gunshot wound to the left knee. Any additional injuries incurred in the resulting fall will be assessed after transport."

"I'll call the hospital to expect us before long." Rich hurried into the house one step behind his partner.

"She made bail all of an hour ago," Cal muttered.

Rich recognized a tone of defeat in his partner's words and agreed in silence. Today the shooter was apprehended and the victim was alive and alert. The contrast to other interactions with the principles should be seen as positive. But Rich couldn't shake a sense of futility.

"I want a lawyer." The petite woman with unnaturally blonde hair called her request from a plain kitchen chair. She kept her arms crossed over her chest and glared at the detectives.

Wife number three. Janet's moniker for the woman intruded. Rich blinked away the nickname. The person in front of him had been in the motel room with Al the night he was murdered. The Miami police detained her on a material witness warrant the moment she deplaned. In addition to the local and state accusations for financial crimes, federal authorities filed charges for traveling under a false passport.

For the first time, Rich stood face-to-face with Pam. Until the call arrived twenty minutes ago, he categorized her as non-violent based on interview transcripts and a tangle of property records revealing partial ownership in the motel.

Stepping over a nine-millimeter handgun lying on the carpet inches from the kitchen vinyl, he stopped beside her. "Pamela M. Cork." He spoke her legal name and touched her arm. "Please stand. You are under arrest for assault with a deadly weapon." He recited the entire Miranda warning. "Do you understand these rights?"

"I want a lawyer," she yelled.

Rich guided her toward a uniformed officer. "Please confine her in the back of your patrol car."

"My lawyer—I need to call my lawyer." Her voice pierced the soft sounds of police officers working the scene as she was escorted toward the street.

"She works fast." Cal tugged his gloves into place and slid the handgun into an evidence bag. "Her brother posted her bond. My gut tells me the weapon traces to him."

"In this case—network of cases—with this cast of characters—anything's possible. Zwingel's lived in the house six days since he made bail. He's demonstrated more poor judgment than most people, but bringing a gun into his residence would put him in a special class." Rich pulled on his gloves, stepped close to the dining room table, and looked into an open purse. He beckoned a crime scene tech. "Let's get a few official photos before I dump the contents."

Two hours later, Rich blotted out the scent of disinfectant as he entered the hospital room. "Good evening, Mr. Zwingel."

Greg opened one eye and rolled his head toward the detective. "Go away."

"Doc tells me you'll be fine. Bullet missed the most vital parts. You'll be moving on crutches and discharged in the morning."

"Leg hurts like a—"

"I imagine it does. However, we didn't come to discuss your pain level." Rich leaned forward and read the label on the single IV bag. Assured no narcotics were flowing into the victim's veins, he straightened and signaled Cal to take the lead.

Making considerably more noise than necessary, Cal set a small audio recorder on the movable tray table. Once he positioned the equipment, he extracted a notebook and recited a scripted introduction. "Talk us through the incident, Mr. Zwingel. Tell us every move you made after noon today."

Greg scrubbed his face with a hand. "I've been minding my own business—worked until a quarter to two. I put in honest work, at the restaurant, breakfast and lunch both."

Rich maintained eye contact with Greg. "Did you make any stops on the way home? Which route did you take?"

"One question at a time fellas. My head has a brass band inside." Greg's voice faded.

"We want your exact route home, including any stops. Tell us where, why, and expand on any purchases." Cal poised his pen above a nearly blank page.

Greg shifted his gaze to Cal. "And I want my next dose of pain meds."

During the following moments of silence, Rich focused on a corner of Greg's pillow and listened to the muted sounds of voices and phones beyond the closed door.

Greg sighed. "I stopped at the Gas Mart a couple blocks from work. Intersection of Major and Lily, I think. I bought gas and a six pack. Do you need the brand name?"

"Did you make any other stops?" Rich shifted his attention to the patient armband.

"How will I explain this mess to my boss? I'm scheduled to go in at four—breakfast prep—short staff for morning shift." Greg's eyes drifted shut.

"Stay awake. Keep talking." Cal rapped his pen on the lowered bed rail.

"Where were you standing when your wife entered the house?" Rich hurried to the heart of their question list.

"Living room…I was sitting…enjoying the first beer of my six pack."

Rich allowed silence to settle over the trio.

"She comes in from the garage. Guess I left the door up. Words were exchanged." Greg rubbed his eyes and looked toward Rich.

Shifting his weight to the other foot, Rich leaned forward. "Be more specific."

"She…she…blamed me for Al's death. Babbled on about how I ruined everything. Then she pulled the gun out of her purse. I was standing by then. I remember backing a step. The conversation stayed short." Greg pushed up in the bed and winced. "Did you arrest her? I'll sign all the charges you want. Will the judge revoke my bail?"

Rich ignored the questions and the short silences between them. Working from a mental list, he focused on the conversation between Greg and Pam at the house. Several questions and contradictions later, Rich stepped back and signaled Cal to end the audio recording.

"Our additional questions will wait until tomorrow. Consider your bail temporarily cancelled. The officer posted in the hall will escort you to the station after the doc signs your discharge." Cal hesitated before he shut the notebook.

Greg settled his gaze on Rich and moved his lips.

"Please repeat. I didn't hear your last comment." Rich cupped one ear.

"Just go. Let me suffer alone."

At the doorway, Rich beckoned a nurse and gestured toward Greg. "We're done. He complained of pain."

Cal matched Rich's quick steps the entire walk to the elevator bank. "Speaking of Zwingels...how's your conflict of interest?"

"Out of town." Rich pushed the button for the lobby and hid a sigh. No matter how often he reinforced his barrier between work and personal life, thoughts and images of Janet surfaced in stray moments. He resisted the urge to cross fingers for luck in exploiting their arrangement's loophole. "Uncooperative."

****

Janet moved her gaze from the sparkling lights of San Francisco outside the large window to her immediate surroundings. She missed Sims. The group around the table was too small. Four women left more elbow room than comfortable. She skimmed a finger down the stem of her glass and frowned. Her drink was gone—again. She took a quick glance around the table and confirmed her three companions were in a similar condition. She turned to locate and signal the hotel restaurant server.

An instant later, Carter stood and snatched the empty margarita pitcher.

"What's on her mind?" Janet floated the comment across a nearly empty platter of chicken nachos. She shifted her gaze in time to see Carter take the three final steps to the sleek marble and mirror bar.

Holt, now wearing civilian designer jeans and a cable pullover, popped a small nacho chip into her mouth. "You need to admit facts. He's got magnificent hair. She's available—and we're living in the twenty-first century."

Janet turned her attention to the hotel bartender. From his profile, he appeared mature, within the range of late forties to sixty. He stood tall and slender, shaking a cocktail and participating in conversation with Carter. His head, crowned with long, dark, thick hair conjured images of pirates—or survivalists. "He looks interesting…but not my flavor."

"Your flavor would be?" Baker shifted her gaze from the bartender to Janet.

"Short…silver…no comb required." She skidded her lips to a halt and swallowed before another careless word emerged. Maybe she could blame the alcohol—or the stress of the commitment service. She closed her eyes for a moment. *I'm safe—among friends.*

Baker lifted her glass and tipped the last few drops of sweet liquid into her mouth. "Tell us more."

"What are we telling?" Carter slid into her seat at

the round table. With one easy swipe of her hand, she swished a stray portion of long, curly, black hair into place.

Without hesitation Baker slanted her glass toward Janet. "Johnson has developed a fondness for silver hair on men."

Carter nudged Janet with her elbow. "Interesting—we need details—no secrets allowed."

"I've nothing more to add. Nothing capable of working, anyway." She selected a chip and held it above the platter. "I'd need more than my current amount of alcohol to tell…and then my words get unreliable."

"No problem. I requested another pitcher and order of nachos. Zack is putting a rush on both." Carter collected salt from the rim of her glass on her index finger.

Baker lowered red-framed readers from among her blonde curls and peered across at Carter. "Zack. Will you be needing the hotel room to yourself tonight?"

"Negative." Carter licked her salt-encrusted finger. "I gave him my business card, not my room number. Actually, I invited him to contact me for a shoot if he ever visits San Diego. I really would love to photograph him."

"At least you have an original pick-up line." Holt laughed.

"Ladies." Zack arrived with a generous pitcher of margaritas. "May I pour?"

The women raised four glasses simultaneously.

When he stepped to his right to fill Holt's glass, Janet noticed the mark on his neck. A port wine stain too large to be completely covered with his abundant hair touched the bottom of his ear and disappeared below his collar. The instant he walked out of easy earshot, she leaned to Carter. "I see you're going for a perfect imperfection."

"Aim high. Whoops—wrong service branch." Carter touched two fingers to her lips.

"We heard you." Baker and Holt spoke in unison.

Carter sighed. "You remember the stories of Carlo—my first love. When I see a birthmark on a man, my mind tends to visit the past. Those were some good times."

Taking a careful sip from her full glass, Janet stared at Carter's delicate hand.

Carter paused and looked at each of them in turn. "You don't need to worry. I'm in contact with reality and aware I'm not nineteen." She paused for a sip. "On the bright side, his death propelled me straight to the recruiter. I took the oath six days after Carlo was murdered."

"Ah." Janet filed a minor correction of timeline concerning the life-changing incident rarely spoken of. "Refresh our memories—was the shooter convicted?"

"I'm afraid not." Carter's frown was brief, but definite. "According to my brother, he died on the streets about a year later."

"The close timing clarifies your first day on the rifle range." Baker centered her glass on a black napkin.

"Personalization did wonders for my aim—still does." Carter leaned back.

"I agree." Holt lowered her glass. "My shooting scores trend upward after an argument. Not the ones with hubby." She shook her head until her short brunette strands quivered. "A fresh from OCS ensign or

J.G. gets imagined on my targets. New officers are the most frustrating creatures. What about you, Johnson? Do you put your ex on the bulls-eye?"

"I haven't been shooting for a long time. I can't imagine going again, after…" She stared at the edge of the table, swallowed, and willed the memory of Al's sightless eyes and bloody chest to vanish.

"After?" Baker lifted her glass and sipped.

Janet raised her gaze and looked at each of her three true friends in turn. She was safe here. Face-to-face was the only way to tell the whole story. Her Navy buddies deserved more than the bits and pieces she'd shared in emails or video chat. She drew a steadying breath. "Earlier this month…the first day I was doing installations…at the motel."

"One moment." Holt lifted the empty nacho platter while the server placed a fresh, warm batch in the center of the table.

Sealing her lips, Janet sorted the various places to begin. Her friends already had an outline. Tonight she needed to supply details. After the server left, she let the words flow. "The sight shook me. I didn't expect to find a murder victim when I opened the door. I'd been a little afraid of…well, finding the room occupied with the living."

Janet sipped her drink and savored the cold, sweet liquid. She drew confidence from their small nods. Her friends understood exactly the trouble she'd envisioned. "The emergency services operator asked more questions than I expected. A uniformed officer arrived a few minutes later with another list. Then the detectives arrived. The moment Rich stepped from the black police sedan, I knew I was in trouble." She glanced at the table and recalled the mixture of astonishment and embarrassment which swept over her during her return from the dumpster area. "His partner asked me dozens of questions. Thank God Rich wasn't present during most of my interview."

"A detective?" Carter looked straight into Janet's eyes.

"Rich." Janet gulped. The detail she'd considered holding back was released and replaced with relief.

Holt leaned back and slapped the table edge. "A detective with a first name. Does he have short, silver hair?"

"He does." Heat rolled up Janet's neck so fast she figured her skin turned brighter than Zack's birthmark. She delayed speaking by crunching a chip covered in shredded chicken and melted cheese.

In a flash, an image of Rich's hazel eyes, the indicator of playful or serious, popped into her mind. Her skin tingled at the memory of his hands full of electric magic tricks. Lips… She squeezed her eyes shut and counted to three. Blaming the alcohol for her boldness, she shared a fact omitted from her email. "He arrested Greg."

"For murder?" Holt bumped her glass and captured the flare after a few drops spilled.

"Close enough." Janet crushed a stray cocktail napkin in one hand. For a moment, she gathered courage and arranged the words wrestling in her throat. "The charges, as of three days ago, are burglary and manslaughter."

Baker picked a hot pepper slice off the platter. "I'd expect you to cheer."

"I've met your ex. I'm giving your detective kudos

for arresting him." Carter topped off their glasses.

"He's not my detective." Janet dabbed her lips with the mangled napkin. "The situation's complicated. Daniel, Ashley's fiancé, is his nephew. He'll attend the wedding and maybe other family events. Henry, his father, is a charming old man—and my dad's new, best friend." She lifted her glass and set it down without drinking. "What? I've told the truth."

"We don't need biographies of his relatives." Carter leaned forward. "What's the problem with having the ex arrested? I seem to recall occasions when you rambled on about running him over in a dark alley."

"Never myself." Janet shook her head. "You must be thinking of the times I would have applauded the driver if Greg stepped in front of a speeding garbage truck. Excuse me, but I was young and foolish. I believed child support payments should be paid on time and in full. I realize now Greg couldn't money manage his way into a free concert."

"And before the arrest?" Holt lifted a chip covered with shredded chicken. "Mr. Detective sounds identical to your new friend fond of desserts and mini-golf. How did you feel about Rich with the silver hair then?"

"Comfortable." Janet snapped her mouth shut and reached for her drink. She narrowed her eyes and for a brief moment viewed her friends as traitors. Her friends—her parents—Ashley—Henry, and all the other amateur matchmakers experimenting on her should go find a different target.

"Ahhh." Holt leaned back and curved her lips.

"You can stop with giving me morning inspection, Chief Petty Officer Holt." Janet studied her friend's wise-woman smile and rubbed her arms to banish a sudden chill under her long sleeves.

"I think we need more information. We can't give solid advice without knowledge." Carter smiled small.

"Spill—all of it." Baker traced the rim of her glass.

Janet pushed a hand through her hair and organized swirling thoughts along the way. "Did I mention he arrested my boss?" She waited for the head shakes and mummers to taper. "After the arrests, I didn't want to hear from him. So I ignored his messages. Monday, he appeared at my door. I figured one conversation might clear the air. Victory was short-lived when he found a loophole in the promise to stop the emails and phone calls."

"Continue." Baker rotated a hand above the table.

Janet drew in her lower lip for an instant. "When did you last get a card from a man? Your husband doesn't count, Holt. A card sent in the mail—not even for a holiday—a pretty drawing and a short verse with a signature. The next day, another greeting card arrived with a generic phrase handwritten above his name."

"Do you want my opinion?" Carter reached for a chip.

Janet settled her gaze on Carter's hand. "Do I have a choice?"

"He's sincere…a keeper."

"I'll second Carter's assessment."

"Make the vote unanimous."

Janet propped her chin on her hand and reviewed the comments. Was she blind to something obvious to her friends? "I'm doomed. You welded me to his side before I had a chance to tell you about the third card." If she closed her eyes, she could see the little word search puzzle in the hand-drawn grid. The number of words contained in the thirty-six squares boggled her mind. "For all I know, cards have overrun my mailbox by now. He plans to take me to dinner Monday night."

"Definitely a keeper." Baker lifted her glass in a toast. "To freedom…and love…and the freedom to love after the kids move out."

Holt touched her glass to Baker's. "I'll drink to that. One more year and the youngest will be stashed at college."

"I had plans." Janet remembered the adventure travel brochures waiting for her decision. "Plans with gusto…adventure…inspired by Sims. My initial ideas don't…didn't…include a man."

"Seize the opportunity—isn't taking advantage of the situation the whole purpose of gusto?" Carter straightened into the posture of her twenty-year Navy veteran persona.

Janet warmed with affection for every woman at the table. She paused her gaze on each face in turn, lifted her glass, and touched the rim to the others. "Thank you, my friends. To life with gusto—and whatever tomorrow brings."

Chapter Twenty-One

Under a gloomy Monday morning sky, Janet stifled a yawn and braked for a traffic light. She refused to blame yesterday's flight half way across the country for her exhaustion. She placed the majority of the blame on the late Saturday night filled with alcohol and conversation. Images and snippets of the wide-ranging discussion at their table in the hotel bar circled whether she was awake or attempting sleep.

Entering the Comfort On Call property, she exhaled relief at the sight of Pat's familiar truck. All the regular vehicles, including those of the two techs who were never early, sat in a ragged row by the fence. Did management change the hours without leaving her a message? Checking the dashboard clock, she confirmed her usual ten minutes early arrival.

"Welcome back." Tim called from the second open warehouse door.

"Are things the same?" She slammed her truck door and took three steps toward him.

He shrugged.

"I see Pat's truck. Isn't that a good sign?" She avoided mentioning the SUV parked next to the building. During the three days before she left for California, the outside auditor used Mike's former parking spot.

"Oh, he's here—with some factory guy." Tim

scuffed a toe on the packed gravel. "I wrote a resume yesterday. Lots of procedure changes since I got this job. Everything's online applications—not many firms hiring at the moment."

"I don't see a 'Closed' sign on the door." *Yet.* Janet tucked her worries deeper behind a cheerful exterior. Silence concerning overheard portions of conversations appeared the best strategy. She wouldn't blab about Pat's difficulty obtaining a payroll loan because his voice leaked through thin walls.

"I don't like it—too much drama these last couple of weeks." Tim looked beyond her, toward the slow-moving clouds. "By the way, some of the guys and I are going over to The Watering Hole after work. You're invited."

"Thanks—but no thanks. I've got other plans." The pub, a scant two miles away, tended to be the first choice for Happy Hour. In addition to an extensive selection of local craft brews, the kitchen served some of the best waffle cut fries in the area.

She mentally reviewed this morning's text message from Rich. The entire contents consisted of a suggested time and the name of a popular Italian restaurant followed by question marks. Her reply, a thumbs-up emoticon, echoed simplicity. Face-to-face remained the only way she saw to express her side of the situation. She held serious doubts of any relationship beyond polite acquaintance.

Maybe tonight she'd get answers to questions. Half a dozen of the pesky things shared time with weekend events during yesterday's flight. After she checked over her mail last night, the messages on Rich's cards joined the comments from her friends and circled in her mind.

She wanted answers. However, Rich demonstrated more skill making inquiries than giving meaningful responses.

"Another time, then?" Tim mimed drinking.

"Hang tough, Tim." Janet resumed her walk into the office. She took extra care and fastened her invisible cloak of optimism. A few moments later, she handed Kim a gift of San Francisco chocolate.

"Send Janet in as soon as she arrives. Please." Pat's voice interrupted via the intercom.

"Will do—she just walked in." Kim released the key on the old-fashioned apparatus. "I think you've been summoned."

"Payback for my vacation day, I suspect." She sent Kim a forced smile and walked toward the office. Getting singled out was unsettling at any time. Since Mike's arrest, and subsequent release on bond, the sensation amplified to dread. After two light raps, she opened the office door and stepped inside. Pulling the latch until it clicked, she settled her gaze on the two men seated behind the desk.

Pat beckoned her forward. "Welcome back. Did the memorial service go as expected?"

"Like my grandfather used to say, 'We got the job done.'" She turned her attention to the stranger. Her first impression was of an athletic man near her age. His build reminded her of a swimmer, with shoulders and arms one size too large for the rest of his body.

He pushed to his feet and extended a long arm across the uneven stacks of files. "John Shaw, Midwest manager for Silver Star Enterprises."

After introductions were complete, Mr. Shaw tapped a manila folder laid on the corner of the desk.

"I've been reading your personnel file, Ms. Zwingel. I'm impressed. The industry needs more people with your dedication."

Get to it. Why am I here? She nodded and kept her questions silent.

With a casual wave, Pat gestured her to sit in the visitor's chair. "I'm retiring—effective the minute I walk out the door this afternoon. My brother dragged me into the edges of his mess. The best thing for Comfort On Call is for me to step away entirely."

Janet blinked, sealed her lips, and lowered into the chair. Recalling some of the convoluted reports she'd failed to make sense of a month ago, she hesitated a moment before trusting her voice. "How bad is it? How much did Mike skim, or embezzle, or whatever current word fits?"

"Two million plus," Mr. Shaw supplied.

Janet opened, closed, and opened her mouth again. Swallowing, she added a drop of calm to her roiling stomach. The inheritance, the assurance of financial stability, came within inches of vanishing. Her retirement dollars would have vanished in a whirlpool with the building improvement funds and a good deal more—never to be seen again. Moistening her lips, she found her voice. "More than I expected."

"Mr. Maguire tells me you're not the sort to speak out of turn. Is he right?"

"Yes, sir. Gossip's not my vice." She paused. This meeting was a poor time and place to admit to any failing. She'd keep quiet about the simple weakness of chocolate—and certainly the complicated one of tangled emotions for a certain silver-haired detective.

"Silver Star wants to keep a dealership in this

portion of the metro area." Mr. Shaw sipped from a coffee cup with a popular, local logo. "We've multiple reasons. Corporate plans to purchase the inventory, lease the current facility, and retain most of the employees. One of our most immediate requirements is an on-site manager. We want a person who knows the people and the area." He stilled the pen in his hand and looked her straight in the face. "Do you want the position?"

Resisting the urge to rub her ear, Janet blinked. Her hearing was fine. Dare she believe him? She studied his face and found a serious set to his mouth. "Would I report directly to the factory?"

She ignored a twinge too small to be called pain at her knees and lower spine—a reminder of on-the-job abuse. The balance between practical experience and physical aging tipped another degree from level each year. The physical demands of her occupation required pretty much all her body had left to maintain current strength and agility.

A moment later, Mr. Shaw nodded.

She floated her next question. "Will I get some training on the business side? I'm willing to enroll for classes at our community college—or attend a factory school. How much commitment do you need this minute?"

"Corporate wants you to succeed. Training is key to both long-term and short-term plans. How are you at webinars?" He eased back in his chair.

"I've had some recent experience with them." Janet recalled the last module of training videos.

"Pull your chair closer, and we'll go over these balance sheets."

She moved the visitor's chair to the end of the desk. Excitement echoed in her chest with every heartbeat. An unexpected opportunity, a challenge, lay before her. *Accept it. Live with gusto.* Bits of Saturday's conversation reinforced her instinct to accept. She opened her purse, removed her half-glasses, and cleared her throat. "Where do we start?"

****

Monday evening Rich glanced toward the small blue gift bag on the passenger seat before he lifted his gaze to his sedan's visors. *I hope tonight works.* After snatching the present, he walked to Janet's front door with long strides. Would tonight begin a new, happy chapter in his life? Or would she slam an invisible barrier between them? *Be an optimist.* He gripped an invisible thread of hope.

As the chimes faded, Janet opened the door. "You're prompt."

Drawing in a breath, he skimmed his gaze over her. He delighted in her casual smile, admired a blue-and-white dress which flattered her curves, and contained a laugh at the sight of her bare feet tipped with bright red nail polish. Returning his attention to her face, he noticed caution in her sapphire eyes. "I attempt to be punctual."

"Come in. I need another minute."

He extended the bag toward her. "For you—welcome back, traveler."

"A gift isn't necessary."

"Are you discouraging generosity?" Naturally wary of grand gestures, he preferred to give small, more frequent gifts and surprises. "It will look better on you than on me."

She accepted the bag and poked two fingers in the white, glittered tissue paper.

Watching her face, he felt warm satisfaction when her mouth curved. She pulled the scarf from among the generous amount of packing. In an instant, her eyes sparkled more than the glitter on the tissue. He moistened his lips. "I think blue looks good on you."

"Nice to confirm we agree on at least one thing." Janet set the bag on the floor and examined the variegated blue, silk infinity scarf. Small clock faces, showing various hours, added interest to the fabric. "It's beautiful. Thank you."

"My pleasure." Dare he give in to impulse? He shifted his weight and decided to wait. He'd allow her to make the first touch.

She dropped the scarf over her head, made a second loop, and adjusted the front. "Perfect, exactly the accessory for tonight. Now excuse me, I need to get shoes and a sweater."

A moment later, he watched her vanish toward her bedroom. Turning his attention to the dining table, the piece of furniture which appeared to be the heart of her home he inspected the surface. Three stacks of mail occupied the near end. The tallest pile consisted of flyers and the other unsolicited paper every mailbox received. A smaller collection bore logos from banks and utilities. At the sight of the third stack, he smiled. White, cream, and pastel envelopes lay in a tidy group with his handwriting exposed on the top one.

"Are you detecting?" She spoke from three feet away.

He shrugged before turning to face her. "A habit which is difficult to turn off. I see you got most of them."

"Ten—how many did you send?" She widened her eyes.

"Eleven—expect one more in tomorrow's mail."

"Do you send cards, notes, and puzzles to all your lady friends?" She smoothed the white sweater draped over an arm.

"Only the special ones. The ones I'm…" *courting.* He silenced the word in time. *Slow down.* He should relax and wait for her cues. Clenching and releasing his left hand, he reminded himself her emotions might not have blossomed to match his own. He stepped toward her and presented his elbow as if he escorted her at a formal affair. "Since your response looked positive, shall we depart for the Italian restaurant I suggested?"

"Yes, please. I apologize again for needing to change the time." She opened her purse and retrieved her keys without a second glance at his gesture. "Work was…well…very unusual today. I even had to ask Jeremy to take a ride share to the airport."

"Unusual—do you want to expand on the topic?" He lowered his arm to his side and hid his disappointment.

"Not tonight—maybe after things settle into a pattern."

He led them to the front steps and waited for her to secure the deadbolt and test the knob. Touch—her warm skin against his—sent excitement up his arm the instant she laced fingers with him. He didn't realize how much he missed casual contact until she came into his life. Now he craved human touch—Janet's touch.

Following an unwritten script, he selected safe subjects including the hassle of airline travel and the weather in San Francisco during the drive to the restaurant. Rich sorted and discarded several openings to the topic which circled in the back of his throat. First the sight, and then her touch, confirmed his recent decision. In his typical fashion, he pursued with determination—mixed with a drop of caution. If he frightened her away, he feared a fall back into despair.

After settling side-by-side in the restaurant booth, he slid his fingers across her hand. He rubbed a thumb across her soft, warm flesh. "I missed you—every day."

"Do the puzzles have a special meaning? How do I know if I found all the words?"

"The number in the lower left corner is the word total. I figured you were smart enough not to need a complete list."

"People keep giving me more credit than I deserve." She lowered her gaze.

Rich studied her with one raised brow and filed her comment for further exploration.

"Welcome to Mario's Patio. Would you like to start with a beverage from our bar?" A server wearing a red, white, and green tie with her black shirt stopped at the end of the table.

"No wine for me. I had an entire month's alcohol allotment Saturday night." Janet ordered ice tea with extra lemon.

"The lady has spoken. I'll take diet cola, and we'll start with the toasted ravioli." He waited until the server left their table before he spoke again. "A month's worth of drinking in one night? Remind me never to challenge you."

"My friends and I got a little carried away. Mourning turned to visiting and then to celebrating.

Too much time since all five…four…of us were together." She blinked rapidly.

"Did you plan the next gathering?"

She stilled her finger on the menu's photo of vegetarian lasagna. "Carter is attending Ashley's wedding. Holt and Baker are uncertain if they can get time off in December. We didn't set a firm date for our trip to Mount Rushmore."

"Good to know you've not cancelled your adventure." He lowered the menu. "Are these group trips you've mentioned what you call gusto?"

She nodded.

"Is the term gusto confined to Navy buddies?" He slipped quiet words under the commotion as two couples took seats in the next booth.

"Absolutely not."

"Good." He steadied his gaze on her face. "Any objections if I use 'living with gusto' to define any sort of welcome change?"

****

Living with gusto. Janet enjoyed the sound of the phrase from Rich's mouth. She didn't realize how much she enjoyed his presence until he'd stood in her doorway. In addition to underlining the fact he listened, the words confirmed her decision to take the manager's position. She pressed her lips and arranged possible responses.

"Are you ready to order?" The server returned with their drinks.

After placing her order, Janet squeezed lemon into her tea, sampled the drink, and reached for a second lemon wedge. With her beverage adjusted to the tartness she favored, she leaned back and discarded several possible conversation topics. Portions of the reunion clearly were best left in San Francisco—pretty much everything from the middle of the second margarita pitcher until the end of the third.

Work, another item front and center in her thoughts, deserved a delay before sharing. The longer she'd spent with Mr. Shaw, the more sensible Rich's fence between vocation and the rest of life became. "Did I miss any important events since we last talked?"

He leaned back and rested his head for an instant against the high booth back. "That answer depends on your definition of important. How much did your family keep you informed?"

"Phone calls with Mom and Jeremy kept me up to date on Dad's progress. On the way home from the airport, Ashley clued me in about Greg's location."

"Henry went to visit Joe." He moved his glass to make room for the server to set down the appetizer.

"What?" She froze mid-swallow. "I knew they hit it off, but I didn't expect a visit. Did you take him?"

"He figured out the bus…or rather, buses. Friday afternoon, I got home and found a note on the table. Living with Dad can be similar to having a teen in the house."

Retrieving a mental image of the rehab center's front entrance, she expanded the view and remembered a small group of employees waiting at the end of the block. "I hope he traveled in daylight."

Rich released his flatware from the black, cloth napkin. "He did. Now he's talking about the next time. Claims he needs a re-match in dominos. Have I told you he tends to be a stubborn old man?"

"Henry's not the only one. Reasoning with either

Mother or Dad drains my energy. Last night, Jeremy told me he's eager to get back to work to recover. Then in the next breath, he reported remarkable progress on the to-do list. The house will be ready for Dad when his stay at the rehab center ends."

"Are you limited by insurance rules?"

While dipping a warm, toasted ravioli into red sauce, she nodded. "The original plan authorized three weeks, but his neurologist got a one-week extension. The coverage also includes a bunch of outpatient visits. I'd have to check the information sheet for the exact number."

"You know what the media calls us."

She bit into the spiced treat. "Sandwiches—pressed between duties for parents on one side and children on the other." She chewed and savored the contrasting textures before she swallowed. "You and I are in a better situation than many. Our children don't actually live with us."

He reached for a warm ravioli. "Your inherent optimism is only one of many reasons I enjoy your company."

"Optimism's a thin candy shell." The words flew free before her mind got organized.

Laughing, he touched her hand. A moment later the server returned with their meals. "The lady shows a sense of humor...all the more reason to polish my skills."

Skills? Janet reserved her questions until after the first delicious bites of spaghetti carbonara. Words from the puzzles in the greeting cards returned in random order. Charm...pursue...explore...awaken...sunshine. She saw plenty of optimism and compliments but not a clear theme. "What sort of talents are you polishing?"

"Courtship."

She stilled with a bite of pasta in her throat. Concentrating on completing the swallow and taking her next breath, she examined the word. Courtship—his response laid large and whole behind her ribs. What happened to the friendship she was beginning to enjoy? She tipped her head and studied him.

Continuing to wind angel hair pasta on his fork, he glanced in her direction.

Failing to see unease with the old-fashioned word choice, she moistened her lips. "Sorry." She blinked to delay another instant. "You don't need to repeat. I heard you fine. But I need a moment to digest."

He waited until she'd swallowed a drink of tea before speaking. "During the break in electronic communication, I thought about us. I'd like to be more than casual friends."

"Best friends forever? Impossible. You lack the qualifications for the Navy buddy group."

"Nor would I want to join. I rather expect I'd get vivisected."

She raised the napkin to hide her grin. "You exaggerate our skills. Will it reassure you to know none of us are in medical related professions?"

"Enlighten me. What sort of day jobs do the others have?"

"May I save a discussion of Navy buddies for another time?" Lifting her drink, she surprised herself at how easy she assumed they would speak again— laugh together—and share a meal. "Can you tell me which charges are sticking against Greg?"

He narrowed his mouth before turning. "How

much did Ashley tell you?"

"After years of practice, she stayed light on the details. I know he made bail, hurt his knee, and moved in with one of the cooks from the restaurant. I got confused when she mentioned he filed charges against Pam. This strikes me as odd timing for a divorce."

"Greg's charges against his wife are not marriage related." He rested a forkful of Marinara-coated pasta against his dish's edge. "I'll only tell you the public portion, what you could find on the website I gave you a week ago."

She nodded. "Public information is all I expect. When Jeremy calls in the morning with the recap on his flight, I plan to correct a wrong assumption or two."

"You lied to your brother?" He raised both brows.

Ignoring his impression of a high school actor, she shook her head. "I failed to clarify a topic with him. I intended to make the correction during the drive to the airport. Our opportunities to talk without fear of being overheard were limited." Janet reached for her glass and silently admitted she'd not taken full advantage of their few private moments. "Mother believes a maid found the body. I'm not stirring up unnecessary drama with her. Jeremy, well, he can handle the truth."

For the next ten minutes, with interruptions for questions, and fresh drinks from the server, Rich released the public information. He summarized the charges against Greg and Mike before stating the true nature of Greg's knee injury.

Janet burst into laughter. "Oh, I'd have paid to witness the scene."

One of the men from the neighboring booth turned and frowned.

"No problem." Janet arranged her mouth in a small smile and gave the stranger a miniature wave.

An instant later, Janet lowered her voice. "Will his case go to trial? Or is Greg getting a deal from the prosecutor? Will I need to testify? Dare I talk amongst friends?"

"You won't know about a trial for weeks—or longer. Did you write down everything the first evening?"

"Detective Collins stressed the importance of notes." She visualized the spiral notebook pages she filled during one of the worst evenings of her life.

"You'll be fine. As to deals"—he wiped drops of sauce from the table top with his napkin—"I expect the prosecutor will present an offer to Greg. I'm not privy to details."

Janet leaned back against the soft, padded vinyl and pictured Greg in prison. In her imagined scenarios after the burglary, he served either a suspended sentence or probation, whichever fit the situation. If convicted of manslaughter, he'd certainly spend time in a state facility. Her ex chaffed at both routine and authority. *Let it go.* She sighed. At age fifty-two, Greg needed to face consequences for any illegal actions.

"Are you ready to go?" Rich tucked bills into the check folder.

During the ride home, Janet kept the conversation on mundane topics. While speculating on the next baseball game, she stayed conscious of a hum of electricity between them. She wanted his touch. Rubbing her arms increased her longing to be held. She hesitated to imagine more than one kiss. When she remembered leaning against his chest, she became aware of her hard-won independence and his offered protection wrestling.

"Let me practice my manners." Rich parked the car in her driveway and turned to her for an instant.

She nodded and fussed with her seat belt longer than usual.

When they stood on the front porch, he stepped close and framed her face with both hands. "May I?"

With her skin tingling in anticipation, she curved her mouth. "Affirmative."

He closed the small space and matched her smile perfectly to his lips.

Closing her eyes, Janet tumbled into pleasure. She savored.

He probed.

She welcomed—explored. Shivers of excitement skipped along her spine. Emotions long dormant surged to the surface. "I...I...don't stop." She abandoned his lips and melted into his chest. Time faded and the world shrank to his strong, steady heartbeat. The rhythm calmed and reassured her. His embrace offered a safe harbor for her thrashing emotions.

"Do you know what I want?" He traced little circles on the back of her neck.

"Don't tell me. Not tonight. I...I'm...not thinking right." To be entirely truthful, she wasn't thinking at all. Stray words flitted about in her head like hummingbirds bumping against the interior of a red box—risk...reward...gusto.

"Soon—I'll put my words in proper order." He backed half a step and raised her chin until they stared into each other's eyes.

She blinked, uncertain of pending tears. Listening

to her heart begin to settle, she whispered, "Come inside for a bit."

"After you." He swept a hand for her to enter.

After she walked to the center of the living room, she turned to face him. In an instant, she wrapped her arms around his steady body. "I…I want…hold me."

He pulled her close and sent one hand to toy in her hair.

Clocks ticked almost in time to the heart close to her ear. She sensed clumps of tension slide away. The world contracted to the two of them in a comforting embrace.

Later, she became aware of sitting. During her daze, he settled into a corner of the couch and nestled her on his lap.

"Feel better?"

"Much," she whispered.

"Are you upset about work?"

She sighed and shook her head. Grabbing a thought swirling past, she steadied her breath. "I'm sorry. You were doing your job. I didn't think Greg and Mike's arrests would bother me."

"We had evidence."

"Mike's arrest hit me hard. I didn't realize how much I cared." The entire atmosphere at work felt clouded since Mike's absence. She refused to imagine how Pat's retirement would change the conversations in the break room. "Greg…" She stilled her lips before more unfiltered words slipped out. Rich could put together facts. Examining clues was his job. Had she been married to a murderer? Had she lived with a man capable of shooting another human—not in war?

"Do you want me to leave?"

She eased away and stood. At the moment, she found it impossible to keep track of all the moving pieces in her life. What would happen if he stayed? No, she wouldn't risk taking that path. She moistened her lips. "For tonight, yes."

"Will you think about what I said? Can I expect answers to voice mails and texts?"

"Absolutely." She punctuated the word with a soft, quick kiss on his cheek. "I'm confused at the moment—and tired."

"At the lady's request." He stood before her, touched her chin, and dusted a kiss on her forehead. "I bid you farewell. I'll see you soon. Stay safe."

For a long moment, Janet remained standing beside the sofa before following him to the door. She stared at his back and allowed random phrases from tonight's conversation to parade through her mind. *More than friends. Courtship. Stay safe.*

He turned, raised an arm, and waved before sliding into the driver's seat.

After latching the door, she leaned against the smooth wood. A simple dinner—no, an evening with Rich was far from simple—rolled her world in a new direction. The steady, stable independent life she enjoyed a few months ago tumbled out of control.

Closing her eyes, she recalled the determination in his face tonight. *Once I make a decision.* She worried her lower lip. Why am I so sure his decision will change my life?

Chapter Twenty-Two

Thursday evening Janet blocked her yawn from the receptionist's view with a hand and signed the Oak Leaf Center visitor log. She wouldn't stay long. If she remembered the correct schedule, the staff settled Joe for the night within a quarter hour. *Hardly worth the drive.* She shook away the thought. She promised her mother to visit Joe after work. Giving her word to visit was one of the few ways to get Marie back to her own house for a decent amount of sleep.

A burst of male laughter from the end of the long, narrow, community room got Janet's attention.

In the center of the room, a housekeeper wiped tables and arranged chairs.

Farther down, two familiar men sat at a round table. While walking toward the pair, she caught portions of the conversation.

"And then…by crackers…the boy darted up a big, old pine tree quicker than a squirrel. Patches, the hound, stayed on him close enough to keep him honest. Dog snagged himself a shoe." Henry wiped away laughter spittle with a frayed handkerchief.

"Good one," Joe replied, slurring over the words.

"I see you already have a visitor. How are you doing, Dad?" Janet leaned over and dusted a kiss on Joe's cheek.

"'Kay." Joe grasped her wrist with his good hand.

"Dressshed fancy."

"Just for you." She smiled. If her mother got word how much the job shift to management stressed her limited business wardrobe, Marie would insist on a shopping trip. Janet preferred to juggle her current garments for another week or two. She gave a nod of greeting to Henry before addressing Joe again. "Did you have a long day? Did the therapists work you hard?"

Joe nodded and paused before attempting a verbal answer. "Walk better—bumped wall once."

Hiding pride at his understandable speech this late in the day behind a small smile, she eased into a chair. A moment later, she lifted his good hand and inspected his knuckles. "You need to pick your battles carefully. You know walls usually win."

"I won." Joe pointed toward Henry.

"Sounds like a good day." She turned her attention to the other man. "Does Dad's win mean the great domino tournament continues?"

"He beat me three out of four. I need a rematch." Henry tapped the worn and faded storage box.

"No surprise. Dad's good at table games. But I must admit, I didn't expect to see you here tonight, Henry."

"I lost track of time—missed my bus." He lifted one hand in the general direction of a large wall clock.

"Do you need a ride? I know where you live." She studied the elderly man's face for a moment and decided he tried too hard to appear casual.

Henry pursed his lips for a long moment before he slid the domino box back and forth between his hands. "I called Rich an hour ago. He's working late—too many criminals."

"Well, if he's not here in a little bit, you call again, and I'll be your private taxi."

One of the young aides approached and parked a wheelchair beside Joe. "Mr. Johnson, time for bed."

"Daughter." Joe smeared the word and squeezed Janet's hand. "Go with."

"I'll walk you to your room. You're old enough to put on your own pajamas."

Joe laughed.

"Yeah, I know. You'd love to put on your pants by yourself." She pressed her lips and decided to stay on light topics. "I see Mom brought you new Cardinals sweatpants."

The aide reached to help Joe transfer.

Joe nodded and grunted.

"He's trying for best dressed." The aide released the brake.

"Dad cleans up good. Give him a fresh shave, put him in his Sunday suit, and he could pass for a millionaire." Smiling, she recalled the fresh, mint scent of his favorite aftershave.

"Not now. No suit." Joe rubbed at the uneven stubble on his chin.

Janet walked beside him and provided a running commentary about traffic and a problem getting parts for one of her clocks. She touched on the plans for Joe's scheduled Saturday morning discharge. The topics she omitted included the changes at Comfort On Call. Yesterday, she'd given her parents a broad outline of the changes in her job description and minimized the underlying reasons. Specifics could wait a few days. In less than a week, Joe would be settled at home, and she would have a better understanding of her new duties. Ten minutes later, she returned to the community room.

Henry folded the flip phone and smiled. "We're good. You have permission to drive me home."

"Great. I'll get the truck and meet you at the entrance." She strode toward the front door and gave the receptionist a smile and wave as she passed.

Half a mile from the rehab center, Henry launched into an unprompted monologue.

Janet drove the familiar streets and listened to a convoluted tale involving Rich, the grandson Brian, and selling furniture during last year's downsizing. When stopped at a traffic light, she stole a glance at him. *Matchmaker or devil's advocate.* The dim lighting in the truck cab made subtle differences undetectable. She took advantage of a longer than usual pause. "I think Brian avoided me at the party."

"My grandson is smart and dense at the same time. He's self-centered…and slow to accept his mother's death."

"Death's a difficult situation to deal with." She'd lost count of the times her heart ached for Sims in recent weeks. The memorial service, seeing her other friends face-to-face, and a little time coated the memories with a fragile layer of acceptance. "Has the rest of the family done better?"

Henry sighed. "During the early months, we all worried about Rich. Then, near the end of the first year, he pulled his act together and moved forward. Brian's the only one with a still-obvious blind spot. Did you know he came into town for an interview early this week? I overheard Rich telling him to face facts— again."

A moment later, Janet flicked on her turn signal and eased to a brief pause at the red light. Pressing her lips tight to prevent asking further questions, she glanced at her passenger. Rich's conversations with his son were none of her business. Yet, a bit of comfort lodged in her chest with the knowledge she wasn't over-reacting to Brian's behavior.

"Do you want my opinion?"

She checked her mirrors. "Why do I think you'll tell me regardless?"

"You're good for Rich. I advise you to ignore the rest of the family—me included. I'm just a grumpy old man with arthritis. Follow his lead—he's solid."

Changing lanes, she recalled the end of Monday's dinner date when Rich filled the air with too many unsaid words. He wanted more than she could possibly think about at the moment. "Don't get wild ideas. I have neither the time nor inclination to train a man. Anyway, my track record isn't good."

"Don't under-rate yourself. Ashley's father is carved from rotten wood. You did a fine job with your daughter." He shifted his cane to rest against the corner of his seat. "I hear you have fabulous friends. Do some of them go back to your stint in the Navy?"

"Affirmative." She pulled to a stop at the end of the Taylor driveway. An incident from the recent gathering with her friends in the hotel bar flashed in her mind. At the beginning of the first pitcher, they stood, touched full glasses, and proclaimed to the near-empty room. *To life with gusto.*

Henry unlatched the door and turned. "Thanks for the lift—and for listening to an old man."

Giving him a smile, she shifted her gaze to the

house. Rich stood in the open doorway. *He's here.* With her heart pounding double-time, she scrambled for a greeting.

****

Rich opened the front door and hesitated. The sight of Henry stepping from Janet's truck halted the sharp comment he'd been rehearsing for the previous half hour. The old man was meddling—and getting obvious. He exhaled worry wrapped in exasperation. A serious conversation with Henry was overdue. Rich needed to remind his father of a few facts.

One—he was capable of determining his own path in life.

Two—concerns and pressures multiplied when making decisions at his age.

Three—he wasn't the only adult involved.

Recognizing an unplanned opportunity to see Janet, he smiled. During his workday, she'd crept into his thoughts during every minute not spent concentrating on a case. Monday night confirmed his emotions for her exceeded the wispy smoke of friendship. During the week without electronic communication, he decided exactly which direction he wanted their relationship to travel. The dinner date clarified his decision. But he doubted she'd reached the same conclusion. Pushing too fast might scare her away. Then again, he didn't intend to waste any opportunity to speak in person. He stepped off the porch and walked toward her truck. "The wanderer returns."

"Or the bad penny." Henry slammed the truck door and straightened.

Dad knows I'm on to him. He maintained his stride. "Excuse me, I'd like a word with your chauffeur."

"Go ahead. Take your time." Henry paused in the middle of the driveway, leaning on his cane.

A dozen hurried steps later, Rich stood at the driver's door. He raised a hand to tap on the window. An instant before his knuckles would touch the glass, he realized the window was lowered. "Have you time for a word?"

She tipped her head toward Henry. "Is he playing you—or me?"

Rich breathed in excitement and longing. While pleasant, the phone calls and emails exchanged since Monday night paled when compared to actually seeing her. He restrained his inclination to reach in and give her a hug. Placing one hand on the sill, he determined to mind his manners, and gave her space. "Both—he's a cunning old man."

"He's also a decent actor. Tell me, did he really call you half an hour ago?" She settled her gaze on his face.

"He did. According to him, you volunteered to bring him home."

Following a short laugh with a sigh, she shook her head. "Technically, he's correct. But I suspect he missed his bus on purpose."

"Should we let him savor the situation?" He lingered his gaze on her face, enjoying the gentle lines in her profile. In the soft illumination of the street light, her blue eyes shone large, framed by dark brows. Flexing his hands, he stifled the desire to push his fingers into her short hair and play among the soft strands. He licked his lips and fought the urge to kiss her. "Have you eaten?"

"I need to get home. I've at least a dozen things to

do before the morning."

"You didn't answer the question." He moved a hand to rest lightly on her forearm. In an instant, warmth seeped into his skin through her suit jacket and soothed his breathing. "Will you meet me at the hamburger place up the street in ten?"

She frowned and shook her head. "Not tonight— call me tomorrow. I should be off work after five—no, better to plan on after six. I'll keep some time open."

"You're making me work for every minute." He skimmed a hand up to her shoulder, jumped it over to her chin, and steadied her face. Leaning forward, he placed a gentle kiss on her lips. In his next breath, the kiss morphed from chaste—to eager—to urgent. The instant she opened to him a sip of heaven surged all the way to his heart. Panting, he backed off a portion of an inch. "Tomorrow."

Nodding, she tucked in her lower lip. "Tomorrow."

Backing away, he supported her chin and caressed her smooth skin with a thumb. "I'm an all-or-nothing sort of person. I want you, Janet. In my life...all the way. I'd marry you next week if you gave the word."

Janet opened and closed her mouth without a sound. With her eyes wide and brows stalled near her hairline, she swallowed.

He pressed his lips and shut his eyes for a moment. *Stupid to move so fast.* For an instant, he saw his younger self dropping a ring on a softball infield while proposing to Mary. "I'm sorry. I didn't intend to scare you." He opened his eyes, lifted her left hand, and scattered kisses on the back. "Tomorrow—I'll call— after six."

"I should go."

Her voice emerged all warm, soft, and confused to settle on his shoulders. "Yeah, we've put on enough of a show for the neighbors." He placed one more kiss at the base of her thumb and surrendered her hand. "I'll call. You control the time and place. I warned you my courtship skills needed work. Please think about what I said so poorly."

"I…I'll think about…what you said." She tilted up her head for an instant before glancing away and touching the transmission lever.

"Janet, I love you. I'd like you in my life. I want you to stand by my side. Kick my butt when necessary." He paused for a quick breath. Thinking too much tended to ruin simple statements and get him all tangled in the expectations of others. The little flashes of clarity visiting him since the Labor Day party glowed steady now. Janet shined like a beacon to his lost emotions. He eased away from the truck and raised a hand. "Stay safe."

Chapter Twenty-Three

Sunday evening, Janet pressed a palm against her stomach and surveyed her kitchen. *Calm down.* She breathed in the competing scents of warm cinnamon and fresh coffee and nodded approval at the clean countertops and scrubbed floor. After a busy day, her house was prepared for a visitor.

She glanced at the calendar and thought of Mr. Shaw, her trainer from Silver Star Enterprises. Friday afternoon he shook her hand and assured her he was a mere email away before he drove toward the airport.

Official site manager of Comfort On Call. She tested the phrase in silence, adjusted her shoulders under her light sweater, and swallowed the lump of responsibility—again. *Is this gusto?* A better question would be to ask about the eventual results—soar or crash?

While her clocks ticked in near unison, she thumbed a lighter and held the flame to the first candle in an autumn centerpiece. "I can do the job," she whispered to the empty house as the wick caught. "The other techs respect me."

She moved the flame to the second candle. "Greg's sentencing is tomorrow." The steadiness in her hand and voice startled her. Either Greg, or his lawyer, got sensible and entered a guilty plea to the manslaughter charge. In exchange, the prosecutor dropped several of the associated charges. The best-case scenario would be ten years until parole.

"Mike." While her mind whirred, she pressed her lips. Sorting fact from fiction in the activities of her boss—former boss—proved difficult. Working only with the public information gave an incomplete picture. Evidently, Mike entered the room after Al's death, removed the gun, and hid the weapon in his vehicle. He also faced numerous tax and fraud charges involving both state and federal authorities. His legal battles were at the beginning. Janet sighed. She sincerely hoped Mike's crimes didn't drown Pat and other family members.

"Pam." Janet spit the name into the silence and shook her head. Greg's third wife faced weapons, assault, and fraud charges. Yesterday, when Janet checked the website, a tentative trial date was set for late spring.

"Then there's the turmoil in my private life." She touched the tip of the lighter to the third candle. Three flames swelled and steadied as she watched. She spun conversation topics and directions to steer them through her mind. The same choices circled every night, all night. Three short days—and long nights—after Rich stood beside her truck and spoke the word marriage, the idea refused to settle. She lay awake during the dark hours while past and present opinions of a second marriage wrestled in her chest.

Is Rich serious? Can a person be sure after two months? How long is long enough? Equally unsettling was the fact each episode ended with five champagne flutes touching above a table.

Glancing around her modest home, she absorbed

satisfaction from the framed family photos, multiple mantel clocks, and functional, comfortable furniture. She viewed the material things as symbols of deeper, more important values. Since Joe's stroke, she treasured family more than ever. Books on the shelves and possessions in the cupboards symbolized education and hard work. Independence felt good—satisfying.

"And then Rich strolled into my life." She turned her gaze to the deck slider and saw her reflection. Stepping over to close the vertical blinds, she indulged in one more comment to the quiet house. "I didn't expect to find a man."

The doorbell chimed and jerked her thoughts to the present. Brushing lint from her tailored black pants, she hurried toward the door. "In a moment."

"Take three."

She smiled. Rich's voice and low-key sense of humor packaged in simple words lifted her spirits.

The moment the door opened shoulder width, Rich thrust six red roses, stems bundled in clear plastic, forward. "Good evening, these are for you."

"Thank you. Come in. Coffee's hot." A warm blush inched up her neck. Roses—the last time a man gave her roses, or flowers of any kind, the gift had been tainted by insincere apologies and promises. "Let me find a vase for these. They're…beautiful."

"No more lovely than the recipient."

She froze and stared at the tips of his shoes while fire surged across her skin.

"Honest. I mean every word." He backed one step and drew a noisy breath. "You are pretty, smart…and dressed…very professional tonight."

"Hostess attire." She flicked a hand to direct

attention to her high-neck red sweater. A moment later, she led him to the dining area.

"Allow me to modify the compliment. I'll say you look very welcoming." Pausing at the end of the table, he studied the candles a moment before again directing his attention to her.

Delaying a reply, she pulled a milk glass vase from a cabinet and filled it from the tap. She was naturally wary of compliments. "You sound very confident."

"How are your new duties at work going?"

She pulled the flowers from the plastic sleeve and alternated her gaze between Rich and the floral gift on the counter. "Everyone's very supportive, at least for the moment. The new normal is document, document, and document. Most of the techs are okay with the changes. I'm sure a few are checking out other employers. The question is when, rather than if, the shine will wear off the dozens of new procedures. I've…well…I've never imagined myself as a boss. I'm used to taking orders, not giving them."

"You used lots of independent thinking on your service calls." He rested his hands on the back of a chair.

"Some of them." She held back a simple truth. A great majority of her tech work followed memorized flowcharts and checklists. Step-by-step procedures diagnosed an overwhelming number of mechanical failures.

Shaking his head, he rubbed his neck with one hand. "Are you trying to tarnish my sterling opinion?"

A short laugh escaped as she trimmed rose stems to a slant with the kitchen shears. "I'm a realist. By now, I thought you realized I have a large, practical core."

"I have. I'd say you keep at least one foot in reality at all times. Just for the record, I find honesty and practicality charming."

She allowed his words to slide in and quiet the hummingbird flitting behind her ribs. She studied his face for a moment before she set the flowers beside the glowing centerpiece.

With a neutral expression to his mouth, he settled a look on her without an obvious stare. She decided to use Carter's word from the snail mail cards incident—sincere. "For the record, you've often exhibited a practical side. I think…well…the timing of your…"

"My declaration the other night was a proposal." He sighed and shifted his weight. "My words were miserable, inarticulate, and ill-timed. I intended to wait a few days and present my request in complete sentences without a truck door between us. Then Henry ignored bus schedules. Brian sent another email full of opinions disguised as reasons. I'm not living like a monk to please him. I couldn't help myself. I warned you my courtship skills were rusty."

"Courtship." She widened her smile while pouring coffee into a pair of bright red mugs. "Do you often use old-fashioned words for…non-conventional actions?" She would have missed his shrug if not watching intently. "Okay, in hindsight I see a proposal tucked into your comments. About the other part—did you mean the declaration at the end?"

"I do love you. I want you in my life—ever and always." He opened his hands and displayed them on the chair back.

She set both mugs of coffee and a plate of fresh cookies on the table and motioned him to sit. "You surprised me…maybe shocked is a better word. I've not stopped thinking about your…offer."

Pulling out the chair, he glanced toward the front door and eased to his seat. "Has all your thinking resulted in any conclusions?"

"I like you." *Be honest.* She glanced at his left hand resting on the table. Gripping her mug firmly, she conquered the urge to caress his skin. Before Rich entered her life, she didn't remember craving touch. Blowing across her steaming drink, she organized swirling words. "I enjoy your company. I visualize a mountain of obstacles in any future together. Are we too old for such a major change? Do we drag too much baggage everywhere we go?"

"Personally, my definition of old has changed a few times." He rubbed a finger on the mug handle. "Do you mind if I use the phrase 'life experience' instead of 'baggage'? I'd rather imagine our pasts as warm coats instead of pieces of luggage."

Nodding, she studied the mixture of seriousness and humor in his eyes. "Please don't tell me which side of your private age line I fall on."

"The correct side." He grinned before raising his cup.

She sipped coffee and minimized her smile. A few well-chosen words from him lit her internal flame. Aware of every movement in his face, from pale eyelashes during a blink to a minute tremble at the left corner of his mouth, she surveyed him from behind her mug. "You're being diplomatic. Is that a skill you've developed for investigations?"

"Truth wrapped in kindness proves useful in all sorts of situations." He selected a sugar-and-cinnamon-coated cookie and set the treat on a napkin without taking a bite. "For the record, I meant the proposal. I'll take you to the courthouse and get married this week, if you want."

"Not this week—or next." She shook her head. An interior flutter tickled—the imaginary hummingbird left a phantom perch and flitted in her chest.

"Shall we talk practical? Or would you prefer I embarrass myself while expressing emotions?" He bit into the cookie.

"Hmmm." A memory of his kiss three nights ago, in front of his house, hovered behind her ribs. When he kissed her, held her, or even touched her, rational thought turned in a vacation request. "I enjoy my independence. I won't be easy to live with."

He nodded and swallowed. "I'm not looking for easy. I'm very aware a successful marriage is work. Being half of an equal pair can be difficult to a point beyond frustrating. But I'm also confident the benefits will more than cancel the bumps."

"Benefits, now there's a modern word." She became very conscious of a line he'd not crossed during the intense moments of kisses and caresses. He granted her requests to slow. The words he whispered remained suitable for publication. No matter the amount of heat and excitement generated, she sensed safety in his arms—protection from the winds and waves life constantly tossed at her.

"I want to be more than friends." He gathered her right hand in both of his. "I'm serious about certain things. I believe my stance on important aspects of the marriage relationship overlap with yours. I know I'm impatient. Compare me to an exuberant, half-trained puppy. But puppies mature and become dependable, vital members of the family."

Janet turned her smile into a grin and added her left hand to the stack. "Benefits within marriage—I like the meaning." She held his gaze for a long moment and let the phrase turn a slow somersault in her brain. Did she love him? Was she daring enough to risk her scarred heart? "I think we need to come to agreement on some of the practical, mundane portions of our relationship before I can commit."

"Ask me questions." Leaning close, he whispered. "I'll give honest answers."

She pressed her lips and contained the words balanced on the back of her tongue. *Gusto. Gusto. Gusto.* She could almost hear Sim's voice urging her to take the risk. "I'm fond of you. I trust you to keep a confidence. I enjoy your touch." She straightened, increasing the distance between them, and focused on their stacked hands. Heat pooled at her neck, like a blush at the starting line. I crave your presence when I'm alone. I want to keep you in my life. But I don't want to feel smothered." She tipped her head and met his steady gaze. "Do you understand what I'm saying? Does independence conflict with your definition of love?"

"I don't see any purpose to interfering with your professional advancement. I expect my own career will present a number of problems for you with the irregular hours. I'm not the sort of person to insist on knowing your every move or expenditure."

"What if I revert to my maiden name?"

He shrugged before he stood and pulled a slim, flat box from an interior jacket pocket. A moment later, he set the ribbon-clad gift on the table. Squatting beside her chair and grasping her hands, he gazed at her face. "I don't want to stifle you. I love you, Janet. I want you to grow and bloom by my side. Stand where we can be both individuals and a team. Marry me—make us happy."

"Us—I like your phrasing." *Was her imaginary hummingbird dancing?* She hesitated while words crowded behind her teeth. She leaned forward until their brows touched. "Rich Taylor, I love you. You've made imagining a future without you impossible." She paused, drew a tiny breath, and adjusted her hands within his. "I'll marry you. I'll love you until my dying day."

Her world consisted of his light, warm breath and the soft, steady rhythm of her clocks. Suspended in space, she floated into his kiss—a soft, warm, urgent kiss. *More. Give me more.* She frowned when she no longer felt his lips.

"I have a gift for you." He stood and guided her hand to the box on the table. "Open it."

Standing, she followed directions and revealed a single strand of uniform, quarter inch, cultured pearls. "Oh…they're…beautiful."

"Since I've never seen you wear any sort of ring, I purchased an alternate engagement gift. Will you accept?" He lifted his gaze until he stared into her eyes.

"I can't imagine anything more perfect." She lifted the necklace, held the polished pearls against her red turtleneck, and expected her heart was a serious competitor for a world speed record. After her divorce, she never wore rings because the ones with raised settings snagged on pockets, gears, and access panels.

She could wear a simple, short necklace always. Pearls would be suitable on display with any of her management outfits. When she went into the field, she could slip the necklace under a uniform shirt.

"You...you make me...happy." He fastened the necklace and scattered light kisses along her hairline between his words.

Turning to face him, she matched his grin, rested her arms on his shoulders, and stroked his neck with one hand. "I love you, Rich." She blinked at the ease of the declaration. "You have a generous soul."

He gave a soft laugh. "You need to go easy with the praise. My greedy parts want you—all to myself."

Janet pressed into him to begin the next kiss. Savoring, and exalting in his taste, she felt her interior hummingbird soar. Nibbling along his jaw, she teased a sensitive spot behind his ear. She tingled from scalp to toes as his hands performed a dance of love in time to the chiming of every clock in the house. *Gusto, gusto, gusto.*

Chapter Twenty-Four

December 26

With a crushed tissue in one hand, Janet blinked away another tear. Ignoring the couple kneeling for a final blessing, she focused on the church Christmas tree. The seasonal decoration stood tall and proud. Hundreds of tiny white lights and dozens of red, white, and golden globes prompted pleasant memories. She lifted the tissue and wicked away more threatening tears. Ashley and Daniel deserved the best today. She raised her gaze to the ceiling and gathered her emotions into a tidy bundle. Red-rimmed eyes on the mother-of-the-bride made poor photos.

Breathing deep, she renewed her determination to be clear-eyed with a genuine smile for the receiving line. She glanced across the aisle and then back several rows. How many people did the church seat? When Jeremy escorted her to the front pew, she estimated enough guests to overrun the reception arrangements.

She stole a glance to Joe and Marie farther down the pew. Pride for their granddaughter showed in their straight posture and small smiles. Joe gripped his cane, the only walking aid necessary after months of therapy. Marie lifted a lace-edged handkerchief with one hand. Sensing a secret in the air, she suppressed a sigh as a tingle wove up her spine.

"And now."

The pastor's voice brought Janet's attention back to the wedding couple.

"The bride has asked to say a few words before the recessional."

Janet raised her brows. The moment she glanced to her brother, seated beside her, he shrugged.

"Thank you for attending our wedding ceremony today." Ashley paused and fumbled with the switch on the cordless mic. "I think it's turned on now. Will someone in the last pew wave if you can hear me?"

A ripple of laughter rose and fell behind Janet.

Glancing across the aisle, she discovered Daniel's father hid a chuckle behind his hand. *What's happening?* She remembered Ashley, Daniel, and his parents huddled in a brief, but definitely private, conversation in the narthex before sending the bride to don her dress in a small classroom.

"As many of you are aware, a very special couple is seated among you today. I'll ask them to come forward in a moment. You see, my husband and I have discussed a family situation at length." Ashley squeezed Daniel's hand. "With the aid of Pastor Gilmore, you will witness a second wedding. Mom—Rich—you did get the license last week, didn't you?"

Janet dipped her head, blinked, and brought the tips of new white pumps into focus. She sensed every drop of blood pooling in her feet, freezing her in place. *Today?* She and Rich arranged for a very quiet ceremony tomorrow.

"Go." Jeremy nudged her ribs and stage whispered.

Dragging in air, she raised her head and looked across the aisle.

Rich pushed to his feet and wagged a finger at Henry.

The simple ceremony plans so carefully discussed vanished quicker than warm rolls on Christmas morning.

"My dear." Rich stepped to the end of her pew and offered an arm.

After one glance at the twinkle in his warm, hazel eyes, Janet curved her mouth into a wide smile. Her internal hummingbirds burst into joyful acrobatics. Standing, she smoothed her gold-and-white satin dress and looped an arm into his elbow. She leaned close. "Did you know?"

"The conspirators didn't leak a word."

She swallowed her doubt, certain no person on earth was more startled than she'd been. "Where are the rings?"

"I suspect the best man has them in his pocket."

Feeling strength return to her limbs, she nodded. "Then let's get married."

With a few deft motions, the pastor signaled the first bridal party to a position left of center.

In another moment, Carter appeared at Janet's side and Daniel's father stepped beside Rich.

Pastor Gilmore eased forward. "Shall we begin?"

Was she living in a hallucination? Janet felt like an observer perched among the rafters. Reality couldn't be standing in front of more than a hundred people, some close to strangers, while pledging to love and cherish the man beside her.

"I, Richard Micah Taylor, take you, Janet Marie, to be my lawful wedded wife for as long as we both shall...live." Rich's voice stalled between the final two words. An instant later, he slid the plain platinum band on her finger.

"And I, Janet Marie Zwingel take you, Richard Micah"—she paused to regain a bit of composure after speaking his formal name—"to be my lawful wedded husband for as long as we both shall live." The matching band hesitated at his knuckle, then eased over in a perfect fit.

Pastor Gilmore raised his right hand in blessing and proclaimed them husband and wife. "You may kiss your bride."

Janet closed her eyes the instant Rich's lips touched her mouth. The world shrank to only the two of them as she savored the reality…perfection…safety contained in the kiss. She reluctantly opened her eyes and couldn't resist giving him a private wink before a public smile.

A short time later, Janet stood between Daniel and Rich in an abbreviated receiving line. The usual collection of relatives, plus friends of her daughter and son-in-law, offered a kind word with brief hand clasps. When Carter, Baker, and Holt reached her, the handshakes turned into sincere hugs. She pulled Holt's husband into an embrace and blinked back a fresh batch of tears. "Thank you for coming…all of you."

Holt stood in front of Rich and gave him a visual inspection from head to toe and back again while gripping his hand. "I've heard good things about you, Mr. Taylor. I hope you live up to your reputation."

"I'll do my best." Rich looked at her straight on.

Janet nudged him with an elbow. "She'll stand there for an hour if you let her."

"She exaggerates." Holt blushed deep rose and

released Rich's hand.

"Not by much." A tall, white-haired man extended his arm. "I'm Holt's husband—also known as Marty. Welcome to the fringes of their club."

The guests continued until Janet suspected some of the police officers came through a second or third time. Her smile felt a permanent fixture, and a quart of water might return her voice to normal. She stepped back to look around Daniel for the length of the line. A person in front of her cleared their throat and got her attention.

"Brian."

Rich's son extended a hand. "I suppose now's the time to be a good sport and wish you well. Don't expect me to call you mother."

"I wouldn't think of it. Janet is fine." *Better than wife number two.* She pressed her lips before the suggestion escaped.

Brian's shoulders relaxed, and his smile grew two sizes. "You'll watch out for him? Will you keep him away from the stove?"

Adding a nod to her grin, Janet relished his softened tone and squeezed his hand a little firmer. "We've got cooking duties covered."

A few moments later, the line ended, and Janet touched Rich's shoulder. "Please, give me a minute."

"Take two. I'll join you by the side door for our ride to the reception."

Janet nodded and hurried toward the restroom before his words penetrated her brain. *Side door?* Where did he park? The front door gave easy access to the main parking lot. Or did one of the many police officers volunteer to chauffeur them? In the hours since she'd arrived with Jeremy and Ashley, a great many plans changed.

A few minutes later, Rich reached for her long, tan coat as she approached the cloak area. "Ah, your reappearance is fashionably timed."

"The side door is... Where are you taking me?" She pointed over her shoulder and lengthened her stride to match his pace.

"I've been informed of a change in transportation plans." He led her through the chapel and down three steps to the alley door.

Janet stepped into cold December sunshine. Less than four paces away, a large, white passenger van idled. Tinted windows prevented her from seeing inside, except for the driver. *Detective Collins?* "What's...did the conspirators not trust us to find the reception hall?"

"I'm not sure. I'm following orders—from my son. I suspect we're victims of a second conspiracy." Rich opened the van's side door.

Janet leaned in and gasped. "All of you?" She skimmed her gaze over her best friends, Marty, plus Rich's sister and brother-in-law. Swallowing surprise, she smiled at her second family—the relatives by choice rather than blood.

"Now get in, sweetie. It's all of twenty degrees out here." Rich adjusted a hand to assist her into the van.

The conversation between the new and old friends churned with good humor. Words and chuckles collided in the air like storm waves against a dock.

Collins drove a wandering, back street route to the reception hall and then circled the block twice to allow the laughter to ebb.

"I think I found it," Janet announced as the van

rolled to a stop.

"Found what?" the entire back row chorused.

"Our new family motto."

Rich released seat belts and circled his arms at her waist. "Spill."

"Life's temporary—live with gusto."

A word about the author…

Raised in a household full of books, it was only natural that Ellen Parker grew up with a book in her hand. She turned to writing as a second career and enjoys spinning the type of story which appeals to more than one generation. She encourages readers to share her work with mother or daughter—or both. When not guiding characters to their "happily ever after" she's likely reading, tending her postage stamp garden, or walking in the neighborhood. She currently lives in St. Louis.

You can find her on the web at:

www.ellenparkerwrites.wordpress.com

or on Facebook at:

www.facebook.com/ellenparkerwrites.

Another title by this author
Stare Down